Praise for the Novels of Cindy Miles

Into Thin Air

"Another sweet paranormal featuring a sparkling lead couple and a supporting cast of ghostly charmers . . . this adorable, otherworldly romp is sure to leave readers feeling warm and fuzzy."　　　　—*Publishers Weekly*

"Filled with humor, romance, mystery, and a lot of ghosts, *Into Thin Air* is a book that is hard to put down."
—Romance Junkies

Spirited Away

"Absolutely delightful! Cindy Miles outshines the genre's best, writing with a charm and verve sure to captivate readers' hearts. *Spirited Away* is pure magic."
—Sue-Ellen Welfonder, *USA Today* bestselling author

"A sparkling debut, reminiscent of favorites like *The Ghost and Mrs. Muir*."　　　—Julie Kenner, *USA Today* bestselling author

"This charming paranormal debut heralds an exciting new voice in the genre. Warm, humorous, fun-filled, magical, and spiced with deadly danger, this ghost story has it all."
—*Romantic Times* (4½ stars)

"Cindy Miles's love for the genre shines through in her endearing, quirky heroines and her larger-than-life heroes. As a reader, I was *Spirited Away* by the magic in each and every word."　　　　—Jolie Mathis, author of *The Sea King*

"This is the most charming story I have come across in some time. It has such a wonderful plot, characters, setting, and dialogue; I eagerly await the next book."
—Romance Readers at Heart

"A charming tale that mixes best what readers enjoy in medieval fantasy and contemporary romance. The less common ghostly theme will appeal to paranormal fans looking for variety, and the quirky, lovable characters will leave readers wanting to revisit the knights

"An energetic, amusing gho
intelligent mortal and a som

Highland Knight

CINDY MILES

A SIGNET ECLIPSE BOOK

SIGNET ECLIPSE
Published by New American Library, a division of
Penguin Group (USA) Inc., 375 Hudson Street,
New York, New York 10014, USA
Penguin Group (Canada), 90 Eglinton Avenue East, Suite 700, Toronto,
Ontario M4P 2Y3, Canada (a division of Pearson Penguin Canada Inc.)
Penguin Books Ltd., 80 Strand, London WC2R 0RL, England
Penguin Ireland, 25 St. Stephen's Green, Dublin 2,
Ireland (a division of Penguin Books Ltd.)
Penguin Group (Australia), 250 Camberwell Road, Camberwell, Victoria 3124,
Australia (a division of Pearson Australia Group Pty. Ltd.)
Penguin Books India Pvt. Ltd., 11 Community Centre, Panchsheel Park,
New Delhi - 110 017, India
Penguin Group (NZ), 67 Apollo Drive, Rosedale, North Shore 0632,
New Zealand (a division of Pearson New Zealand Ltd.)
Penguin Books (South Africa) (Pty.) Ltd., 24 Sturdee Avenue,
Rosebank, Johannesburg 2196, South Africa

Penguin Books Ltd., Registered Offices:
80 Strand, London WC2R 0RL, England

First published by Signet Eclipse, an imprint of New American Library,
a division of Penguin Group (USA) Inc.

First Printing, June 2008
10 9 8 7 6 5 4 3 2 1

For my silly, sweet, funny, confident daughter, Tyler. I wish I'd been more like you when I was a kid. Thanks for still hanging out with me, baking cookies, sitting on the front porch with me whenever I ask you to, and for listening to all of my wacky ideas. You can borrow my shoes anytime. I love you, girl.

Prologue

Munro Keep, 1303
Scotland

"*Munro!*"

Ethan jerked awake and sat up. He shook his head and blinked a time or two, but the chamber remained hazy and blurred. Had someone shouted, or had he dreamed it?

Damn, how his skull throbbed. Pressing his knuckles hard against his temples, he sought to ease the pounding ache. Christ, wed less than a fortnight, yet he must have fallen deep into his cups the night before. He couldn't even recall entering his own chamber. He glanced down. His bed was empty. And he was fully garbed.

"*Murderer!*"

Ethan jumped to his feet and reached for his blade. It was gone. So was his new wife, Devina. Muffled shouts rose from outside the keep, and in two strides he stood at the lone window. Throwing the bolt, he pushed open the shutters and stared out across the black water of the loch. Beside it, the knoll was shrouded in mist. A line of torches flickered at its base in the dim, early-dawn light of morn.

The chamber door swung open and his younger brother stumbled in. "Ethan! Something's amiss!" Rob reached his side and pointed toward the torches. " 'Tis Devina's kin."

Ethan stared at the score of men below. "Her kin left yestermorn."

"They're back."

So it seemed. Ethan stared at the flickering torches below. "Where's my wife?"

"I don't know."

As Ethan took in the scene below, wondering what had made Devina's folk return, something else caught his eye. Atop the knoll and through slips of heavy mist emerged the unmistakable figure of a makeshift gibbet.

Unease gripped Ethan's stomach as he pushed away from the window. Something was indeed amiss. "Wake Aiden and Sorely. Have them find Gilchrist and rouse the others." He cinched his belt and snugged his plaid. "And by Christ, find me a damn sword."

"Aye." Rob ran from the chamber.

Ethan grabbed a dirk, tucked it into his belt, and followed his brother out. Moments later, Aiden met him in the passageway and handed Ethan a sword.

"You look like hell."

Ethan walked the length of the corridor, then took the steps two at a time. He ignored his cousin's jest. "Where's my wife?"

"Your sister has gone to search for Devina at the priory. 'Tis her kin at the knoll," Aidan said, right on his heels. "Mayhap they've returned to make sure the devil hasn't eaten their daughter."

Ethan frowned and started across the great hall. His timid wife had indeed spent the greater portion of their wedded fortnight within the priory, crossing herself and praying for safety. *From him.*

His men were waiting at the door, and he looked each one in the eye. "Dunna make a solitary move without my say. And keep your bluidy tongues in your heads. No need to provoke that superstitious lot." Without another word or glance, Ethan sheathed his borrowed sword, grabbed a torch from the wall, and stepped out into the damp morn. The others followed; the only sounds breaking the stillness were the shuffling of boots across the rushes and torches being lifted from their cradles.

In silence, they crossed the meadow, skirted the loch, and started for the knoll. Several paces from the line of men, they could see that those gathered included the MacEwans, the laird, and Devina's uncle, who let out a shout. "Murdering devil!"

Ethan stopped, glanced up at the gibbet, and noticed then that a short stretch of frayed twine dangled from its end. A scrap of Munro plaid, held in place by his own bluidy sword, lay buried in the gibbet's post. He looked back at Devina's uncle. "What is this madness, Daegus? I know not what you—"

"*Murderer!*" the laird interrupted, his voice an angered sob.

And then his new wife's kinsmen parted.

Behind them, on the ground, a small mound lay still, covered with a MacEwan plaid.

Dread and anger built inside Ethan, and he moved toward the covered body. He knew without looking who lay beneath it.

Devina.

"You'll not touch her again, you bluidy devil!" Daegus bellowed, and he pushed Ethan back. "I shouldna have allowed this union!"

Ethan charged forward, and this time it took several MacEwans to hold him. The Munros became restless and agitated, the air snapped with tension, and the hissing of a sword being drawn from its sheath rang out. Ribbons of mist moved amongst them.

"Nay!" Ethan shouted. He struggled against six large MacEwan lads, and he'd almost broken free when a gust of Highland wind caught the end of the plaid covering the body and lifted it, revealing his wife's ghostly white face. Lifeless eyes glared at him. *Accusing*.

Daegus MacEwan grabbed Ethan's throat and forced him to look away. "You killed my niece, you bluidy Munro," he snarled, his voice choked and raw. The rims of his eyes were red. "My brother made me promise on his deathbed! He insisted on this union, and by Christ, I agreed when I damn well knew I shouldna!" He glared at Ethan. "Your blade, your plaid. Your reluctance to wed. The other lasses who've died because o' you. 'Tis all the proof I need."

" 'Tis a lie!" Rob yelled.

A burst of fury let loose, and Ethan broke free of the MacEwans' strong arms. "You're mad, Daegus! Let me at my wife!"

"You'll die first, Munro."

Daegus unsheathed his sword, let out an anguished scream, and charged Ethan. As Ethan readied his own blade, so did every man on the knoll.

Ethan did his best to ward off Daegus' fury without killing him. 'Twas no use. A battle broke out, and then Ethan reflected attacking blades from all angles. Shouts and cries chimed with the ring of steel as Munro fought MacEwan. The scent of blood tainted the sweet Highland air.

Meanwhile, Devina's lifeless eyes watched.

Then the bite of sharpened steel sliced into Daegus's back, and he sucked in a breath and whirled around, sword raised.

The MacEwan fell to the ground, and Rob yanked his blade out of the older laird's back. Shouts were cried out, and a dozen more MacEwan warriors topped the knoll. With a fierce battle cry, they charged downward.

And then the sheets of mist that had been slipping in and around them thickened to near-blinding, so much that Ethan couldn't see his own hand before his face. His men cursed and shuffled about, drawing closer to one another, until they all huddled together, seemingly shoulder to shoulder. His brothers, Rob and Gilchrist, flanked him.

Somewhere in the whiteness, a voice—not a warrior's voice, but that of a lass—murmured, heavier than a whisper, and carried on the same breeze that had lifted the plaid from Devina's face. A curse? A spell of sorts? Ethan couldna decipher the words.

And then the thick blanket of white turned to pitch, the MacEwan shouts faded away, and all was eerie, unholy, breathless, and still as death . . .

Chapter 1

Charleston, South Carolina
Present day

Amelia Landry stepped through the French doors of her beachside cottage and onto the deck overlooking the Atlantic. She shielded her eyes against the sun's glare and took in the view. What an ideal June day. Sea oats waved in the breeze atop hilly sand dunes. Cornflower blue skies, puffy white clouds, and gulls screamed overhead. *Perfect*. She stretched, walked to the railing, and scratched between the ears of her sunbathing cat, Jack. The lazy fur ball didn't even bother to crack open an eye. With a shrug, Amelia leaned on her elbows and inhaled a lungful of salt-tinged air.

A gull pooped on her arm.

So much for perfect.

Pulling a tissue out of the pocket of her lucky white cotton robe, she wiped her arm, tossed the tissue in the ceramic trash bin in the corner, then from her other pocket lifted a loaded can of Cheez Whiz to her mouth and bent the white tip with a forefinger until a stream of orange paste covered her tongue.

Bliss.

Anything, she thought, to help her forget she'd lost her mojo.

Writing mojo, that is. Gone for nearly a year now. Everything she came up with bored her beyond tears.

She closed her eyes and let the tangy, creamy paste melt in her mouth.

"You are pathetic, you know that?"

All at once, Amelia inhaled with surprise, swallowed, and coughed. Rather, she choked. Congealed fake cheese was torture on the lungs. After she wiped the tears from her eyes, she glared at her best friend. "Jesus, ZuZu. There's this thing called knocking." She coughed once more, and then squirted another mouthful of heavenly paste. Jack meowed, opened his mouth, and she gave him a squirt, too. They both swallowed. "What about ringing a doorbell?"

Zulia Tinkerly—known by all as ZuZu—set her handbag on the deck, tucked her jaw-length auburn hair behind her ear, and frowned. "Okay, Meelie, this has got to stop. Not only is that disgusting, but it's not nutritious at all. For you or Jack."

Jack meowed and nudged the can with his nose.

Amelia, whom ZuZu had called Meelie since childhood, lifted the Whiz and wagged it at her friend. "It's a full dairy serving, smarty-pants."

ZuZu grabbed the can, hung it over the rail, and squirted until it sputtered empty. Jack jumped down, following the stream of cheese. Then ZuZu threw the can in the bin. "You're ridiculous. Now sit down. I've got something to tell you."

"You just littered."

"Jack and the gulls will eat it." ZuZu guided Amelia to one of the Adirondacks and pushed her into it, then perched on the railing. "Any new ideas lately?"

"No."

"Great. That's what I hoped you'd say."

Amelia glared at her friend. She always knew when ZuZu was up to something rotten. Her lips twitched. "Why?"

"Because I'm sick and tired of seeing you mope, eat horrible, nasty by-products of God-knows-what, and just . . . mope. You need a change, Amelia. Your hair needs a trim, your nails need a manicure, and you definitely need some new clothes. You've been in that ratty robe now for what? A week?"

"A month."

ZuZu grabbed her by the hands and pulled. "Stand up."

"You just made me sit down."

With a hard yank, ZuZu succeeded. She untied the knot in the sash and pulled the robe off Amelia's shoulders.

"What are you doing?" Amelia asked. "I wash it twice a week."

"You need an intervention before your publisher lets you go." Reaching into her handbag, she withdrew a big pair of scissors and made a cut in the collar of the robe. Gripping the scissor handles with her teeth, ZuZu ripped the material right down the middle.

"So your idea of an intervention is cutting my lucky robe into shreds?"

"Give me that hideous T-shirt."

Amelia glanced down at her beloved garment, then scowled at ZuZu. "No way. You're not getting it." She crossed her arms over her chest. "Over my dead body."

"*That* can be arranged. Now, give it here before I cut if off of you."

ZuZu's lips twitched.

With a gusty sigh, Amelia made a vow to herself to get that oh-so-beloved garment back, yanked the cotton T over her head, and plopped it into ZuZu's outstretched hand. "Do not cut it up. It's my favorite shirt. My lucky shirt. I *love* that shirt." Black in color, it had a pair of fluorescent fangs on the top, and in a dripping-blood font the words *Bram Stoker Rocks!*, also in fluorescent. It glowed in the dark, and she adored it.

"We know. You love that old bikini top that you've been wearing for the past month, too. God, Meelie, your boobs are going to sag to your kneecaps if you don't wear more support." She pushed Amelia back into the chair, and then started to pace the deck. "Now, here's the deal. You're going on a little vacation this summer. It's already arranged, so you've got no choice but to suck it up and go. I used your business account Visa and booked your flight, lodgings, and rental car. You leave in two days."

Amelia blinked. "Have you lost your mind? I've got a book due, on my editor's desk, *completed*, in three months. That's twelve weeks. I can't go on a vacation." She shoved her fingers through her hair. "Good Lord, ZuZu. That's credit card theft, you know. I could report you."

ZuZu didn't even bat an eye. "I'm your assistant, ding-dong. You can't report me. Besides, your editor is all for it. And let me remind you that you've had an entire year to start, finish, and complete a book. Your fault."

"What'd she say?"

ZuZu tapped her chin with a perfectly manicured

fingernail. "Let's see. I think her exact words were, 'Anything to get her sorry ass moving.' Now, I pulled a lot of strings to get you this place for the summer. Lucky for you, I *know* people."

Amelia narrowed her gaze. "What place?"

ZuZu stopped pacing, squatted in front of Amelia, and grinned. "A remote, creepy, supposedly haunted fourteenth-century tower house."

Amelia lifted a brow. "Where?"

"The Highlands of Scotland."

"You're lying."

"I'm not."

"What about Jack?" Amelia asked. She wasn't, by any means, the cat lady. Not that there's anything *wrong* with it, mind you. But she liked Jack's companionship. He was a quiet presence during times of extreme solitude. And he *adored* her.

Twenty-eight years old, no children, not even the prospect of a relationship in sight, and her constant companion was a cat.

God, she *was* the cat lady.

"Amelia!" ZuZu hollered, snapping a finger in front of her face. "Did you hear a thing I said?"

Amelia glanced down at her bare feet, wiggled her toes, and noticed the pink polish that had started to chip off a week ago. "The Highlands of Scotland?"

"The remote, secluded, *haunted* Highlands of Scotland."

A grin tugged at Amelia's mouth. "I like haunted."

"I know you do." ZuZu reached into that big bag she'd dug the scissors from and pulled out a book. "Here. Read this on the way over. I've dog-eared a section I think you'll find very interesting."

Amelia took the book. *Haunted Scotland*. She flipped

to the page ZuZu had tagged and read the chapter heading out loud. "The Bluidy Munro."

"Cool, huh?"

"Definitely."

The idea did sound fascinating. She'd never been to Scotland before, but she'd certainly seen pictures and watched movies, and the scenery was breathtaking. Throw in a haunted castle and a Bluidy Munro to boot? Maybe that was just what she needed to jump-start her imagination. She grinned. "When do we leave?"

ZuZu pulled the book out of Amelia's hands, tucked it under her arm, and pulled Amelia to her feet once more. "*We* don't. Just you."

"Jack?"

"Luckily, Jack. If you hadn't made that trip to Bermuda in February, he would have had to stay. But he's been microchipped and vaccinated, so he's good to go. Just a quickie trip to the vet, which I've already arranged."

Amelia glanced out over the sea and watched a pelican nosedive into the water. "Indoor plumbing? Please tell me I don't have to use an outhouse for three months."

ZuZu laughed and guided Amelia into the house. "Yes, indoor plumbing. It's been moderately renovated over the past ten years. Nothing fancy, mind you, but your necessities will be taken care of. You're not froufrou, so you shouldn't have a care in the world, other than getting your work done. The castle is secure. Gorgeous, too. Now," she said, giving Amelia a push toward her bedroom, "get showered and dressed. We've got some shopping to do."

At the doorway to her room, Amelia turned.

"Won't you come to keep me company? Buy me Cheez Whiz?"

ZuZu gave her a stern look and shook a finger. "Once you're nearly finished with your new project, yes. Say, in August?"

Amelia blew out a breath. "You drive a hard bargain, Tinkerly." She nodded. "Done. And ZuZu?"

"Yeah?"

"Thanks. You're the best."

ZuZu smiled. "I know. Now, get ready. The mall is calling us."

"Lass, you've missed your turnoff, is all."

Amelia groaned out loud. She was going to kill ZuZu. What had made her think driving in the Highlands would be a good thing? *It's a snap, Amelia. Easy peasy.* Right. She blew out a breath. "That's only the fifth time I've been told that since leaving Ten Mile Burn, where this wild-haired woman on a horse pointed me in the right direction. Twice."

The store owner, a tall, wiry man with a full head of wavy copper hair, chuckled and walked around the counter, stopped at the wide front window, and peered over the rim of his glasses. "Next time, lass, fly straight into Inverness instead of Edinburgh. Now . . . go eighteen meters that way"—he pointed—"and you'll see a wee single-track lane to your left. It's unmarked, so watch carefully for it. That lane will take you right to the Munro keep." He glanced down at her. "Are you the new owner, then?"

Amelia shook her head. She liked the way his O's sounded like *ooh*s. "I'm leasing it for the summer. Why, is it for sale?"

The man grinned, revealing a slight gap between his front teeth. "Oh, aye. 'Tis always for sale."

ZuZu had forgotten to mention that.

After purchasing as much junk food as possible, which included a handful of orange chocolate bars, several sleeves of chocolate-coated digestibles, a large bag of potato chips, and two six-packs of chocolate drinks that resembled Yoo-hoo, she thanked the store owner, whose name was Hewitt, and left.

That Hewitt had offered his and his wife's phone number, "in case you find yourself in need of aid whilst on the Black Isle," was something else to consider. But later. For now, her only concern was getting to her destination without leaving the fender of her rental car embedded in the rocky Highland walls hugging either side of the very, *very* narrow lane.

Several miles later—kilometers, rather, as Hewitt had been quick to point out the difference—with the afternoon waning, Amelia spotted the barely visible single lane and turned onto it. It was no more than a narrow strip of gravel, with tall, ancient-looking trees canopying it from each side, and it seemed more like a footpath winding up the rocky incline. Pines and oaks and other Highland flora surrounded the area, so thick that Amelia caught only mere glimpses of the sky. The shadows certainly made for an eerie atmosphere. Long branches tangled above the road like lanky, bony arms. She drove at a snail's pace for what seemed an hour. In the back of the rental, inside the pet carrier, Jack meowed with what Amelia could only imagine was impatience.

Suddenly, the trees parted, and Amelia slowed as she topped the incline. The sight left her breathless. She stopped, put the car in park, and stared.

Across a green-meadowed clearing, dotted with clumps of thistle, rose an enormous gray-stoned tower. A tall, single tower. No fairy-tale turrets, no Cinderella castle, no merry flag waving from atop the pointed roof. Just a tower, powerful, probably a hundred feet tall, with a massive double door. One word came to mind when Amelia tried to sum it up.

Masculine.

On one side of the tower stood the darkest body of water Amelia had ever laid eyes on. A Highland loch, she supposed, and it was black as pitch against the bright green of the grass. Behind it was a hill covered in purple heather.

Suddenly something banged on the window of the rental car, and Amelia jumped. When she turned, an old, craggy-faced man stood just on the other side of the glass, peering in. He scowled.

Amelia screamed.

He tapped on the window with the end of a walking stick, frown still affixed. Through the open sunroof, his deep brogue, R's rolling, floated in. "You're late." And then he turned and started off toward the castle, a noticeable hitch in his step.

Amelia blinked, drew a breath, lowered the window, and poked her head out. "Um, hello?" she said, slowly accelerating but keeping a safe distance behind him. She could only guess he was the castle keeper ZuZu had told her about. She hadn't bothered to mention that he was such a grump. "Mr. McAllister?"

He kept walking. "Guthrie."

"Right. Guthrie. Um, late for what?"

At first he ignored her. He just kept right on walking toward the tall tower house, until his footsteps fell within its long shadows. Up close, the castle appeared even more imposing, and the great double doors were easily thirty feet high. Big. Daunting. "Late for what?" Amelia repeated. She stopped, put the car in park, and opened the door.

Guthrie walked up to the great doors, slid back an enormous bolt, and then turned toward her. A soft brown hat was cocked sideways upon thick white hair. Brown trousers, a brownish plaid, long-sleeved shirt, and a pair of much-worn leather boots made him look every part the Highland shepherd. Only there were no sheep.

One of his bushy white brows lifted. "We've been waiting for you."

Chapter 2

We? What did that mean? As far as Amelia knew, only the castle keeper, she, and Jack would be living at the tower house for the summer. Maybe old Guthrie had a wife?

Amelia hopped out of the rental and opened the hatchback. Jack's big yellow eyes stared at her from inside the pet carrier; then he blinked, let out a big meow, and Amelia flipped open the latch. Jack nudged the carrier's door with his little pink nose and jumped out. In a flash of pitch-black fur, he disappeared around the corner and into the shadows of the tower. Pausing, Amelia turned in a slow circle and looked around. She fought the urge to run inside.

A peculiar silence enveloped the castle and grounds. No birds tweeted, no dogs barked. At least three or four miles off the main road, which was out in the middle of nowhere to begin with, the ordinary sounds of cars and horns tooting and simple everyday noises just didn't exist. Only the wind rustled the leaves. Out of the ordinary, she thought. Uncanny. *Perfect.*

Perfect, but still creepy.

Amelia heaved her suitcase out of the car and grabbed two more duffel bags, her laptop bag, and her purse, and then slammed the trunk. With the late-afternoon light fading fast, she hurried to the yawning doors of the tower. "Come on, Jack!" she called. Rolling—rather, dragging—her suitcase, which was the size of a small car, she struggled across the gravel. As she stepped in, Jack scooted between her feet and ran inside.

The door banged shut behind her, and Amelia jumped. And squeaked. "Hello? Guthrie?" Where had the guy gone? Dropping her duffels and purse to the floor, she laid her computer bag down and took in the massive room. Although June, a chill seeped into the skin of her bare arms. She supposed the tank top, overall shorts, and flip-flops just wouldn't do unless the heat was turned on. Rubbing her arms, she continued her inspection.

No fluff, no frills, no fuss. Purely male. Gray stone walls, a dark-stained, wood-planked floor with various throw rugs, an enormous hearth with a stag's rack high above it, and wood beams crisscrossing the ceiling definitely summed up ZuZu's *moderately renovated* description. Two mammoth light fixtures made of more antlers hung from opposite ends of the room. Two substantial leather sofas, separated by a large chunk of wood serving as a center table, along with two overstuffed chairs sat before the wide mouth of the hearth. A ladder-back chair perched against the wall. A door near the rear, a large wooden chest pushed into the corner, and a spiral set of steps leading to the rooms above made up the most gigantic living room Amelia had ever seen. Very medieval. *Cool.*

More than seven hundred years before, big, strong medieval hands had laid every stone in mortar that made up the enormous Munro tower. The very thought gave Amelia the chills.

"What are ye waiting for, girl?"

Amelia jumped—again—at the unexpected sound of Guthrie's voice. "Hi, well, I wasn't sure where to go."

"Follow me, then," Guthrie said. He ambled over, grabbed the handle to the suitcase before Amelia could protest, and pulled it to the spiral steps. Without much effort, he started up. "This way."

Stronger than he looks, Amelia thought as she gathered her duffels and laptop case and followed old Guthrie, Jack right on her heels. Dim lights embedded into the stone barely lit the passageways. The higher they got, the cooler it became. They climbed two more floors before Guthrie, who'd managed to get way ahead of Amelia, stopped in front of a half-cracked-open, large wooden door. The old Scotsman wasn't the least bit winded.

Amelia wheezed. "Thanks."

"Aye." Guthrie moved past her and headed back the way they'd come. "You've free run of the tower, lass, so unpack and help yourself. Watch your step, though. The closest infirmary isn't so verra close at all. Supper's every eve at seven. Breakfast is at eight. Lunch, you're on your own." With that, he disappeared into the shadowy corridor.

Amelia blinked and shook her head. "Man of few words, huh, Jack?"

Jack just looked at her.

She gave the door a push, and it creaked open on ancient hinges. Amelia stepped inside her room. The faint glow from a table lamp in the far corner shed very little light, especially with the one lone window closed, but enough for her to make her way inside without bumping into things. Then a cool breeze grazed her neck and ruffled her ponytail. Amelia jumped and looked behind her.

Jack arched his back, flattened his ears, and hissed.

Amelia blew out a shaky sigh. "Stop it, Jack, you big scaredy-cat. It's just a drafty old castle." Giving the room a hasty once-over, she found it, of course, empty. Her heart still pounded hard and fast. "God, I love that fright-induced adrenaline rush."

After a close inspection, Amelia found three more lamps and turned them all on. No wall switches, she noticed, just lamps. Which was fine. She loved lamplight. It gave off just the right ambience for writing spooky, bloody mysteries. When plopped in a fourteenth-century tower house for the summer, one that had a Bluidy Munro legend to boot? Well, that sort of mood would surely give decent fodder for her imagination . . .

The candle flame blew out. Jack squalled and scooted under the bed.

Amelia grinned. She felt like she'd been thrown in the middle of an Abbot and Costello meet Frankenstein movie.

She couldn't wait to go to bed and read over the *Haunted Scotland* book ZuZu had given her. Already, she felt inspired and enthusiastic. Scared, a little, but in a good, *boo!* sort of way.

With a quick glance at her watch, Amelia then pushed her big suitcase over onto its side and unzipped it. It was almost seven, and her stomach rumbled at the thought of supper. She'd unpack, wash up, change, eat, and then do a little investigating.

If she was lucky enough, she'd bump into a ghost or two.

"Well? Was she frightened or no'?"

Ethan stared into the empty mouth of the hearth. He scratched his head. "Aye."

The men grumbled.

Turning, Ethan met their scowls with one of his own. "And nay."

His younger brother cocked his head. "What mean you? How can it be aye and nay?"

Ethan shrugged. "She was afraid, but she liked it. I think."

"Fetching lass, methinks," Aiden said. "The tallest I've ever seen, and by the cross, I canna get over how modern women expose vast amounts of their skin." He grinned. "Quite a pair of legs, she has, and ample hips for breedin'."

"Aye," Sorely said, nodding his big head. "Nice white teeth, too."

Ethan frowned deeper. "She's no' a brood mare, for Christ's sake."

"Big, heavy bosoms, too," Sorely muttered under his breath.

The men chuckled. Ethan almost did. 'Twas her eyes, though, that had caught him unawares . . .

"Is she receptive?" Rob asked.

Adjusting his belt, Ethan rubbed his chin. "I'm no' positive, but 'tis verra likely. She flinched a time or two, and her heart raced. Her cat knew I was there." He palmed the hilt of his sword. "We'll know more by tomorrow."

"Why do you think she liked it? Being scared, I mean?" Rob asked.

"Aye, indeed, most lasses are squeamish and would have run like a hare," Torloch, who had only one working eye, said.

Ethan shrugged. "She mentioned enjoying a rush of sorts. Of adrenaline. I looked about but saw nothing of the sort. 'Twas only her and the cat." Not that he had any bluidy idea what adrenaline was, but he felt fairly sure he'd know it if he saw it.

"Strange lass," Sorely said, and a few agreeing grunts accompanied him. "Bonny, but strange, and wearing those flip-flop slippers. Think you she's a bit addled?" He tapped the side of his head with a forefinger.

Ethan nodded. "Possibly. But mayhap what we need *is* strange and addled, aye?"

The men grunted.

Rob rubbed the back of his neck. "Did Guthrie find anything else out?"

"Nay," Ethan said. "Only that she's a bard of sorts. From *America*. And that she's here for the whole of the summer." The girl was fetching. Strikingly so. Never had he met a woman quite so tall. Compared to himself, that is. Most barely reached his chest. This one—Amelia—came easily to his shoulder. A lad would have to be damn near dead not to notice the tanned skin and peculiar eyes. Large, green, and shaped in such a way that it reminded Ethan of a pair of half-moons. Despite the fact that she wore her fair hair pulled high into a horse's tail, she was indeed . . . unusual. He scraped a hand over his jaw. "Dunna get your hopes up. We've had others who were receptive over the years, and proved to be of very little use."

"Aye," Sorely said. "But those were passersby, hill walkers, stopping just long enough to explore the keep. Now that it has been restored and she'll be staying on, mayhap the lass will warm up to us?"

"Especially since she'll be here for so long," Rob said. "No one's ever stayed more than a sennight—especially if they're receptive to us."

Ethan nodded. "Mayhap. But 'tis a lot to hope for. Mortals are a scary lot." He paced, considering, then stopped and glanced at his kin. "Dunna show yourselves to her. Not yet. We dunna want to scare her off. We'll wait and see if she can sense us whilst she explores the keep."

"And if she senses us?" Aiden asked.

Ethan met his stare. "Then I'll give her a few thoughts to ponder. Tonight."

Refreshed from a shower and full from Guthrie's surprisingly good supper of potato soup and a hard roll, Amelia stood in the great hall. Staring. In awe and completely spooked. Guthrie had driven into the village for a game of cards and wouldn't be home until the wee hours, he'd said. Leaving her all alone to "explore the fortress, or whatever it is you storytellers do," he'd added, with a cheerful slam of the great hall door. Although not dark outside, and it wouldn't be, Guthrie had said, until well after eleven p.m., the interior of the castle—rather, the keep—had very little light at all, being that it had no windows. Only the faint glow from the wall sconces and overhead light fixtures gave off the tiniest bit of yellowed light. The hall sat empty. No TV, no stereo, no suits of armor, no crossed swords hanging from the wall. Nothing. Not even one of those medieval spiky ball things on the end of a chained club. Not even a dust bunny.

She walked over to the only splash of color, a long length of plaid, the interwoven colors brown, black, and a deep, deep red, casually draped across the high mantel on the hearth. Amelia reached up and grasped the end between her fingers and rubbed. Coarse and heavy, the cloth seemed very old.

All in all, the place reeked of centuries gone by, and of something Amelia couldn't quite put a finger on. It seemed harmless enough, though. No boogeymen, no ghosts, no malevolent beings, all bloody guts and headless and festering wounds . . .

Yet the long shadows stretching from darkened corners and alcoves made her skin prickle into goose bumps, and she had the overwhelming urge to look over her shoulder and hurry. Constantly.

Perfect.

Where should she go first? She'd already seen the kitchen. Simple, neat, a place for everything. A long wooden table with a bench on either side, a walk-in pantry, sink, fridge, several cabinets. Cut-and-dry. No froufrou as ZuZu would say.

Amelia let her gaze roam over the hall once more, and just as she was about to head upstairs to check the other chambers out, she saw something she'd missed before. A single door, in the far corner.

"Aha," she said to no one, and headed for that nearly hidden entrance to *somewhere*. Her rubber-soled red wedgies, which were part of her Power Outfits ensemble she'd bought with ZuZu, who'd said, "If you want to be successful, you've got to feel and dress the part. Burn that hideous Dracula T-shirt, for God's sake, and buy some decent clothes!" didn't make a sound as she crossed the wood plank floor. She stopped in front of the ancient-looking wooden door. A long bolt locked it tightly shut. Wiping her clammy palms against the thighs of her jeans, Amelia smoothed the front of the gauzy red baby-doll blouse she'd traded her beloved Stoker T for and reached for the bolt.

Nay, woman.

Amelia jumped and squeaked, and turned around fast. "Who's there?" Her heart pounded in her chest as she waited.

Not a sound came.

Sliding a glance slowly around the room, Amelia's breath quickened as her gaze settled on every single shadowy fourteenth-century corner. When the hall proved empty, she took a deep breath and blew out a gusty sigh. "Ha! Like I thought. Nothing." She meant it, too. Sincerely.

Flexing her fingers, she gripped the bolt and pushed up.

Stay oot o' there, lass!

Amelia jumped and looked around. "Guthrie? Is that you?" A long strand of hair fell from her clip, and she blew it out of her eyes. What the heck did *oot* mean, anyway? "Now," she said, extraloud to prove to Guthrie or who/whatever that, while she was indeed a grade-A chicken, she would not let her overactive writer's imagination get in the way of her castle exploration. Already, she was feeling inspired, and the only way to stay inspired was to roam the spooky old keep. Right? As she started for the spiral stairs at the other end of the great hall, her steps, unavoidably, became a tiny bit faster.

Without looking back, Amelia made it to the staircase leading to the upper chambers, and just as her red wedgie heel touched the first step, a shiver shimmied down her spine. She looked behind, over her shoulder and down, at the back of her waist.

The ties to her blouse lifted in midair, and one began to slowly tug out of its bow. *As if someone were pulling it.*

Not Guthrie.

With a strangled yelp, Amelia ran up the winding steps. She hit the second-floor passageway at almost full speed. Well, as full speed as one can manage in a pair of red wedgies. Later, she'd remind herself that she *loved* the rush of being scared out of her wits and that the whole experience, when recalled to mind, would make for some kick-butt suspense in her book that she had only three months to write. For now, though, she couldn't get away fast enough.

Get away from *what*, exactly, she didn't know.

With a brave, if she said so herself, glance over her shoulder, just to see if some blood-dripping, sword-wielding ghost in armor chased her, Amelia ran to her room, hurried inside, and slammed the door. Leaning her back against it, she drew in large gulps of air.

From the foot of the bed, where he lay curled up into a big, happy, black ball of fur, Jack lifted his head, looked at her, and meowed.

Amelia frowned. "Some help you are."

Jack stretched and yawned.

After several minutes of just leaning against the

door, breathing and trying to slow her racing heart, she glanced at her watch. Already ten thirty p.m. Perhaps she shouldn't try to cram all of her explorations into one night. What with the exhaustion of jet lag and the five-hour time change, she was beat. Besides, she had three months, for God's sake. It'd be much wiser to space it out, savor the experience, and absorb each and every detail. She nodded to herself in agreement.

Amelia pressed her ear to the smooth, cool wood and listened. Not a sound came from the other side. With a deep breath, she eased from the door, crossed the room to the bed, and scratched between Jack's ears. "I should have gotten a dog. A big one."

Not taking any chances, Amelia searched the room until she found the only thing she could drag and wedge against the door: an empty trunk. She pushed it hard against the only entrance into her room, and then locked the door.

Taking several minutes to unpack, and finding no closet to speak of, Amelia neatly stashed her clothes in the lone empty trunk that now had a duel use as a garment keeper/doorstop. Good thing she'd brought her liquid wrinkle release, anyway. She laid out her pajamas, kicked off her heels and clothes, and then scooted into the small bathroom and brushed her teeth. Finished, she realized just how cool it was in Scotland in the summertime. Especially in the keep. Drafty, really, as she kept feeling a brush of coolness against the skin of her neck. Discarding her bra with a firm fling, slingshot style, Amelia pulled on her favorite black yoga pants and black tank, and then dug through her bag once more and pulled out the book ZuZu had given her. Maybe she'd read up on the legend of the Munro Keep. Get herself in the mood to write.

Settled into bed, with the covers pulled up to her waist and Jack curled up at the foot, Amelia cracked open the book to the page ZuZu had dog-eared.

The Bluidy Munro, 'tis rumored, haunts the old stone walls of the keep, yearning for a chance to swing his claymore and hack off a few more heads . . .

Amelia pulled the coverlet up to her ears. She wasn't taking any chances.

Chapter 3

Ethan stared down at the sleeping form and frowned.

Why did it have to be a woman?

Amelia. Bedcovers pulled up to her ears and a book gripped tightly in one hand, she breathed deeply as she slumbered. He turned his head sideways and squinted at the text. *Haunted Scotland.*

Odd lass, in truth. Comely, but verra odd. And so far, verra receptive to his presence. Then again, so was old Guthrie, and the scores of others through the centuries who'd wandered upon Munro land and ventured into the keep. As soon as he tried to make contact, to see if they were receptive enough to his presence to help him and his brothers, they'd hightail it. Fast. No one, save the castle keeper, had ever stayed as long as the American planned on staying. Not even the new owners. The rest had run off, terrified of the ghosts. Fearing the legend was true. Centuries went by before anyone even dared step foot into the keep of the Bluidy Munro. And of all people, it had to be a damn lass.

Mayhap he shouldn't frighten her quite so much?

A snore erupted from beneath the coverlet, and

then the woman muttered something Ethan could not understand. With a shake of his head, he peered about the room. That the girl had shoved the trunk against the door and had gone to sleep with every lamp blazing left light aplenty in the chamber— enough for him to do a bit of exploration himself.

Moving over to a long table in the corner, Ethan considered the gear the girl had set atop it: A thin, flat black square, along with a book of parchment and pens. Aye, he'd recognized those, the pens, since Guthrie used one oft. On the chair beside the long table, her satchel. He itched to look through it, to see what marvels the modern lass had stashed within its flowery depths. Mayhap, he thought, he'd be better off not knowing.

Turned on their sides and thrown casually on the floor, her shoes. Garnet in color, with what looked like braided twigs for the sole. Again, he shook his head.

The next thing that caught his eye needed no explanation, no matter that he'd never seen anything of the sort. At least, not so little of it. Hanging off the edge of the bed, it was indeed a strange garment. One he'd surely investigate further at a later time. One solid piece of black cloth, a loophole for each arm, no doubt to help bind the girl's heavy breasts—

"Damnation, Ethan, what have you there?" Sorely said, suddenly next to him. He bent his head over the black swath of lace. "Saints."

Ethan thought the very same thing.

"By Christ, man," Aiden said, emerging from the garderobe. "The undergarments in yon bathing chamber aren't big enough to fit a bairn's arse." He shook his head. "I vow the lass has no modesty." One side of his mouth lifted. "I like her."

"Look you how she slumbers," Sorely said. He glanced at Ethan. " 'Tis time, aye?"

Ethan nodded. "Now, keep quiet. We dunna want her to awaken." If she caught the three of them ogling her underclothes, 'twould be much hollering, no doubt.

It was then the cat, curled up at the foot of the bed, sensed their presence. Its ears lay flat against its shiny black head, and a low growl sounded from its throat.

"S-shush, Jack. You big scaredy-cat," the girl said, her voice sleepy and muffled.

Ethan's eyes darted to the heap beneath the bedcovers. He stared, waiting for her to rouse fully. Not that she could see them in their present state . . .

With one hand, the girl pulled the coverlet down to her waist, but her eyes remained closed. Soon, she relaxed, another tiny snore escaped, and then her breathing became long and deep. Her black tunic, sleeveless as it was, had ridden halfway up her stomach, exposing a goodly amount of soft flesh.

"By the rood, she's bonny," Aiden said, mostly to himself.

Ethan frowned. "Shut up or you'll wake her." He didna want to take notice of her bonniness. 'Twas too much of a distraction. By the cross, his men already acted like idiots in her presence, and she'd been in the keep naught for a solid day.

"Ethan?" urged Sorely.

With a deep breath, Ethan fastened his gaze on the girl's face, slowly released the air in his lungs, and then closed his eyes . . .

*   *   *

Murderer!

Amelia sat straight up in bed. Drenched in perspiration, her heart thumping hard, she shook her head to gather her whereabouts. After a few deep breaths, a quick glance at her bedside clock, which read six a.m., she settled down and considered. Scotland. Fourteenth-century keep. Ghosts.

A very big warrior.

"Now *that* was some dream," she said. Amelia recalled what she could before it all faded away. Unsure of the century, although by the looks of the seasoned warriors and their weapons, she was pretty sure it had been hundreds of years before—medieval, maybe. Two groups of men, each wrapped in a different fashion of plaid, fought each other with very big swords. A body lay on the ground, covered in one of the plaids. One older man fought a big, younger, *handsome* man. The younger one had turned briefly and stared straight at her.

Handsome? No, scratch that. Average men were handsome. This was by far anything but an average man. More like knee-numbingly *sexy*. She obviously had seen him on some movie because she certainly hadn't met him in life. As a matter of fact, she didn't think she'd *ever* seen such a man in her life. There were good-looking guys all over the place. Her brothers were very handsome. Butt-heads, but handsome. But those were her brothers and she was prone to take a biased opinion where her own family members were concerned. No other man that she'd seen or met came even a shade close to possessing the breath-robbing factor her dream man emanated. All that from a reverie? God, she was pathetic.

Well, pathetic or not, she didn't want the vision of that wild Highland warrior to leave her. Perhaps she could use his likeness in her book. Historicals weren't her genre, but she could certainly borrow a sexy warrior for a main character. Squeezing her eyes tightly shut, Amelia called forth the memory before it scattered into so many bits of dream dust and disappeared.

Big. No, make that huge. Very broad shoulders, an even broader chest, draped in a rough-looking plaid of various reds, browns, and blacks, and a pair of thick, well-defined calves that disappeared into a set of crisscross-laced leather boots. Dark hair hung in thick long hanks, nearly to the middle of his back, a narrow braid hanging from each temple. A wide silver band encircled each chiseled bicep. Something was etched into the metal, but she couldn't tell what. Dark brows—the right slashed through the middle by a silvery white scar—furrowed over the most amazing pair of pewter-colored eyes. Beneath the right eye, at the outer corner and almost at the cheekbone, another scar, white and crescent-shaped. Lips—Lord have mercy, the lips. Both full, the bottom one fuller than the top. Strong, firm, masculine lips. And gripped in both hands, a very, *very* big sword . . .

I'm called Ethan . . .

Jack hissed, leaped down, and darted under the bed.

Amelia tried hard not to follow suit. Was she hearing things? Had she really imagined the deep-voiced brogue? As far as that thought went, had she imagined all of the weird things that had raised the hair on her neck and made her shove a trunk in front of her door the night before?

She hoped not.

Ethan? Characters had spoken to her in the past, had even dragged her from sleep before. Who's to say Ethan wasn't one of her new potential characters, and that he was indeed speaking and dragging? She'd wanted inspiration, was desperate for it, even, and she was certainly getting a whopping dose of it now. Too bad the dream had been so short-lived. Maybe she should write it all down before she forgot.

Slipping from the bedcovers, Amelia crossed the floor to the table, grabbed her laptop, fluffed a few pillows against the tall oak headboard, and settled back into bed. She powered up, opened a new file, and quickly typed everything she could remember about the dream, including a full description of the gorgeous warrior. Jack, who'd eased out from under his hiding place, jumped up on the bed and curled up next to her, heaved a kitty-cat sigh, and started his outboard-motor purring. She scratched between his silky black ears.

"Jack old boy, you'd better tighten up that soft backbone of yours. I have a feeling we're in for a long, spooky summer, and you can't just go dust bunny diving beneath the bed every time you get scared."

Jack snored.

Amelia stared at her computer screen until her vision blurred. Nothing else would come to her. She tried to imagine the sexy warrior, along with the other men, in a bloody confrontation over . . . something. Her mind, as was its nature over the past year, drew a complete and utterly ridiculous big fat blank.

Maybe she just needed more inspiration. Or a good workout to get the circulation flowing in her brain.

Since she was wide-awake and it was too early for breakfast, she might as well. Then she'd shower, have a bite to eat, and then maybe explore the castle grounds. According to ZuZu, there were acres and acres to investigate.

Happy with a solid plan that would take up at least a quarter of her day, Amelia shut off and closed the laptop, then dug through the clothes chest until she found her black sports bra. It was big, binding, and came nearly to her belly button. Hopefully, she wouldn't give Guthrie a heart attack if he happened in and caught her doing her tae kwon do routine.

After giving her teeth a good brushing, she gargled some mouthwash, bound her hair in a knot, pulled on her lightweight yoga shoes, and squeezed past the trunk she'd pushed against the door of her room. Out in the dim light of the corridor, Amelia stood and listened. Hearing nothing whatsoever, she eased down the stony passageway, soundless, in case the ghosties were sleeping, and made her way to the great hall.

"What in the bluidy hell is she doin'?" asked Sorely.

Ethan watched, intrigued. He had no clue.

Aiden scratched his jaw. "Mayhap she's mad? Look you how she fights invisible enemies."

"Aye, as if there's a soul really there, fightin' back," said Rob.

Ethan had to agree. The lass was indeed odd. She had managed to move the big sofa and flanking chairs off of the long, wide rug before the hearth, stood in the middle of that rug, and then ensued to work up a fierce lather, kicking and striking at the air, with an occasional *Hi-yah!* amidst even more fierce grunts.

"Damn me, but look at the girl's belly," Torloch said. "She's got bluidy muscles there."

"More likely than no', 'tis because of how she kicks her leg so high and punches with such fierceness," Gilchrist, who'd been unusually quiet since the American had arrived, said. He glanced at Ethan. "She's the one."

In truth, Ethan agreed with his brother. He had never seen anyone—not even a warrior—fight so ferociously with no weapons in hand, no' to mention no opponent. 'Twas as though an invisible source attacked her thusly, one only she could see. Intrigued even more, Ethan, along with his kin, moved closer.

With one final shout and spinning kick in the air, the lass landed in a crouched position, slowly rose, and bowed. Breathing heavily, she bent over at the waist, her head hanging down, her hands braced against her knees. The revealing black tunic, hacked off at the midriff, left almost as little to the male imagination as the skintight black trews she wore. Damn him, but he couldn't help how his gaze froze to that round, lush backside.

Until the girl tensed, bent even farther over at the waist, and peered at him from betwixt her knees.

"Och, hell, Ethan. She's spied us," Sorely said under his breath.

"Think you she can hear us, as well?" Rob said. He gave a low whistle and scratched his head. "Damn receptive, she is."

Ethan closed his eyes and called forth a rather pleasant image: himself, strangling his two bumbling kinsmen. Even so, he opened his eyes and stared at the girl, still bent over, round rump in the air. Saints, what a sight. Then she slowly rose, until her posture stood as erect as a stone statue, shoulders back, chest heaving with each breath. Scared? Aye, she was. But strangely enough, she wasn't running. He exchanged a brief glance with Aiden, whose amused look irritated him for some reason, and then he had no other choice but to clear his bluidy throat and address the lass, before she thought them all a big lot of idiots and left Munro Keep for good.

Ethan took a step forward, crossed his arms over his chest, and stared at the girl's head. He cleared his throat. "Lass, we've need to have speech with you."

The girl's shoulders began to shake.

Ethan took yet another step forward. "Er, lass?"

This time, a snort escaped her. Then she turned and faced him. Was that a bluidy grin on her face? After a deep breath, she walked toward him, stopped, and looked up. Her already-wide eyes widened even more, but still she did not bolt.

"Hello. I realize you're a powerful figment of my lonely, haven't-had-sex-in-way-too-long imagination"— her eyebrows lifted as she looked at him from boot tip to eyelash—"but I'd prefer you to stay nice and safe in my dreams, if you please." She smiled wide, showing scores of straight, white teeth. "All of you."

She stepped around Ethan, dodged Sorely and Gilchrist, gave Torloch a wide berth, and even smiled at Rob. But as she approached that smiling jackass, Aiden, by the cross, he sidestepped, as did she, once, twice—until the lass huffed and stormed ahead.

And walked straight through him.

With a squeak, the American stopped, her jaw slid open, and she made a strangled sound that Ethan did not fancy in the least. Then she took off at a dead run, straight to the great hall door.

"Stop her, Ethan, before she gets away!" Rob shouted, looking as though he may just take off after her.

"Nay," Ethan said. He kept his eyes trained on the storyteller until she was out of sight. "Let her alone for now. She'll come to us."

Gilchrist walked up and stood next to him. "How do you know?"

Ethan recalled the girl's intriguing eyes. "She will."

And he prayed mightily that she would.

Chapter 4

A week later, and no matter what Amelia did, she couldn't get the vision out of her head. You know: *that* vision. Even though she'd seen nothing more of said vision—or of those amazing pewter-colored eyes, swarthy skin, and long, dark hair of the leader of said vision, the memory remained. Embedded. Emblazoned. Digging deep into her thoughts like an unwavering, gritty worm chewing its way to the core of an apple. Her brain was the apple.

That warrior—Ethan—was the worm.

Chomp chomp, chomp chomp . . .

Of course, had she not been busy dreaming of fourteenth-century Scottish warriors every single night since, perhaps she would have been able to exile the memory. Not only was she thinking about those same six big warriors who had watched her work out, but she was thinking about the fact that she'd run straight through one of them. All big, all wearing the same colored and patterned plaid wraps, all armed with very big swords, all ferocious-looking.

"You are a nutcase, Landry," Amelia said to herself in the mirror. She smeared on a few more globs of green clay facial mask, leaving only her eyes, nostrils, and lips exposed. So intense were the nightly dreams that not only had they completely exhausted her during the waking hours of the day, but they'd provided excellent fodder for her new novel.

Not that it was in any way, shape, or form organized, that novel. But she had an idea. And it was unlike anything she'd ever written before. The idea was still fermenting in her brain, but hopefully she'd have a *Eureka!* moment very soon. If only the dreams didn't have so many plot holes . . .

Finished applying the clay mask, Amelia turned out the bathroom light, fished her thinking ball—which was a tennis ball with the words *Think, dammit, think!* written on it—out of the trunk, slipped on her sneakers, and started for the door. A nice walk through the cool, creepy corridors, in her comfy yoga pants and long-sleeved MonsterCon T-shirt, while the mask worked miracles on her pores would be just the thing to get her mind working before bedtime. After a hearty supper of Guthrie's pot roast and potatoes, she needed to walk anyway. A too-full belly would no doubt lead to horrible nightmares. At least that's what her granny had always told her.

Slipping into the passageway, Amelia turned right out of her room and walked slowly, tossing the tennis ball in the air and catching it as she let her mind wander.

She'd read the book ZuZu had given her from cover to cover. The Bluidy Munro was truly a fearful specter to be reckoned with. According to lore, the Munro and his clansmen, in cahoots with the devil, mind you, murdered innocent young women in an attempt to steal their souls—so they could live forever—and then would hang their soulless bodies out for the villagers to see. Merciless. Cold-blooded. Psychos. She hadn't felt any of those things. Sure, there'd been pranky-pranks played on her, like the string of her shirt being tugged. But malevolent threats? Not a single one.

Amelia tossed the ball high.

It didn't come back down.

Amelia peered into the shadows of the ceiling above but didn't see anything. No ball. No Bluidy Munro. No sexy Highland warrior. Nothing.

For some reason, that made her wonder a big, fat *something*.

Were the guys real? Were they ghosts? Sheesh, she'd never had a ghostly encounter before, but she'd not dismissed the phenomenon, either. Haunted stuff fascinated her. She loved it. Every October she was glued to the History Channel, which had dozens of episodes of *Scariest Places on Earth* running the entire month. So why did she have such a hard time believing she'd seen six big warriors in the great hall?

Amelia blew out a breath. "Okay. *Uncle.* I give up," she said, tight-lipped since the mask had dried into concrete. She peeked around without moving her head. "I'm an educated woman with a third-degree black belt in tae kwon do." God, she sounded like an idiot, talking out loud to no one. "So. If you're there, show me. *Educate* me. Because right now, all the silly little pranks you've been playing on me are not helping . . . your, er, . . . cause." She blinked as the word died on her lips. The ball dropped down and bounced into an alcove.

The warrior from her dreams walked out of that same shadowy alcove and stopped not three feet away, and Amelia's lips went numb. He looked quite solid, and the dim light from the wall lamp did little to reveal anything other than half his face, half his body, which included one of his arms crossed over one side of his chest, that silver band encircling a big rocky bicep, and the monster-sized sword strapped to his back. Shadows colored the other half of him black.

Two dark brows pulled together into a fierce scowl as he drew closer and peered at her face. "Dunna run away, lass. I willna hurt you." He cocked his head. "What the bluidy hell is that?"

Amelia, now only able to purse her lips, squeaked out a response. "Clay." Adrenaline slammed through her veins and her heart slammed inside her chest, she was so scared. Too scared to run, for sure. Too scared to *move*, much less anything else.

The man nodded. "Good. 'Twill keep you quiet whilst I speak."

Amelia tried to frown, but the clay did indeed keep her face in check. "Who are you?" God, she wanted to run screaming down the corridor, but she was glued to the very stones of the passageway floor. She'd called him forth, and now she didn't know what on earth to do with him. "*What* are you? A ghost?" In the back of her sick, demented mind, she wished for a pad of paper, or better yet, her laptop, to jot everything down, just to make sure she didn't forget a single detail of the insane moment. Although it was probably just a bad case of castle fever, and she was imagining the whole thing in her slowly deteriorating mind. Next she'd be chasing poor Guthrie around the castle with an ax, maniacal grin plastered to her face, shouting "Here's Meelie!"

"I'm no' a spirit." He eyed her, frowning. "Are you going to bolt, lass?"

Amelia gave a shaky laugh, and she felt the hard clay on her face crack. "I'm not sure just yet." She wasn't sure if knowing he wasn't a ghost made her feel better, or worse. If he wasn't a ghost, then . . . *what* was he?

"Fair enough, girl. Mayhap 'twould be best if we had speech in the hall." His mouth quirked at the corners. "Space aplenty for you to run, if the notion strikes you."

Drawing a deep breath, Amelia blew it slowly out. "Okay." She turned and glanced behind her, at the direction she'd come from. "I've got to wash this off . . ."

When she turned back around, the big warrior had disappeared.

A shiver ran through Amelia as she hurried to her room, glancing at every darkened shadowy alcove and cubby space she passed. If he wasn't a ghost, which made her give pause and question her own sanity for even considering such, then what *was* he? He'd just disappeared before her eyes. Well, almost, but no way could a man that big run away without her noticing. He had to be every inch of six foot seven. She was a tall girl herself at five foot ten, and she'd had to lean her head way back to look him in the eye.

As Amelia slipped inside her room, she paused. Had the whole thing really happened? Maybe all the seclusion was driving her insane. Maybe she'd thought the whole thing up.

Dunna keep me waiting, lass . . .

Amelia gulped as she checked the sexy voice that had suddenly appeared inside her head. With an apprehension she'd never experienced, except for that one time she and her brothers had been caught by the school principal lighting Black Cats and throwing them into a big metal trash can behind the band room, Amelia hurried through the washing of her face and then slipped out of the room.

Only then did she give a brief thought to just how bossy the no-ghost warrior was.

Minutes later, Amelia, stomach in knots, took the last step off the staircase and entered the great hall. She scanned the spacious, dim room, until her gaze found his. And that's when her breath jammed in her lungs, and she did everything in her power not to wheeze or fall into a coughing spell. Partially because she knew in her heart she was looking at someone of the supernatural nature, or at least someone from another century who'd somehow become trapped. That was her guess, anyway. Partially, too, because the enormous man taking up quite a lot of space near the hearth was, hands down, the most enigmatic, potent male she'd ever been in the presence of—even if he was a figment of her imagination. Or trapped in some odd supernatural gap in time. All of her peculiar critiques of the situation made her feel somewhat comforted. Enough not to run screaming out the front door, anyway.

Amelia took a deep breath and walked across the hall. The plaid-draped warrior stood with a wide, masculine stance, an arrogant lift to his square chin, and with a muscle clinching at his jaw. His arms were folded across his massive chest, biceps cut out of stone and sheathed by wide bands of silver. Piercing pewter eyes remained trained on hers, unflinching as she took each fake-brave step, and even if she'd wanted to, Amelia didn't have the strength to look away. The word *mesmerized* came to mind. Finally, she stopped, keeping the sofa between them. To say her throat was tight and the air wouldn't even budge from her lungs was an understatement. She sincerely hoped she didn't wheeze out loud.

She was freaking petrified out of her gourd.

And the fact that this guy—Ethan—studied her with such scrutinizing intensity made her fight the urge to squirm where she stood. Inconspicuously shifting her weight, Amelia clenched her hands together behind her back, kept her own gaze glued to his, and waited for him to speak first. Finally, he did.

"You've heard of me, aye?" he said.

The words sounded almost unintelligible, so heavy and deep the accent. Amelia concentrated and thought a moment. "I'm not even sure you're standing there."

She thought his mouth tipped up at the corner, but she couldn't be sure.

The big guy continued to stare. "I'm Ethan Munro." He inclined his head slightly. "You're in my keep, lass. Know you not who the owner is?"

Amelia shrugged. "Mr. and Mrs. Conaway?" That's the couple ZuZu claimed owned it, anyhow, and she'd shucked out a pretty penny for the summer lease, too.

"No' the true owners." He cocked his head and frowned. "Need I convince you of my presence?"

Amelia considered. And then considered some more. Rubbing her chin, she asked the question that she darn well knew the answer to. "Was it you who warned me away from that door over there?" She pointed at the door. "And pulled my shirt strings? Scared my cat?"

He moved toward her. "And blew on yer neck scores of times, aye." Again, the corner of his very sexy mouth tipped up—barely noticeable, even, but it was there. *Amusement.* "You, lass, snore like a seasoned warrior."

Amelia stared, skeptical, of course. If she were making the whole vision of Ethan Munro up, then by God, her visions had certainly improved. From what she could recall, her last vision involved a Whopper and large fries. Extra onions.

Ethan came around the sofa, edged closer to Amelia, and stopped a few feet away. He had those big arms crossed at the chest, legs braced wide, and the hilt of that big sword poking out of a leather sheath over his right shoulder. *Which means he'd reach for the sword with his left hand, which means he's a southpaw . . .*

With absolutely no shame whatsoever, Ethan openly watched every move Amelia made. He studied her, those unusual silvery eyes inspecting her feet, her legs, waist, breasts—where he spent a little too much linger time—and finally, her face. Being a professional people watcher, which had given her access to various and sundry personality traits for her characters, Amelia got the immediate sense that Ethan was scared of no one, that he did what he pleased, and he didn't care a bit what people thought of him.

Amelia liked that.

"You're a verra big lass."

Hmm. Apparently, he spoke his mind without pause, too. She frowned. "Well, that proves it."

He cocked a dark brow. "Proves what?"

Amelia stepped forward and looked up. "You must be real, because a figment of my imagination would gush about my beauty. Not voice their opinion about my largeness."

"I didna say you were large. I said verra big."

"Well, then." She fought the urge to tug her T-shirt down over her obviously big behind. Damn her daddy for passing on the bubble-butt gene. "That certainly clears it all up." She chanced a look at his face, and he had that darn almost-smirk on again. Better to change gears, she thought, from her *verra big* physique—whatever—to something a little less embarrassing. "The name's Amelia, by the way." She extended her hand. "Amelia Landry." Although she thought the use of the word *lass* was pretty darn cute.

Her hand hung in midair. Ethan didn't reach for it. Looked at it, but didn't reach for it.

He inclined his head to her outstretched hand. "Odd, the customs you modern maids possess." Ethan's gaze moved to hers. "But with regret, I cannot accept your greeting."

Dropping her hand, Amelia crossed her arms over her chest and shifted her weight. "Why not?"

"Because, Ms. Landry," he said, his voice heavy, thick, his gaze intense. "I've no substance."

Giving his incredible physique another once-over, Amelia had a difficult time believing he lacked substance. As a matter of fact, Ethan Munro all but leaked substance all over the great hall floor. "Who are you, exactly? I mean, I've seen you. Before." She shrugged one shoulder. "In a dream."

The naughty grin that lifted both corners of his mouth made Amelia's throat go very dry.

"I've been the object of many a lass's dream, Ms. Landry."

Gulp.

Taking in an inconspicuous breath, Amelia blew it out slowly, then narrowed her gaze. "Well, Mr. Munro—"

"Ethan."

"Ethan"—she took a brave step in his direction—"you've yet to answer even one of my questions in full. Why is that, if you were so adamant about speaking with me?"

The grin disappeared from the warrior's face, an intense, stern one in its stead. " 'Tis not my intention to play games with you, Ms. Landry. I had to make sure you could stomach the truth."

"Which is?"

After a second of solid staring into her eyes, which more than set Amelia on edge, Ethan turned and paced, with an occasional swipe of his hand to his jaw. Finally, he stopped by the hearth, facing its empty depths. "What sort of dreams have you been having of late, lass?"

Amelia considered. "Well, you're in them, for one. Perfect detail, right down to that half-moon scar by your eye." She shook her head. "Bizarre."

Ethan didn't move a muscle. "What else?"

Over the past week, Amelia in fact had dreamed the most strangest of dreams involving the big man standing in front of the fireplace. "It's all disjointed, really," she said. "Lacking coherence to the point of frustration." She shrugged. "But it's given me great ideas." Moving around the sofa, she started toward the hearth. "Do you know why I'm here?"

Still, he didn't look at her. "I heard you're a bard of sorts."

"Right." A *bard*. She liked that. "In the dream, I see you, and others dressed like you, in the same color plaids. You're fighting another group of guys." She thought for a moment. "I think there's a dead body on the ground between the two groups of men. The rest is mostly a lot of sword fighting and battle scenes." She looked at his profile. Strong jaw, straight nose, long dark hair, a muscle clenching in his cheek. "I wonder if I haven't gone crazy. Am I really here alone? Have I just imagined you, Guthrie, the other non-ghosts?" She ducked her head, to get a better view of his face. "Am I? Crazy?"

Ethan drew in a hearty breath, then turned to look at her. "Touch me."

Amelia blinked. "Excuse me?"

He inclined his head. "Touch me. It doesna matter where."

She quirked a brow. "You do realize that you're giving perfect permission to an almost-thirty-year-old female with a vivid imagination to touch you anywhere?"

The tenseness in his features eased a bit, a tiny spark flashed in his silvery eyes, but he said nothing. Only gave a short nod.

Not that she couldn't promise *not* to cop a feel. Even if Ethan Munro was only a figment of her imagination, she couldn't promise not to try.

So, she copped a feel.

Rather, she *tried* to.

Even as Amelia reached for that big, cut-from-granite bicep, the reality of what was about to happen registered in her brain before she grasped the signal said pitiful brain was trying to send.

Like touching an image cast by an old movie projector, Amelia's hand slipped right through Ethan.

She could do nothing but stare wide-eyed at what she thought to be a living, breathing man. She'd obviously thought wrong. The words she wanted desperately to say simply wouldn't form, instead getting all jumbled up in her mouth and forming nothing that made a lick of sense.

Ethan held up a hand to shush her. "Nay, girl, I'm no' a ghost. I told you that."

"Well," Amelia said, finding her tongue useful once more, and taking a few swipes through his person to make sure she'd seen correctly, "what the heck are you, then?"

"Enchanted," he said. "We're all bluidy enchanted."

Amelia stared at him a moment. Had he said *we're*?

Ethan's gaze fell behind her, and she turned just as the other warriors appeared.

Chapter 5

"At least Jack Torrence had a freaking ax . . ." But what good would an ax do if it'd pass straight through the body you were hacking at?

"Easy, lass," Ethan said, his voice deep, soothing. " 'Tis naught but my kin, from before. They willna hurt you."

Amelia met each warrior with a shaky breath. Just like before, when she'd been caught doing her tae kwon do sets, they looked real enough, the same as Ethan. Each carried a giant sword over his shoulder, long hair, midcalf boots, and the same plaid pattern and color as Ethan's. They were the same guys from before.

The one, Aiden, looked as though he'd love to have her for supper, *one slow lick at a time . . .*

"Ms. Landry?" Ethan said.

Amelia jumped from her naughty thoughts and blew out a gusty breath. "Well." She managed to squeeze through two of the warriors and start mindlessly walking. "Well."

Without really thinking, she headed straight across the great hall and out the door.

*   *   *

"Who the bluidy hell is Jack Torrence?"

Ethan stared at the front door for a moment longer, and then glanced at Torloch. "Damned if I know. But she thinks he's armed."

"I dunna fancy that pasty look affixed to her face," said Sorely. He took a step toward the door. "Mayhap I should go after her?"

Aiden grabbed him by the arm. "Nay, little lad. No doubt you've scared her with that jagged scar across your jaw." He nodded and slapped Sorely on the back. "I'll go."

"None of you fools are going anywhere," Ethan said. He scrubbed his chin, then shifted his belt. "Where's Guthrie?"

"He went to see Widow Malcolm," Rob said. "He willna be back until he's eaten every crumb of her pound cake, no doubt."

The men chuckled.

"Stay here, ye ken?" Ethan said. "I'll go find her."

"Why you?" asked Gilchrist, frowning.

Ethan shrugged. "I've had more speech with her than the lot of you." He met each man's stare. "Now that she's seen you, I'll try to coax her back inside."

As Ethan left the great hall, five sets of grumbles and various curses followed him out. Not that he blamed a one of them. They'd not had the pleasure of having a lass about the keep for centuries. One that stayed, anyway.

Sifting through the front doorway, Ethan stopped just outside on the gravel drive. As the midsummer-evening light shone a filtered, yellowish hue, even at such a late hour, he searched for the fetching bard.

She hadn't run away scared. More likely to consider things. She did quite a lot of that, he thought.

Not seeing her out front, he started around the side of the keep, toward the loch. 'Twas there, at the bank, that he found her, facing the black water.

Ethan stood and watched her for some time. Modern maids were indeed something unique to consider. He'd seen a few over time, those who'd wandered onto his land before the keep was restored, and those who'd purchased it in the years that followed.

Not a one had stayed more than a fortnight.

And, he noticed, not a one was nearly as intriguing as the one presently throwing rocks into his loch.

He considered the reason she'd come. She'd said 'twas to write her story. Mayhap the quiet beauty of the Highlands, or the sweet scent of the clover, or the craggy ruggedness of his land, urged her to come and stay. Mayhap it helped her pen her stories. For him, the Munro, even in his enchanted state, 'twas his birthright. He needed the Highlands, and especially his own land, as much as he needed air to breathe.

The lass was sitting now upon a big rock close to the shoreline. He briefly wondered what ran through her mind. Had she an inkling of the horrors he and his men were accused of? Probably not in detail, for even *they* didn't know everything. It pained him now to even think on it. But he'd placed a portion of those horrors in her dreams.

A *plop* broke the quiet as the girl threw a stone into the water. She heaved a big, exaggerated sigh, pulled her knees to her chest, and wrapped her arms about her ankles. After settling her chin atop those knees, she spoke.

She continued to stare out across the loch. "You're the Bluidy Munro."

Ethan sat down on the ground beside her. "Aye."

"I thought so." She turned her head to look at him, now resting her ear against her knees. For several moments, she studied him with those unusual eyes. "You don't seem so horrible to me."

Relief washed over him, for whatever odd notion, and he gave a nod. "That you haven't left the keep yet is a wonder in itself."

"Why is that?"

Ethan shrugged. "Most run screaming in terror."

One nicely shaped brow lifted. "Do you frighten them on purpose?"

A smile pulled at his mouth. "No more than what you experienced."

She brushed her long, fair hair back, grinned, and tossed another stone into the loch. "I happen to like scary things. I write scary things." She scowled at him, although Ethan thought it was in play. "And I don't frighten easy."

This time, he laughed. "Well, lass—"

"Amelia."

For some reason, Ethan nearly choked on the name. "Amelia. I suppose you've proven yourself a mighty warrior, then." He cocked his head and studied her in the waning light. "Why do you like to write scary things?"

She shrugged. "I don't know. It fascinates me, I guess. You know, things that are unexplained, phenomenal? Too fantastic for the brain to wrap around?" A grin split her face. "Sort of like you."

Ethan tried to imagine anyone's innards—especially a brain—wrapping about any one part of his body. He couldn't. "I see." He didn't really, but that she thought him *fantastic*, whatever that meant, was something to consider.

"So you're enchanted?" she asked.

Ethan nodded. "I can't think of anything else, save cursed, that would fit our state of being." He reached over his shoulder and shifted his blade, which was poking him in the back. "We didn't die, or so we all believe, and each eve during the gloaming, we gain substance, so we know we're not ghosts. Otherwise, we sift about, flimsy as specters, drifting through walls and—"

"You do what?"

Ethan blinked. "We drift through walls."

"No, the other thing."

Ethan nodded. "Aye, we gain substance each eve at the gloaming hour. We cannot leave Munro land, but we do gain substance. We know not why, but 'tis true enough."

"You can eat, drink? Touch?" she asked.

"Aye."

With a long forefinger, she rubbed her chin. "Guthrie can see you, can't he?"

Ethan considered. "Aye, old Guthrie can see us. Not all can, though. 'Tis why we're forced to, er, play tricks, as you say, to find out who can and canna see. Who might sense our presence." He met her gaze. "You're quite receptive, by the by."

"I'll just add that to my résumé." Amelia slapped at her neck. "What *are* these bugs eating me alive?"

"Midges. Ferocious no matter the century." He inclined his head to the keep. "Much more so than those fools inside."

Amelia clasped her hands about her ankles, her

gaze not once leaving his. "I didn't leave because I was scared."

Ethan nodded. " 'Tis obvious."

"I was just processing. You know? Being *receptive* is a unique experience."

He quite imagined so.

"Actually, I think I might still be processing."

This time, Ethan chuckled. "No doubt, lass." He stood. "I'll see you inside, and tomorrow, we'll continue." He adjusted his sword. "Does that suit?"

"Sure." She rose, brushed off her backside, and stepped off the rock.

Together, side by side, they started for the keep. As they walked, Ethan measured in his mind just how unusual their situation was—he, from the fourteenth century, she from the present, walking together. More than out of the ordinary, to be true. Being a big lad himself, he towered over Amelia— no matter that she was a tall woman. The top of her head still reached to only just below his shoulders. He considered the advantages of that height difference and slid his gaze downward. With little caution, the lass picked her way over the scattered rock and mounds of thistle dotting the meadow between the keep and the loch. Far from being a prissy sort, she carried herself with a confidence he would admire in anyone, warrior or maid. And she did it whilst garbed in the most intriguing, modern fashion. He wasn't quite sure he'd ever get used to seeing women not clothed in bolts of linen. Those snug black trews she wore, now, he rather fancied those.

As if you've a right to fancy anything, Munro . . .

"Well, it's late, so I guess I'll be going now."

Ethan snapped from his thoughts and looked

down at Amelia. Those wide almond-shaped eyes flashed dark in the summer eve's uncanny light. He stepped away from her and clasped his hands behind his back. "Aye. Get some rest, girl, and we'll have speech in the morn."

A throat cleared then. "What's wrong with having a bit of speech now?"

Amelia's swift intake of breath, not to mention an odd noise from deep in her throat that sounded much like a field mouse, made him notice Rob, who had just poked his big enchanted head right through the door. His brother flashed Amelia a grin—one Ethan would have liked to remove thusly and more than likely would. Later. He gave him a frown. "The lass was just headed off to her chambers."

"I don't mind saying hello to everyone," Amelia said. "That way, I won't be quite as nervous tomorrow." She heaved a big sigh. "I hope."

Ethan studied her for a moment, and then gave a curt nod. "Verra well, then." He inclined his head toward the door. "To the great hall, Amelia. Mayhap you can stomach the knowing of my kin after all." He raised an eyebrow. " 'Tis rumored we're a bloodthirsty lot."

Amelia shrugged. "Guess I'll take my chances." She grinned.

"And she fights like a bluidy berserker," Rob said, giving an enthusiastic nod. "Come in, then, lass, and meet the Munros."

Rob's head disappeared through the oak.

Amelia visibly shivered. "Man. That is just freaky." She eyed him with caution. "Inside?"

A feeling bunched up in his throat, an odd sort of mood that, until verra recently, he'd not experienced in quite some time. 'Twas laughter. Damn him, the lass made him laugh.

He, Ethan Munro. The Bluidy Munro, for Christ's sake.

Still, he fought the sensation the girl easily caused within him. 'Twas best to show as little weakness as possible. And mirth was, indeed, a weakness. It stood for ease of friendship, trust—mayhap more. None of which he had to give.

How matters would turn out was as much a mystery as Devina's death.

With a nod, he inclined his head once more to the door. "After you."

Amelia gave him a bold inspection, those strange eyes assessing his as though she could see far deeper than what she let on. "I'm looking forward to a little more in-depth info about those crazy dreams." She gave the door a push and grinned. "I'm starting to think there's a heck of a lot more to Ethan Munro than even he knows."

With that, she stepped into the great hall to face his kin.

And with a gusty sigh, Ethan followed.

The lass had no idea just how verra true her wise words rang.

He only hoped she could withstand that truth.

Chapter 6

Wow. Talk about a reality check. Or maybe an *unreality* check. Freaky. Honest-to-God *Twilight Zone* freaky.

She loved it.

Amelia considered all the experiences she'd had in her twenty-eight years of life. Quite a number of them, truth be told. There'd been several she could recall with extreme fondness—most of those involving her nutty siblings, along with her kooky friend ZuZu. Boy, they'd all gotten into so much trouble as kids. Funny trouble. The kind that made you enjoy remembering and retelling the core of the trouble to anyone who'd listen. Firecrackers-in-the-trash-can-at-school kind of funny trouble.

Then there were those certain extraordinary experiences you preferred to keep solely to yourself, unwilling to share the moment with anyone. Like the time Billy Morgan had kissed her on the Ferris wheel at the fall fair when she was twelve (Billy had a lisp and somehow, it had *worked* for her). Or the time her granny had sent her down to the river to cast a net for shrimp early one morning, and a dolphin and her baby swam right up to the floating dock and surfaced, and they'd all stared at one another, shared a few surreal moments in time. The baby had played a bit, diving all around its mama and then popping up to see if Amelia had noticed. She'd wanted to reach out and touch that cute little baby, with its slick, gray skin, so badly, but she hadn't. She'd just sat there in her cutoff jeans and tank top, feet dangling in the water, watching in total awe. Amelia had been fourteen that summer. What a slice of magic that'd been, those dolphins. And she'd never told a soul about it. Not even ZuZu.

This experience, Amelia decided, was definitely being added to that particular list of keep-to-your-greedy-self, surreal experiences. Had she a photo of it, she'd hide it beneath a secret panel in her dresser, where she'd take it out at least once a day to look at it, then put it back so no one else could see.

Never would she forget the midsummer night in the Scottish Highlands, where she'd entered a fourteenth-century castle and encountered five of the biggest, burliest, surliest, *sexiest* guys she'd ever seen—not including the biggest and surliest of the bunch, who'd followed her inside. Six men in all. They encircled her, making her feel slightly puny, but not really. She'd seen them before—first, in her dreams, then in what she thought was real life.

They claimed to be from the fourteenth century.

She had the inclination to fully believe them, too.

Even in their flimsy state of enchantedness, the primitive male power that poured from each warrior left her with little doubt that they were who, and from when, they claimed. No man she'd ever met had come within an inch of putting out the sort of male vibes these guys were putting out. Sort of like being in the midst of a pack of alpha wolves, she supposed, yet not in a threatening way. She found it quite hard to explain, really—even if to just herself.

Finally, Ethan spoke. "Amelia, my kinsmen." He nodded in the direction of each one, starting from her right "Sorely. Aiden. Rob. Torloch. Gilchrist." He glanced at her. "Rob and Gil are my brothers. Sorely and Aiden are cousins, from my father's brother."

Amelia met each one's stare. Fierce, all of them, and the resemblance between Ethan and his brothers— even his cousins—was uncanny. All with various shades of dark hair, all worn long, all with a thin braid to each temple. Ethan was the only one, though, with those pewter gray eyes.

Her eyes clapped on Torloch, and he stared right back. He looked different from the rest, with hanks of dark blond hair, high cheekbones, and a pair of eyes she'd not soon forget: one brown, the other nearly white-blue. Before she could say anything, Rob answered her silent question.

"Tor there was a wild bairn. Our da found him in the wood whilst on a hunt. Half starved, he was, and barely walkin'."

"Aye," said Gilchrist. "An' givin' Da's leg a good once-over, as if he thought 'twas mutton for supper."

Tor gave Amelia a gentle smile and a curt nod. "Lass, I'm no' nearly as wild as all that anymore, I promise."

"Mayhap no', but I've seen him tear a man's arm clean—"

" 'Tis enough for tonight, lads," Ethan interrupted Rob. "The girl needs her rest."

Tor continued to look at her, but with a glint of mischief in his mismatched eyes.

Aiden nodded. "So right, Ethan. I'll make sure she gets to her chambers safely. Come along, lass."

He winked at Amelia.

Ethan gave Aiden a big, mean scowl. "You'll stay down here with the others, fool." He glanced at Amelia. "Come, girl. Whilst you still can."

Amelia gave the five warriors a smile. "Good night. Even if I'm making you all up in my head, it was very nice meeting you all. If I wake up and you're still here, I'll talk to you some more."

The men chuckled.

Just as she and Ethan reached the stairs, the front door swung open and Guthrie walked in. He stopped, Amelia and Ethan stopped, and everyone stared at one another.

" 'Bout time," Guthrie muttered, yanking off his soft cap. " 'Twas getting' damn near suffocatin', hidin' you big louts from the lass." He shuffled off across the hall. "Breakfast's at eight sharp, girl. Dunna be late."

Well, if she was crazy, at least she had company. She fought a giggle. "I won't. Good night."

Guthrie muttered as he disappeared into the kitchen.

With a final wave to the warriors, Amelia started up the stairs, Ethan close behind.

Once in the passageway, Amelia looked at Ethan, who now walked beside her. "Why at sundown?"

The big man stared straight ahead, his brows pulled together. Finally, he shrugged, but didn't look at her. "I canna tell you most of what's happened. Especially about our existence."

Amelia noticed how his yards of plaid swished

around his muscular legs as he walked. "How come?"

With one heavily chiseled arm, he adjusted the sword poking out of its sheath over one shoulder. Again, she observed the wide band of silver encircling his bicep, as well as the intricate carvings engraved in the metal.

He stopped, and it was then Amelia noticed that they'd already made it to her room. Ethan looked down at her, his ghostly form very real and taking up quite a lot of space in the tight corridor. "Because one minute, lass, we were fightin' for our lives. The next minute"—he waved his hand, the muscles flinching with the movement—"we were surrounded by a thick cloud of mist. And then, darkness."

Amelia liked to hear his strange accent, so heavy and thick she could barely understand him at times. She suspected it was the combination of medieval and Scottish that was so intriguing. His O's sounded like *oo*'s; so instead of *down*, it was *doon*. And instead of *don't*, he said *dunna*. And *canna* instead of *can't*. More times than not, she found herself wishing he'd carry on a long conversation, just like she'd done in high school with the foreign exchange student from Norway who'd sat behind her in World History. She'd thought his accent was pretty darn cool.

Ethan's was downright charming. Sexy-charming, at that. As in melt-in-your-shoes sexy-charming . . .

"Amelia?"

She blinked. "Yes?"

A grin, one Ethan apparently fought, pulled at the corners of his mouth. "You were rollin' in heather."

Did she forget to mention how incredibly sexy it

was when he rolled his R's? "What's rollin' in heather mean?"

Those silvery eyes bore into hers. "It means your inner thoughts overcame you."

Amelia smiled. So he knew—suspected, at least— that she was ogling him in some way. So what? She was a grown woman with plenty of ogling rights, she thought. "That's what writers do, Mr. Munro. Lots and lots of heather rollin'."

This time, he grinned. "Verra well, lass." He leaned a bit closer. "The name's Ethan."

She gulped. And she was pretty sure he saw that, too. "Okay, Ethan." She pushed open her door. "I'll see you tomorrow, okay?"

Just then, Jack scooted out of her room. As he neared Ethan, the black cat skidded to a halt, arched his back, and hissed.

Amelia scolded him. "Jack, it's just Ethan, so you might as well stop getting all wacky crazy and be nice."

Jack meowed and scooted down the dark passageway, disappearing into the shadows.

Amelia frowned. "Scaredy-cat." She glanced at Ethan before stepping through the door. He leaned against the passageway wall now, arms crossed, just . . . staring. "Are you going to make me dream again?"

He studied her for some time. "Do you want me to?"

She considered. "Yeah. I do."

Ethan gave a slight nod. "Verra well, then."

"And one more thing," she said. "During that space of time that you gain substance? Do you guys run around eating everything Guthrie can fix, take showers, take naps? What do you do?"

Ethan pushed off the wall and came closer, and Amelia had to tip her head back to keep eye contact. "Until now, aye, we did all of those things. Now go to bed, girl. I promise, you'll need your rest for the morn."

She nodded. "Okay. Good night."

"And to you."

With that, Amelia shut the door. Right away, she noticed her breath came faster, and her heart thumped heavy. Now, how on earth can a seven-hundred-year-old enchanted guy make her have *that* sort of reaction? She shook her head.

You're rollin' in heather again, lass . . .

Amelia jumped. "Stop that!"

Ethan's laugh echoed, whether in her head only, or from just outside the door, she couldn't quite tell.

She didn't quite care. It was a deep, hypnotic sound that rolled smooth and heavy from his tongue and was extremely male, and she decided she could certainly make do with hearing it as often as possible. But for some reason, even though she'd forced the sound out of him a few times already, she felt like it wasn't all that easy to make Ethan Munro laugh.

How she loved a good challenge.

She might have a serious case of writer's block, but she hardly ever lacked the wit to make some-one laugh.

Kicking off her shoes, she changed back into her yoga pants and tank top, brushed her teeth, wrapped her hair into a ball with a scrunchie, and climbed into bed. Lying there, she stared at the ceiling and thought about everything that had happened since she'd slid behind the wheel of her rental car at the airport in Edinburgh. Mostly, since she'd set foot on Munro land.

She'd come to the Highlands in search of inspiration, peace, tranquillity—anything to jump-start her brain, which had turned to a mushy, useless, Cream of Wheat sort of thing lately. Well, over the past year, anyway. Perhaps her major brain cramp had a little something to do with finding out the one guy she'd trusted with her heart—Dillon—had not only found himself another girlfriend, but had decided to relocate. To Italy. With the new girlfriend. And their new baby.

Amelia kicked off the covers and blew out a gusty sigh. She wasn't a bitter person, not by any means. Really, she'd only wished that Dillon's wein—er, ahem—his *masculinity* would shrivel up and fall off like some aged old prune the first three months after the breakup. She'd cried, she'd gotten mad, and she'd poked the Dillon doll ZuZu had made her at least three times each day with very sharp pins. It had made her feel better. After that, she'd decided to think of the entire ugly situation as a big fat learning curve in her life.

For some reason, though, her brain had decided to stop functioning as a writer. Ideas would come to her, and they'd fizzle out. The thought had struck her, more than once, that just maybe she'd exhausted all of her murderous, who-done-it ideas. Maybe she needed to take her writing in a different direction. Try something new.

Nothing came to mind.

At least, not until she'd found a group of enchanted fourteenth-century warriors semiliving in a dark castle in the Highlands, not to mention the leader of the clan, who was referred to in lore and legend as the Bluidy Munro. She could barely wait to hear the full tale in the morning.

She flipped off the bedside lamp, fluffed her pillow, and clasped her hands behind her head. She no longer worried about Jack—he'd learned where the escape route was through the kitchen door, so if he needed to go out, he would. Otherwise, he'd explore the castle at his leisure. Too many castle rats to chase, she thought with a shudder.

Meanwhile, Amelia wanted to hurry up and go to sleep, just so she could experience another of Ethan's bizarre implanted dreams. She stared at the ceiling some more, turned over, glanced at her Indiglo watch, which read 1:20 a.m., turned *back* over, and then closed her eyes. After a while, drowsiness washed over her and Amelia felt herself drifting off to sleep . . .

'Twill be you next, lass . . .

With a gasp, Amelia woke up. Sitting straight up in bed, she found herself breathless, her forehead beaded with sweat, her heart slamming against her ribs. Only the light she'd left on in the bathroom cast a slit of dim glow across the chamber floor. Everything looked murky still.

She shook her head. *That dream*, she thought. She tried to remember everything at once, but instead of full scenes, it'd been flashes of . . . something. Something frightening. A man, hooded—no, cloaked—chasing her through the dark walls of a castle. He stopped and stared right at her, but the shadows swallowed him up, and Amelia couldn't make out his features. She wasn't sure exactly why he'd frightened her, but he had. In a big way. In a big panicky way . . .

Just then, the temperature in the room dropped. Amelia's breath puffed out icy white with each exhale. "What the heck?" She jumped out of bed, rubbing her bare arms, her teeth chattering. Turning in a circle, she took a quick inventory of the room. The light in the bathroom went out, and she cursed. Edging over to the bedside lamp, she flipped it on. Then off. Then on again.

Nothing.

The hairs on her neck stiffened, and the room, already cold, grew more frigid. Even the flooring felt like ice beneath her bare feet. An unusual feeling of dread crawled across her spine, made her quicken her steps, and she hurried through the dark to the door.

It wouldn't open.

Shaking the handle, she cursed again under her breath. "What is going on? Ethan?" she hollered. "If you're doing this, it's *not* funny!"

Amelia's throat closed, she clawed at the door, and then through the wall, Ethan sifted to stand beside her.

"What is it, lass?" he bellowed.

Just that fast, the icy frost dissipated, the bathroom light flickered on, as well as the bedside lamp.

Ethan stood over her, his face pulled into a frown. "What are you yelling about?" He inspected her, foot to head. "Why are you shivering? It canna be so cold in here."

Amelia blinked. "What kind of dream was *that*?"

She gave her arms a vigorous rubbing, just to ward off the remaining goose bumps. "Are you trying to test me or something?"

Ethan's brows pulled close. "What are you about, girl? What dream?"

Amelia could do nothing except stare. "You know, the dream you just showed me." Suddenly aware of her braless condition, especially when Ethan's gaze kept dropping from hers to several inches *below*, she crossed her arms over her chest. "Remember, you said you were going to put another dream in my head?"

"Aye, but 'tis the usual fashion to fall into a slumber first, dunna you think?" he said.

Amelia glanced around the room. The room that looked completely normal. Unlike how it'd felt moments before. She returned her gaze to Ethan's. "Yes, and I've been asleep and dreaming now for, well, I don't know how long. But long enough to know you planted one scary dream in my head. I mean, you really could have just saved it to tell me with the others in the morning—"

"Amelia, I didna make you dream." He cocked his head. "You've been abed for only a score of minutes."

With a laugh, Amelia met his puzzled expression. "Don't be ridiculous," she said, then glanced at her Indiglo watch.

The hairs on the back of her neck went rigid once more.

The time read one 1:25 a.m.

She shuddered.

Only five minutes had lapsed.

And Ethan hadn't been the one to lapse them.

Chapter 7

"You lads settle down!" Guthrie hollered from the kitchen archway. "What, by the Bruce's blade, are ye shouting about?"

"Somethin' strange happened to Amelia in her sleeping chamber," Rob answered. "She's a bit out o' her head, by the by, methinks."

"Aye," said Aiden, rubbing his chin. "And she's refusin' to sleep anywhere else save that cursed chamber." He grinned. "I told her I'd be more than happy to guard her whilst she slumbered."

"That'd be like havin' the wolf guard the sheep, aye?" said Torloch.

Aiden kept that idiotic grin affixed.

Ethan studied Amelia. She sat upon one of the long sitting benches before the hearth. She wore some sort of strange headgear, with a slender piece that stretched to her mouth. She'd called it a *microrecorder*. In truth, he'd never seen the like.

At the moment, she seemed verra deep in thought.

Earlier, she'd been talking into that microrecorder, although he couldna warrant what she'd been saying.

At the present, he had other pressing matters, the foremost being what in the king's bluidy hell had happened in her chamber. And with all his kin talking at once, he couldn't make sense of anything. Even old Guthrie was stomping about, muttering and cursing and throwing his hands in the air.

Ethan stepped forward. "Enough, lads. Aiden, for Christ's sake, move away from the girl and give her some bluidy breathing room. And, Guthrie, blast your arse, stop waving your arms about and be silent for a handful of moments." He eyed the others, and they quieted. Scrubbing a hand across his jaw, Ethan studied Amelia. She had her long hair pulled back into some sort of floppy ball, high on her head, and wore the most intriguing tunic and trews—both black, formfitting, with a white stripe down each side. The tunic *zipped* up the front, so Amelia claimed, and she'd shown him a time or two how the contraption worked. Ethan thought to investigate that interesting bit of modern garb later. "Can you remember the whole of the dream, lass?" he asked. The fact that he'd not placed the dream in her mind more than bothered him.

With a quick glance at his kin, Amelia settled her gaze solely on Ethan. "It wasn't a long dream, and had no beginning, no ending." She blew out a hearty breath. "I was being chased by a man in a dark cloak"—she pointed at Ethan—"dressed like all of you, in that long cloth wrap and boots. I'm not sure, but I think he was chasing me through *this* castle."

"Was the man's plaid the same colors as ours?" asked Gilchrist. "Same pattern?"

Amelia studied Gil's plaid for a moment, then shook her head. "He was in shadows, so I really couldn't tell." She stood, stuck her hands on her hips, and paced. "What's bizarre is what woke me up."

Ethan moved closer. "What was that?"

"The voice," she answered, and then she stopped pacing and lifted her gaze to meet his. "It said, *'Twill be you next, lass,* and when I jerked awake, the temperature dropped so low and so fast, I could see my breath frosting out in front of me." She started to pace again, that ball of hair atop her head slipping sideways a bit. "The lights went out, the door wouldn't open, and it just kept getting colder and colder." She stopped again and looked at him. "Until you came in. Then everything went back to normal." She shook her head. "Hands down, the most unusual thing I've ever experienced." She gave a lopsided grin. "Except meeting you guys, of course."

"No doubt 'twas the grandest of experiences, to be sure," Aiden said.

Amelia stifled a yawn, which caused the men to chuckle. "Absolutely, the grandest so far."

Ethan hooked his thumbs in his belt and regarded Amelia Landry. A peculiar maid, in truth, yet more fascinating than any other he'd ever known. Confident, yet unaware of the amount of charm she possessed. Tall, yet moved with grace and poise. Quite a friendly sort, he thought, and brave to the point of madness—or mayhap 'twas madness, indeed, that drove such bravery. The girl insisted on returning to the same chamber, and would take no counsel otherwise.

"Ethan is the only one who can cast imaginings in one's head," Rob said. "So who, by Christ's blood, or what, caused such uproar in Amelia's chamber?"

"An' how did we no' know about it?" said Sorely. He turned to Guthrie. "You've no' seen anything such the like, then?"

Guthrie scratched a place under the bill of his hat and shook his head. "Nay, no' a thing."

Amelia stretched, stifled another yawn, and pulled the microrecorder gear from her head. "Well, I'm going to bed. I don't think I can keep my eyes open for another second."

"You'll have a guard whilst you slumber," Ethan found himself saying. While he admired the girl's boldness and lack of fear of whatever had happened in her bedchamber, he wasna going to allow her to sleep in there alone. He wasna going to allow her to sleep in there at all.

The hardheaded lass had other ideas, by the by.

"I'll be okay, really. *Sincerely*. Besides," she said, a mischievous glint in her strange eyes as she made for the stairs, "if one of you plops down in the room with me, it might not happen again."

Ethan blinked. "You *want* it to happen again?"

Amelia stopped at the stairs. "I'm ready this time. Last time, it took me off guard." She smiled. "This time, I'll be ready for it. And if I need you, I'll just holler."

"You'll have a guard, Amelia. I willna argue about it."

She stopped, turned, looked him in the eye, and grinned. 'Twas a wicked look, indeed. She cocked her head. "Fine. Who's going to be my guard?"

Five idiot Munros all jumped at once.

Ethan made the sixth.

"Verra well," he said, only half sorry. "I'll go."

Five grumbles sounded behind him. One giggle erupted from the staircase.

"Well, come on, then. I'm pooped." With that, Amelia Landry turned and jogged up the steps, that ball of hair atop her head slipping far to one side with each bounce.

Ethan shook his head and followed. Never before had he known such a lass. Modern maids indeed were an odd lot, not that he'd actually had speech with one before now. With what few hill walkers and stragglers had ambled onto Munro land over the centuries, few had ventured into the ruins of his keep. And once the keep had been restored, och— he'd tried aplenty to have speech with lads and maids alike. They'd either lacked the sensitivity to his existence, or they'd run like a frightened bairn if they were receptive. Only Amelia had been brave enough to stay, besides old Guthrie, even while questioning her own sanity. He'd thought on the matter more than once, but found himself fascinated by it each time.

"Okay," Amelia said, standing at her room. Her cat sat just in front, as though a guard himself. "Let's find out if anything funny has happened while we've been downstairs." Without waiting for an answer from him, she pushed open the door and went inside, the cat hurrying ahead of them both. Ethan followed.

Amelia walked around, flipped on a few lamps, and then got on her knees, rump in the air whilst she peeked under her bed.

Ethan thought he'd like to remember that moment for the rest of his enchanted life. Not that he'd ever admit to it.

Standing and brushing off her knees, Amelia gave him a grin. "Well, seems that everything's in order here." She inclined her head. "Are you sure you'll be okay out in the passageway?"

Ethan lifted a brow. "In the passageway?"

Amelia blinked. "Of course. You don't think you're just going to sit in here and stare at me for the rest of the night, do you? No way could I ever fall asleep like that." She grinned. "I barely know you."

He could certainly manage it, the staring of her person all night. "Verra well. I'll remain in the passageway. If you need me, you've only to shout." With a nod, he turned to go.

"Wait," she said, and moved a bit closer when he stopped and turned. "I really do appreciate you watching over me." She met his gaze with a bold one. "I'm still coming to grips with all of this"—she waved her hand—"and trying to convince myself that this is really happening, and that I'm not wacky, but just the lucky recipient of being so, so—"

"Receptive?"

She snapped her fingers. "Receptive. Versus being a complete lunatic."

"I dunna think you're that, Amelia."

The smile she gave made her wide eyes sparkle. "This, everything . . . it just completely fascinates me, you know?" She took off her jacket, leaving only that bare-armed tunic she'd worn to bed earlier, which left little to the imagination as to her shapeliness. "Vlad the Impaler's castle was for sale not long ago, and I seriously, *seriously* wanted to buy it. *Really* bad." She shook her head, that floppy ball of hair sliding almost to the side of her head. "Imagine owning and living in Dracula's castle. How cool would that be?"

Ethan considered. A lad named Vlad the Impaler couldna be too friendly of a person, and although he was fairly sure he'd not heard of Dracula, he supposed he'd been someone of high import, for Amelia to want to purchase his castle.

Amelia laughed out loud, interrupting his thoughts. "What is funny?" he asked.

Pressing her lips together, more likely than no' trying to keep her mirth at bay, she finally lost the battle and flashed him a full smile. "You should see your face. I suppose you don't know who Vlad/Dracula is. Rather, was."

Ethan frowned.

"Let's just say he was after your time, but I'll tell you about him later. It's a great story."

Still she stood, grinning at him like some mischievous youngster who'd just gotten caught doing something naughty and was busy planning the next bit of naughtiness. Ethan couldn't help but focus on her, and when he did, he noticed just how wide her smile was, just how white and straight her teeth were, and how verra lovely Amelia Landry truly was.

And she seemed to be just as lovely on the inside, as well.

This did not bode well for him or the blasted enchanted state he was in.

With that dreary thought in mind, he gave Amelia, that grinning fool, a curt nod and slipped out into the passageway. She gave him a little wave, and closed the door.

Ethan settled down against the wall across from Amelia's chamber, rested his arms on his bent knees, and listened to her bedtime rustlings. He knew no' what she did, but she indeed was busy. The water turned on and off, things clinked about, that miraculous bowl in the garderobe flushed, and parchment crackled. She talked to her cat, Jack, who apparently slept on the bed with her, as she patted the mattress several times, trying to coax the feline to do her bidding. She hollered one more "Good night, Ethan" to him, he answered her likewise, and she quieted down.

Briefly, he wondered why it was that she'd come to his hall to pen a story, yet hadn't done much penning at all. Mayhap he and his men distracted her.

No more than she distracted him.

He'd admit to no one, save his own pitiful self, that he was attracted to her. Hopefully, he kept it well hidden. From the verra first day he'd clapped eyes on her, he'd been drawn to her. Mayhap 'twas her kind spirit, or her wit, he knew no'. Her beauty, aye—'twas a given. Any healthy lad would have a passing hard time ignoring such a lush form, but 'twas her eyes that fascinated him. Not only the unusual shape of them, or their color, but their depth. Amelia appeared to have the ability to see far deeper than most. When she looked at you, she met your gaze directly, and it left the sense of having your entire soul bared. Yet she did so without passing judgment. At least, he sincerely hoped it.

Once she found out just what the Bluidy Munro had supposedly done, she might indeed judge, and he couldna blame her for it. Murdering one's wife wasna something to easily put out of mind.

Shoving his fingers through his hair, Ethan rested his head against the wall and closed his eyes. By the blood of Christ, *had* he done it? 'Twas no' his nature, killing women. Aye, he'd killed men aplenty, but 'twas in battle. He'd fully believed he wasna a murderer.

Until he'd become enchanted.

Never had he been a believer of superstition. He preferred facts, truths grounded in more truths. No' the whisperings of ghosties, or ramblings of witches. Yet he'd become enchanted, aye? In life he'd have never believed such a thing could exist.

Mayhap if an enchantment could occur, so could a bewitching. Or a cursing. Mayhap he'd done the murderous deed, but under the spell of a witch.

With a hearty sigh, he opened his eyes and fixed his gaze on Amelia's closed door. Just the words *under the spell of a witch* from his thoughts sounded idiotic. Yet the possibility was there, true enough. And if he'd been cursed all those centuries ago to kill an innocent lass, who was to say that same curse didna still linger within him?

Mayhap it did linger, lying dormant within his centuries-old self. Mayhap he had the potential to do the verra same thing to Amelia once the gloaming fell, when his body found substance for that short period of time.

If so, Amelia's verra life was in grave danger.

Ethan's mood grew murky at the thought of it, and he found himself scowling, anger torrid within himself. He and the lads had kept away from Amelia purposely during the past several days, especially during twilight. He'd have to make good and sure to do the like this eve, as well, for Amelia Landry was quite looking forward to meeting them in the flesh. The Munro warriors would have to guard their verra own laird against the lass.

Never before had Ethan been quite so grateful that the twilight lasted only about an hour.

Mood definitely darkened, Ethan continued to watch Amelia's door with a frown. 'Twas only at just before sunrise, when he heard the lass moving about and talking to that bluidy cat, did he rise from his position on the passageway's stone floor and seek out his kin.

They'd need to know to remain in his and Amelia's presence at all times during twilight that eve.

No matter how much he'd loathe it.

Just as Ethan disappeared, he heard Amelia's door open, then heard an unfamiliar word pass from her lips.

He was fairly sure 'twas a curse.

Chapter 8

"Some guard he is, huh, Jack?" Amelia said, scratching between Jack's ears. The sleek feline flopped over onto his side and stuck his chin in the air, a sure sign that he actually wanted some attention. After a few under-the-chin scrubs, Amelia patted his head, and then he jumped down and slinked out the door she'd left cracked open for him.

So much for having a familiar presence around to soothe her.

As Amelia made her bed, she considered the night before. Rather, the *morning* before. After she'd gone to bed the second time, she'd slept like a baby. No more weird dreams, no more freezing episodes, nothing. Had it all truly happened? Medieval Scottish warriors, an extra spook floating around, and all that enchantment? It was absurd. *Crazy* absurd.

But yeah, by God, she believed it.

As she tucked in the duvet, she remembered how frigid her room had grown, the threatening whisper, and that icy feeling of dread. She hadn't made that up. No way. And she *definitely* hadn't made up Ethan.

Good Lord, that man could start fires just by scowling. She thought she liked that in a guy.

Fluffing the pillows, Amelia smoothed the spread on the bed and then surveyed the room. On the desk sat her laptop, closed. Beside it, a pad of paper. Empty. Next to that, a pen. Combined, they called to her. *Just grab the pad of paper and pen and start making notes. Or at least take the microrecorder . . .*

With a huff, Amelia walked over to the makeshift office, picked up the pad of paper and pen, and stared at it. *Doodle, girl. Anything! Play hangman with yourself! Tic-tac-toe! Sketch a parrot! A pirate! ANYTHING!*

When she pressed the tip of the pen to the paper, only one thing flowed from that squishy gray blob of matter she called a brain. Just one word. Rather, one name.

Ethan.

She even made the E extra swirly.

With still another huff, she set the pen and pad back on the desk, gave them both the stink eye, and glanced at her watch: 6:21. Perfect. She needed some thinking time, inspiration, a good, lung-expanding walk through the Scottish countryside.

What she really needed was a freaking can of Cheez Whiz. But she'd settle for the walk/lung/thinking thing. After all, she had the perfect inspirational setting. She was right in the middle of some of the most beautiful land in the world. Haunting, chock full of history, murder, mayhem, and did she forget to mention haunting?

With a renewed spring in her step, Amelia dug through her clothes chest, found a pair of warm-up pants, a tangerine-colored tank top, and a pair of socks, and then headed into the bathroom. Correction. The *garderobe*. At least that's what Ethan had called it.

After washing her face, brushing her teeth, and pulling a brush through her hair and putting it into a ponytail, Amelia sat on the floor, yanked on her socks and sneakers, and did a few stretches to loosen her muscles. Finally, she stood, did a few more stretches, grabbed her iPod, and then slipped out into the passageway.

She'd do her very best *not* to think of Ethan Munro all day long. Or his engaging smile, or that intriguing accent, or that fascinating scar beneath his eye shaped like a crescent moon . . .

Or the fact that tonight, during the twilight hour—rather, the *gloaming*—she'd actually be meeting him in live, honest-to-goodness human flesh.

Good grief.

The passageways were dark, all except the dim inserts that cast a very weak glow. It was enough for her to see, thank goodness, because stepping on a rat just wasn't on her agenda for the day. Or any day, actually. As she crept along, she considered just how quiet everything was. Did the enchanted warriors sleep? They must. Either that, or they were somewhere else in the castle. When she reached the bottom of the stairs, Amelia found the hall empty. She stood for a moment, transfixed by the serene oddness of being in a fourteenth-century castle, made of stone and mortar by medieval hands, where those hands cooked, ate, fought, loved.

And apparently still lived.

A shudder ran through her, and for a moment, she

felt as though she'd tumbled back in time. The empty hall transformed into a bustling, giant room, with medieval warriors sharpening their swords, telling naughty jokes, laughing.

Amazing.

Out of nowhere, Jack meowed and bumped against her leg. Amelia glanced at him, and inclined her head. "Come on, boy. Let's go for a walk."

Jack stared at her with wide green cat eyes, and as if he understood her words, slinked over to the door. Amelia followed, and they both slipped outside.

As soon as she stepped out into the crisp Highland air, a sweet, clean scent invaded her nostrils, and she inhaled deeply. Unfamiliar with the flora and fauna of the area, Amelia made a mental note to ask Ethan just what that smell was. Clover, maybe. Heather? Whatever it was, she liked it. She took a few more big whiffs, then started out across the gravel toward the loch.

Amelia regarded the scenery while she walked. So consumed by white-knuckled fear as she'd driven from Edinburgh, she hadn't really enjoyed the view at all. Now that she could really look without the panic of scraping a ton of sod from the bumper of her rental car, she had to swallow hard in awe. Breathtaking didn't quite sum it up, didn't even begin to, actually. An eerie mist slipped through the craggy hills, through the tall pines, over the meadow. A patch of it settled just over the water, creeping closer to the keep as it made its way like a live thing across the Munro land. The closer she walked to the loch, the more the mist swirled and enveloped her. It clung to her skin, a cool, moist dampness that wasn't heavy enough to be rain, but definitely heavy enough to soak her clothes. She thought she liked the sensation. A lot.

Picking her way to the water's rock and pebbled edge, where the black liquid rippled over the gritty soil, Amelia turned on her iPod, scrolled to her selection, and let the soothing, haunting concerto of *The Phantom of the Opera* wash over her as she walked and absorbed the Highlands.

As if she'd lost all control over her own thoughts, the one thing she'd been determined to *not* dwell on rushed back, crowded her brain, and well, darn it, she dwelled.

Ethan Munro. While he exerted more raw male power than any man she'd met in her entire life, he and his clansmen seemed to be a far cry from what the book described. Each had their own unique personality, and not one of them seemed to be the evil soul-stealing monster the book had portrayed them to be. Did they seem capable of hacking someone's head off with their very sharp and pointy swords? Sure. Did they seem like the sort of guys who would kill innocents for their souls? Hardly. Now that she'd met them, even in their enchanted state of existence, the notion seemed more than ridiculous. It seemed idiotic.

Amelia glanced up. She'd walked halfway around the loch. As she moved her gaze over the scene before her, an exhilarated thrill ran through her. As the wispy mist eased in and around the water, it weaved around the tower house keep. Tall and gray and masculine, it reached toward the lightening sky with authority, with a stone-solid presence that left Amelia feeling breathless. Craggy yet beautiful, she almost laughed at herself over the fascination she'd taken with the old castle.

As she stared, a figure emerged from the mist. Her heart thumped a bit faster, and that thrill she'd experienced earlier? *Doubled* now. No, make that *quadrupled*.

As the figure drew closer, Amelia begrudgingly admitted, only to her own stupid self, that she was just as intrigued and fascinated by the castle's owner as she was the castle itself.

Dangit.

Without the first bit of shame, and why would she have any, anyway? She was a woman appreciating the physique of an able-bodied man. That said man was over seven hundred years old was another subject altogether, and one she'd entertain herself with at another time. For now she was busy banking to memory this moment. Amelia watched as Ethan crossed the distance. Why he didn't just blink himself to her, instead of walking when he didn't have to, she didn't know or care. When an opportunity knocked, she was not the type of gal to ignore that knock. She was, in fact, a knock answerer, and proud of it.

With long, assured strides, Ethan crossed over the same stretch of ground she had earlier, only with a sure-footedness Amelia had certainly lacked. And why not? He'd been crossing that land for centuries.

He looked damn good doing it, too.

So good, in fact, that Amelia felt the ogling of the seven-hundred-year-old laird deserved a decent sitting down sort of ogle. So she found a big rock and sat, chin in hands, and nonchalantly ogled. Juvenile of her? Absolutely. But who would know besides her?

Honest to God, no other guy could look anywhere near as sexy wearing a big, long bolt of plaid cloth, as Ethan Munro did. He somehow took one end, started wrapping, until he ended up with just a corner of it, secured with a silver sort of clasp, or brooch, at one shoulder. A thick, wide leather belt cinched loosely around his hips, with a few knives poked in here and there, and then the hem of that plaid—called a kilt in modern times, she supposed—swished in a very manly way around his knees with each swaggering, confident step. Above his right shoulder, the ever-present hilt of the biggest sword she'd ever laid eyes on stuck out like an extra appendage. Did he sleep with that thing on? Sheesh, she'd have to remember to ask him that one.

Okay, she'd admit it: the silver armbands completely intrigued her. If she'd seen them on a male model, perhaps, she'd have scoffed and probably made fun. But on Ethan? Maybe one had to be from the fourteenth century to properly get away with wearing silver arm cuffs, but good grief, they made a very appealing accent to his very cut biceps. She didn't know how heavy that sword of his was, but she'd bet a bag of Dove chocolates it certainly contributed to the size and bulk of Ethan's build, not to mention the extra force it probably took to hack through bone and sinew.

Ah, the head. The one atop his very broad shoulders, that is. Only a guy from medieval Scotland could get away with having hair that long and that wild. Not curly, but not straight, either, it had no other description except wild. Not ratty, mind you, or knotty. Just wild. Dark, with a narrow braid at each temple, he'd gathered it all back in a low ponytail, leaving his features completely unobstructed, which was absolutely fine with her. Strong jaw, eyes just the right distance apart, brows thick but not too bushy, straight nose, and the scars on his face? Her brothers would both kill to have cool, chick-magnet scars like the ones Ethan had. She'd have to ask how he got them . . .

It was then she noticed just how close Ethan had gotten. Close enough for her to see a very cocky, male smirk on his face. The one that screamed "BUSTED!" in a loud, clear, proud voice. She didn't care. She smiled back.

"You can just wipe that grin off your face, Munro. I confess, I was ogling. Sue me." She shrugged and turned off her iPod. "It's not every day a girl gets to watch a fourteenth-century warrior swagger toward her."

Ethan stopped, unwinded, of course, and shook his head, grin still affixed. "I dunna swagger."

Amelia laughed. "You definitely swagger." She stood, brushed off her backside, and mock-cracked her knuckles. "Okay, back up. This is you, swaggering." She proceeded to do her best imitation of, well, Ethan swaggering. She made one pass in front of him, then one more.

With a sound that echoed across the loch, Ethan laughed. A big, loud, guy laugh. He crossed his arms, still shaking his head.

"What?" Amelia asked, unable to stop her own chuckle. "I swear, that is *so* the way you walk." She gave an affirmative nod. "Swagger."

With those pewter eyes, he stared at her. "Verra well, lass. I swagger."

In her earlier assessment of Ethan's attributes, had

she failed to mention the accent? Whuh. She thought she could listen to it all day long. The way he rolled his R's . . .

"What are you doing out so early?" he asked, then pointed at her waist. "And what is that thing you wear about you?"

Amelia glanced down. "This is an iPod. It holds over two hundred songs." She unclipped it from her waistband and brought it closer for Ethan to inspect it. "See here?" She pointed at the screen. "I can scroll through like this and find whichever section of songs I want to listen to, and then I put these things in my ears"—she did so—"and I'm all set to listen to my favorite tunes for the day."

Ethan bent his dark head over the iPod; then he raised and studied Amelia's face with just as much interest. He lifted one dark brow. "In my day, you would already be smolderin' at the witch's stake for having such." A grin tugged at his mouth.

Amelia clipped the iPod back in place. "If you're a good little warrior, I'll let you hold it at twilight. Burn me at the stake?" She waved her hand. "Poof! The iPod goes with me, ashes and all."

Together, they started to walk without really even agreeing to do it. Ethan glanced down at her. "Then I shall endeavor to keep you far away from the kindling, lass." He kept his eye on her. "You never said what you were doing out here."

Amelia nodded, savoring his words as she processed them. "It's my morning ritual back home. I take an early walk on the beach to get my brain working, get the juices flowing."

He cocked a brow. "What juices?"

Amelia laughed. "That's just another term for getting your mind and body in shape, and in my case, my imagination. Plus, I have to walk off all the calories I'd consumed the night before."

Ethan shook his head. "I vow, I'm lost with more than half of what comes from your mouth, Amelia."

Amelia looked up at him. "Calories are naughty things inside naughty foods that make you get fat. When you walk, or exercise, you burn the fat in your body."

With a frown, Ethan nodded. "I think I see, although you must do a vast amount of exercise, for there's no amount of fat on you."

She laughed. "You are now my new best friend, Ethan Munro. Maybe one day you can meet my little cousin Jeremy."

Ethan smiled. "And why would I need to meet him?"

"Because his favorite thing to call me is Aunt Jell-O-Butt."

Ethan slowed enough for Amelia to walk a few steps ahead, where he boldly gave her rear the once-over.

"I'm not verra sure what *Jell-O* is." He caught up with her and looked at her. "What is it, by the by?"

Amelia couldn't help it. She laughed. Hard. "Good God, Munro, you crack me up." She cleared her throat. "Jell-O is something you eat. It's very jiggly, congealed, wiggles when you poke it with a spoon."

A slow, wicked grin picked up the corners of Ethan's very sexy mouth. "I see."

Amelia shook her head. "Great."

"Is that why you do that solitary fighting you were doing?"

Sidestepping a big rock, Amelia nodded. "Partly. And it's a form of martial arts. Tae kwon do, it's called." She smiled. "I'm proud to say I'm a fourth-degree black belt." She glanced at him. "There're several steps in learning the arts, and you celebrate each step by gaining a different colored belt. Black is the highest level, then you have multilevels of black you must earn."

Ethan nodded. " 'Twas intriguing to watch you. My men have begged me to ask if you'll teach it to us."

Amelia looked at him, the mist making his enchanted self even more surreal. "With the big swords you all carry around, why would you need to learn the arts?"

His eyes, already intense, stared. "Why did you?"

"My dad had all of us—my brothers and sisters and I—learn it when we were kids. I just continued on with it. At first, just because my brother did." She smiled. "I hate when he outdoes me in something. So the more he kept at it, the more I did, too." She shrugged. "It's a lot of fun, it's a great workout, and, well, anyway." She looked up at him. "That's really it."

"Can you use it in battle?" he asked.

Amelia eyed the enormous blade strapped to Ethan's back. "As long as the weapons were out of the picture, yes." She grinned. "I'll teach you guys tae kwon do if you teach me how to use that." She pointed at his sword.

Ethan gave a curt nod. "A fine trade, methinks." He grinned. "Done."

Before long, they'd walked the parameter of the loch. Amelia glanced at her watch. "Wow. I'd better shower and get down to the kitchen before Guthrie throws my breakfast out." She crossed her arms over her chest. "Thanks for walking with me."

Another short nod. "Aye, 'twas a fine morn to walk, indeed." He glanced behind her, and for a breadth of a second, his features grew solemn. Just that fast, though, the look vanished. "I'm sure you realize by now that you shall be at the mercy of the lads during the waking hours."

She smiled. "So that means I'll see you at breakfast?"

"Aye. For a certainty." He gave a low bow. "Until."

Then he vanished.

At the great hall door, Amelia stopped and glanced over her shoulder. Through the shroud of mist rose the hill, and at its peak, something she did not remember seeing before. A tall, upside down L-shaped sort of object. "What the heck?"

When she blinked, the mist swallowed it up.

An eerie feeling claimed her then. One that made her shiver clear to the bone.

Chapter 9

"You're taken wi' her, aye?"

Ethan shot Aiden a glare any normal man with half a wit would have backed away from. His cousin, though, was anything but normal.

"Your frightful frown says aye, laird," Aiden said. "Canna say I blame you, though. She's a fetchin' lass, to be true."

"Aiden, shut up." Ethan deepened his glower.

"Och, lad," Guthrie said, shuffling his old self about the larder whilst preparing Amelia's fare, "be careful with that one. She's right ornery, I'd say." The old man grinned over his bony old shoulder. "Unless ye like 'em ornery."

The men chuckled.

"How do you like 'em, Guthrie?" Tor asked. He steepled his big fingers and sat his chin at the point. "I beg you, share."

Guthrie chuckled, a wheezy sound of the elderly. "Oy, I'll no' share my secrets of wooing with the lot of you hooligans, that's for sure." A mischievous glint sparked in the old man's eye. "But it's workin' for me, by the by."

The laughter boomed throughout the larder, and

even Ethan had to join in. That Guthrie was a bleating fool when it came to his women.

"What's so funny?"

All heads turned as Amelia walked through the door. As though she'd been living with a castle full of enchanted Highland knights the whole of her life, she walked right over to the long wooden table where his kin sat in various places, moved a trencher filled with fruit, plucked an apple from its mix, scuffed it on her thigh, and took a big bite. Then she slid the trencher over and eased her bottom onto the table. And sat. And chewed.

Never before had Ethan wanted to be an apple.

All at once, his kin overtook the lass's presence. Ethan could do little but stand back, watch, and continue scowling. Not that anyone paid a bit of attention to him or his glowers, although Aiden glanced at him once, winked, and returned his attentions back to Amelia.

"Is it true, lass?" Gilchrist said. "Ethan tells us that you're willin' to trade a bit of swordplay for a bit of your"—he glanced at Ethan—"what'd you call it again?"

"Tae kwon do," Ethan said.

"Right." Gilchrist grinned. "What say you, Amelia?"

Amelia wiped the corner of her mouth with her thumb and nodded. "Absolutely. Whenever you're ready."

The men all started talking at once.

"*After* I've eaten," she added. "So you guys just simmer down. And"—she glanced at Ethan, who then had a difficult time keeping the frown affixed to his face—"I do want to hear every detail of what you remember first."

For a handful of moments, her gaze remained fixed

to Ethan's, and even the annoying drone of his kin was lost. He shamelessly watched as she bit into her fruit and chewed, followed her finger as she once again wiped away the juice. One lovely eyebrow lifted, but still she stared. A grin, seen by no one save him, touched the corner of her mouth.

By the blood of Christ, he wanted fiercely to kiss the girl. Right then and there, in front of his clansmen and that old smilin' Guthrie.

And she *knew* it.

Damn.

"Well go on, then, Ethan," Sorely said, and threw his big self into a straight-backed chair against the larder wall. "Begin the tale, man, before we all grow weary o' waitin'."

"Yeah, and sit right here," Amelia said, patting the very spot across from her seat. "I don't want to have to watch you pace and talk while I eat." Guthrie set a trencher of steaming eggs, meat, and porridge before her, and Amelia wasted no time digging in.

"You're no' verra shy about eatin', are you, lass?" Ethan said, sitting down across from her. "Most of your ilk would pick about that bit of food and eat as little as warranted."

From two round trenchers, she spooned several heaps of the porridge, and the other, lard. After she stirred the lard into her porridge, she picked up a spoonful, blew, and grinned. "Jell-O-Butt, remember? What can I say? I like to eat. Besides. I grew up with four siblings. I had to practically fight my way to the table."

"Bluidy hell, what is a *Jell-O-Butt*?" asked Rob, who'd propped a hip on the table beside Amelia.

"Never you mind, pup," Ethan said. "I'll never get the tale told if you dunna cease your babbling."

Rob winked at Amelia, thusly ignoring Ethan. "You'll give me the meanin' later, aye?" he asked.

Of course, she grinned right back. "Absolutely." Eyeing Ethan, she gave a nod. "Okay, I'm ready."

With a nod and one last lairdly glare at his men, Ethan began. He told the entire tale, beginning from the unwanted nuptials, and ending with him and his kin being overtaken by the heavy mist, and then awaking some time later, mayhap even a century later, in the Munro Keep—run-down, as it was, with a legend so dreadful, no one would claim the tower until well into the twentieth century. He left nothing out—including the finding of Devina's lifeless body lying on the ground, his family plaid covering her.

Amelia, who'd steadfastly taken her meal at first, had stopped eating, fork discarded, her chin propped atop one fist as her elbow rested against the table. Even after he'd said his piece, she continued to stare, eyes wide, soaking in everything.

Finally, she sat back in her chair, leaned back on the hind legs, and swore under her breath. The men laughed, but Ethan kept his gaze trained on hers.

"I saw it this morning, after you left," she said. "In the mist, atop the knoll."

"What?" Ethan asked.

"The gibbet. At least, I think that's what I saw." She held up her hand, and using a forefinger and a thumb, made a shape. "Like this—sort of an upside down L."

"Damn me, aye," said Aiden, who'd taken a seat at the end of the table. "That's what you saw, 'tis a certainty. Dunna you think so, Ethan?"

Ethan nodded. "What I canna understand, though, is how?" He looked at Amelia. "Why you? No' even Guthrie's ever seen the like."

Guthrie shook his head. "Nope. Never saw a bloody gibbet, I can honestly say." He looked at Amelia and pointed a gnarled finger in her direction. "You a witch, girlie?"

"She's no' a witch, but she can kick your old arse, Guthrie," said Torloch, and the others erupted into laughter. "You should see the lass fight."

"Even though she does it alone," added Rob. "She's going to teach us, right, Amelia?"

Guthrie shook his head. "God help us all."

Somehow, watching Amelia banter with his kin, Ethan held old Guthrie's exact sentiments.

"I can't explain why I saw the gibbet, nor can I explain why I can see and interact with all of you," Amelia said. "I'm not asking questions, though." She looked directly at Ethan. "And I'd like to help you any way I can."

Somehow, Ethan hoped she'd say the like.

Rising from her seat, Amelia gathered her empty trenchers and took them to the sink. Flipping on the faucet, she rinsed them out and set them to dry on a cloth. "What I don't get, though"—she dried her hands on another cloth and turned around—"is why your wife's uncle thought *you'd* killed her, Ethan." She draped the cloth over the dish rack and leaned against the counter, facing him. "Had something happened in the past to make Daegus think you'd actually kill a woman, much less your own wife, regardless that you hadn't wanted the marriage in the first place?"

The entire larder turned deadly quiet as all eyes turned to Ethan. He'd not meant for Amelia to know such intimacy from his old life, only the facts surrounding Devina's death. To dig deeper meant fighting demons he'd already fought—many times over.

He hated bringing to surface such bad memories, but by the blood of Christ, he had no choice. If she were to truly be able to help them, possibly even break the centuries-long enchantment, then she had to know everything.

But somehow, having Amelia Landry know his terrible secret and possibly think poorly of him, didna sit well with him at all. Even though he'd known her for such a short time, to see dread in those wide green eyes made his insides ache.

Then Amelia was at his side. He hadn't even known she'd moved from the sink.

She lifted her hand, as though to touch him, but lowered it and clenched a fist instead. "My grandmother, Granny Dona, always told me, *Last I checked, I wasn't Jesus, so I'm not your judge, either.*"

Ethan met her bold stare, with those exotic green eyes tipped slightly upward at the outer corners. He didna say a word.

"What that means, is," she continued, "you can tell me anything and it's not going to change my opinion of you, Ethan Munro."

Thank the saints, his kin had the grace to remain quiet. Even old Guthrie had busied himself in the cabinet doing some odd bit of work. He'd known exactly what Granny's saying had meant. *She willna judge you,* his inner voice assured. *But you already knew that, did you no'?*

With a confident nod, Ethan met Amelia's expectant stare. He prayed her fervor remained after the confession. "The verra same thing occurred before, Amelia," he said. Dragging a hand across his chin, he swallowed and hoped he could get through the telling of the tale once more. "I was naught but a score and eight at the time, and I'd befriended an older woman." He looked at her. "A widow."

Amelia nodded, and kept silent.

"A friend of my mother's, she'd come here for a short visit that turned into more than a sennight. A beautiful woman, even at more than two score." He cleared his throat. "She came to me one night, and a score of nights afterward." A need to move about came over him, and Ethan paced before the larder hearth. Finally, he stopped and braced his weight with both hands across the mantel. "Her dead body was found one misty morn, and just like with Devina, my effects found with her." He shook his head. "I dunna remember anything, save the last night we were together."

" 'Twas rumored Ethan was cursed," Rob said. "Nearly every maid he courted came up dead."

Ethan heard footsteps, and Rob came to stand beside him. His younger brother clapped him on the back. " 'Tisna true, though. He didna kill those lasses."

"Aye, and the only ones who came up dead were the ones he cared for," Sorely added. "The ones he simply took his ease with lived."

Ethan cringed.

"Aye," Aiden said, and then apparently felt the urge to supply the lass with any sort of medieval language. "That means any maid he bedded—"

"Yeah, big fella," Amelia said, holding up a hand. "Gotcha. No need to explain to me, sister of two brothers who were hornpots from the age of six, what *taking ease with* means."

While Aiden grinned, Ethan was more than surprised to see his big oaf of a cousin turn red-cheeked. He'd thank Amelia for that later.

The girl had a sharp wit, by the by. He found he liked that in a woman. In her, particularly. No' to mention he hadn't laughed as much in seven centuries as he had since meeting Amelia Landry.

"You know," she said, moving closer to where he stood by the larder hearth, "they've written many a story with a plot similar to yours." She shrugged. "A cursed man whose every lover dies, or a man who can't love a woman or else she'll die, or women who just end up dead after being with the cursed guy." She smiled. "See? Not all that uncommon after all. Only difference is, yours appears to have really happened."

Ethan blinked in disbelief. "You're no' the least bit fearful, lass? You're no' scared of what might happen to you?"

The grin that slowly spread from corner to corner on Amelia's lovely mouth reeked of pure, sheer, wickedness. She tapped her chin with one long, slender finger. "Hmm. Let's see. According to your story, I'm pretty safe, right? I mean, we could even have sex and I'd stay safe, as long as we were, what was it? Taking our ease? A quickie?" She batted her long eyelashes several times. "Right?"

One could have heard a kirk mouse belch, so still went the larder. Ethan moved only his eyes as he inspected each of his kinsmen, who'd all gone a bit pasty in the cheek and silent of tongue.

A miracle, to his way of thinking.

While he couldn't exactly say what a *quickie* was, he got the gist of it.

His kin, though, were a bit slower.

Could be why he was laird.

And it was then, he realized, as Amelia Landry and her naughty self burst out laughing, that she was in more trouble than either one of them could possibly imagine.

Ethan stood back and watched his kin as recognition sparked in their eyes, and they all shared a rowdy round of laughter with the quirky storyteller. Even old Guthrie chuckled, and he usually chuckled only at his own poor jests.

One thing stood certain, especially in Ethan's mind: Amelia would need a constant guard, day and night, for since he was in truth enchanted, 'twould certainly make sense that he could be cursed, as well. And if the lasses whom he'd cared for in the past ended up dead, then by the blood of Christ, so verra well could Amelia.

Against his will, he'd become rather fond of the fetching American.

Damn.

"Okay, okay," Amelia said, holding up her hands. "Enough. Sheesh, I feel like I'm in a room with my brothers." She turned and slid Ethan a mischievous glance. "All except you, of course."

Ethan rubbed his temples as his kin made bawdy noises at Amelia's comment, which of course, made her laugh even harder.

Aye. They were in a vast amount of trouble.

Indeed.

Chapter 10

By midmorning, Amelia stood in the field between the keep and the loch, before a line of six big chiseled-from-stone medieval Highland warriors. She cleared her throat, braced herself, and then spoke. "With the accomplishment of tae kwon do comes the practiced attitude of modesty."

"Aiden, you're out."

This, to Amelia's ears, sounded like *Eden, yure oot*. With a roll to the R.

The men burst into laughter. Especially after she heard a noise that sounded a lot like the very noise she and her brothers and sisters had perfected—the one that involved a hand and one's rapidly flapping sweaty armpit. She seriously had to fight a smile herself.

They all laughed, Amelia noticed, but one.

Ethan glared at his kin, held up a hand to Amelia, who returned a short nod, and then she stood in dumbfounded silence as the Munro laird addressed his warriors as he would any serious matter of the day.

And in what Amelia could only assume to be medieval-to-the-hilt Scots Gaelic.

She found it to be absolutely beautiful.

Having no clue whatsoever as to just what Ethan said, Amelia figured it must have been good because not one Munro face—not even Aiden's—carried the first trace of a smirk. Not that she minded smirks. Loved them, actually. Was the Queen of Smirks herself, truth be told. Just ask ZuZu.

But when it came to the arts, Amelia took things seriously. She believed in the respect and discipline the sport taught, and while she liked to cut up and joke as much as the next person, she wanted to make sure, more than anything, that if she taught a group of medieval guys the basics of tae kwon do, she'd teach them properly. And they'd learn it properly. From the basic stance to every ounce of respect owed.

Even if they were, in a sense, at the moment, untouchable.

Being enchanted did have its perks, she suspected.

"Sorry, Amelia," said Rob. "I willna interrupt again."

Amelia made a mental note to thank Ethan later. "I accept your apology, Rob. Now let's try the basic attention stance. Okay, watch me and follow along." As she called out each instruction, she initiated the stance. "Chest facing forward. Arms hanging straight down with open hands facing the body. Feet together and toes pointed forward. Back straight, shoulders back, head up, and eyes looking straight ahead."

Amelia studied every warrior, and to her surprise, each had not only followed perfect direction, but each stood in perfect formation, a smooth, flawless motion as though they'd been taking the attention stance of tae kwon do their entire medieval lives. And not a smirk in sight.

She gave them a bow, they bowed in return, exactly as she'd taught them, and then she clapped. "Nice, guys! I'm impressed!" Sure, they'd just performed the most basic of stances, but still. These guys were over seven hundred years old. She seriously *was* impressed.

They all beamed as though they'd just hacked off a hundred English heads. A piece.

"Is that it for today?" asked Torloch. "We could easily practice a few more hours, aye?"

Which they did. The guys were fast learners, and Amelia went through several stances, even throwing together a small routine. They all performed it perfectly.

Medieval Scots warriors performing a tae kwon do routine. Who would have ever thought it?

Hours later, Amelia shaded her eyes with her hand and stared out across the loch. The sun had started slipping toward the hilltops. It'd be twilight soon.

And she needed a shower.

She turned and faced her new students. "Okay, guys. We'll meet out here, in the meadow, right after my morning walk each day. As quickly as you picked up the beginner's stances, plus the routine, the rest will no doubt come just as easy. Then you can practice yourself."

"Will you show us another of *your* routines, then?" asked Aiden. He gave a grin that reminded Amelia of a wolf.

"Aye, lass," added Gilchrist. " 'Twould inspire us greatly, methinks."

Amelia glanced at Ethan, who simply shrugged.

If anything, she knew a con when she heard one. "Yeah, all right." She shooed them with her hand.

"Back up, little lads, and let me show you what hard work and practice will get you."

Ethan stepped forward before he backed up, a glint in his silvery eye. "Not a shy bone in your body, aye?"

Amelia grinned, although she had to struggle to breathe with him being so close. She hoped he couldn't tell. "Not a single solitary one, I'm afraid."

He flashed a cocky grin, and then fell back with his kin.

Drawing a few good long pulls of fresh Highland air, that sweet clovery scent fresh in her nostrils, Amelia bowed to her group of onlookers, slowly rose, then took the attack stance. As she eased into her routine—the one she used to gain her first black belt—everything fell away except her breathing and the practiced movements. With an occasional "hiyah!," she carried out a series of punches, chops, high kicks, and roundhouse kicks. Landing in an attack stance once more, Amelia slowly rose, and then bowed.

When she looked up, the warriors were silent, drop-jawed, and she was proud to say she found their eyes full of admiration. A woman didn't gain that look from a man easily. Not *that* kind of look, anyway. A wolfish look, sure. But one of admiration? Hardly ever.

Six medieval fighting machines presently stared at her, with *that* look.

Amelia would remember it until the day she died.

"Cease ogling the lass, and move along," Ethan said. "You can ask questions over supper. Now, begone."

A few bawdy things were called over shoulders,

but Amelia was surprised to find the men did exactly what Ethan instructed them to do. Without question.

With that swaggering walk, he came toward her, gaze fixed to hers. "It appears that I'm your guard for the eve, lass," he said, and inclined his head toward the keep. "What say you?"

Amelia wiped her damp brow, tightened her ponytail, and grinned. "Seems to me you awarded yourself that duty, says I." She started for the keep.

"Guilty, by the by." He fell into step beside her. " 'Tis powerfully amazing, to watch you fight, although 'tis not the usual character of a bard in my day. They were more of the . . . timid sort. You're vastly exceptional."

She gave him a sideways glance. "Thanks. I worked really hard at it." Sidestepping a thorny bush, she gave a half laugh. "Know something funny? The art requires a lot of severe dedication and structure." She smiled at him. "That's slightly out of character for me."

"Yet you've become a fine fighting warrior, in truth." He stared straight ahead. "Learning the blades will be equally as challenging. Be you up to it?"

"Absolutely." As they neared the front of the tower, Amelia stopped and stared up at him. "I feel like I'm at camp." She grinned. "Warrior camp, and my brother will be so jealous when he finds I've learned to sword fight." She regarded him. "How is it that you think I'll be able to help you? Do you hope to break whatever spell has you bound here?"

Ethan glanced out across the meadow, back toward the knoll, and then down at her. "I vow, lass, I canna know. But you are, in truth, the only mortal who has been brave enough and sensitive to our presence to interact the way you have."

"What about Guthrie?" Amelia asked, and started walking the remainder of the way to the keep. "He sees and interacts with you all the time."

Ethan shook his head. "He's sensitive to our presence and in fact interacts with us, but he's ne'er had a dream, or encounter, to match the one you had last night. Let alone the vision of the gibbet." He hooked his thumbs in his belt. "You're so highly receptive, another soul is contacting you, and that's not happened before. You can see things, Amelia. 'Tis an important gift to be sure."

They reached the keep and Amelia leaned against the stone wall, cool and rough through the thin cotton material of her tank top. She raised her gaze. "You have no idea who may have wanted to enchant you? An enemy?"

Drawing somewhat closer, Ethan leaned to face her, his shoulder to the wall. "I had many enemies, lass, and some rather unsavory ones at that. Although I canna believe any of them had the wit to enchant me and my kin for centuries."

Amelia cocked her head and grinned. "You know, I've always loved to hear a good British accent, but I suppose I've never stopped long enough to listen to a Scots accent before. Other than Sean Connery's. Or the guy who played Scotty on *Star Trek*. Or the entire cast of *Braveheart*." She knew she sounded dopey, just by the confused expression on Ethan's face. She didn't care. "But honestly, you have the best accent I've ever heard."

That he understood, if the light in those silver eyes meant anything.

"So you find my speech pleasin', aye?" he said. A grin pulled at his mouth.

"Yes, I do. I especially liked to hear you speak your native tongue, like you did earlier with your men. I had no clue what you were saying, of course, but the language is beautiful." She smiled. "Just what *did* you say to them, anyway? They sure clammed up and paid attention really quick, which I thank you for."

Ethan gave a short nod. "Let's just say that the lads badly want to learn to fight as you do, and I reminded them that you had to start out the same way they were." A spark of mischief gleamed in his eye. "A threat or two ne'er hurt, either."

Amelia laughed. "Ah, a man after my own heart."

Ethan's smile eased from his mouth, and in its place came a much more serious expression, where a muscle flinched in his jaw, and his eyes grew a shade darker. He stared, first at her eyes, then dropped a bit lower, to her mouth.

Seconds passed, long, drawn-out seconds where Amelia found herself lacking air in her lungs. Her pulse sped up, so much that she knew Ethan could see her heart pounding beneath her shirt, had he bothered to glance in that direction. Then he blinked, a slow-motion type of blink that one might see in a movie, and then he looked away.

Just that fast, the moment disappeared.

"Well," she said, grateful that she didn't squeak. "I guess I'll run upstairs and get cleaned up." She pasted on a cheerful grin. "I can't be meeting my very first handful of live and substantial medieval warriors all stinky and sweaty. I'll see you in a bit?"

Ethan gave a simple, single nod. "Until."

He turned and disappeared through the wall.

Amelia stared at the empty place the big man had just occupied. Well, sort of occupied, anyway.

A smile pulled at her mouth, and by God, she let it happen. As she went through the front door, she threw a wave in Guthrie's direction, who stared, shrugged, and muttered something under his breath, and then she scooted up the stairs, the smile nearly breaking into a laugh.

At least, she thought, Ethan had experienced the same thing she had. Not that she could identify that experience, but it was a shared moment, she guessed. Sort of.

Hurrying down the passageway, Amelia came to a stop in front of her door, where Jack sat just outside of it. With wide green eyes, he stared up at her.

Amelia reached down and scrubbed him between the ears. "What's wrong, boy? Do you want to go in?" Opening the door, Amelia waited for Jack to scurry past her and into the room. He simply sat and meowed.

Walking in, Amelia moved to the chest, lifted the lid, and dug through her clothes. Picking out a plain white cotton sundress, she laid it across the foot of the bed, grabbed her bottle of wrinkle release, and gave it a few squirts. Quickly, she smoothed the few persistent crinkles left in the material, and then turned back to the half-open doorway.

Jack sat staring in.

Amelia bent over at the waist and patted one hand against her leg. "Come on, boy. Get in here so I can close the door. What's wrong?"

Jack simply sat on the other side of the threshold, *not* budging.

With a grunt, Amelia rose and walked to the door. "Okay. Have it your way." After a good frown, which she was pretty positive the cat didn't notice in the first place, or if he had, wouldn't care, she closed the door.

Glancing at her watch, she then grabbed her undies and strapless bra from the chest, stopped long enough to take that watch off and toss it on the bed, and then hurried to the bathroom. A nice shower, a nickless shave, and some lotion to smooth it all out sounded like a fine idea to her. Even though ZuZu tried to force her to be a bit more froufrou than she normally was, Amelia *did* want to look nice for a change.

Flipping on the shower, Amelia heaved a big sigh. Who was she kidding? Impress? *Hail* yes, she wanted to impress. Why?

Because she was completely attracted to the leader of the bunch, that's why.

Darn it, how could she help it? Ethan Munro was an enigmatic sort of fellow, if you asked her. Enigmatic, as well as several other fascinating and potentially charming characteristics. *Other than* incredibly sexy, of course. Good grief, that was a given. The man hummed with primordial raw male power, confidence, and pure outright strength, incomparable to modern man. Sure, there were those few guys who were big and strong—especially the ones on ESPN's Strong Man Competition. Those guys could pull a tractor with their teeth! Their necks were as big around as her waist!

But ZuZu had been a trauma nurse before becoming her assistant/PR person/all-around greatest-doer-of-everything, and she'd given Amelia the skinny on modern guys. *Two words, Amelia: big weenies—and I'm not referring to any part of their anatomy!*

Apparently, Amelia guessed, most injured guys did quite a lot of whining.

She couldn't imagine any one of the Munro knights being weenies. All except Aiden, and it would totally be put-on, just to get the nurse's attention . . .

Stripping off her workout clothes, Amelia kicked them into a pile and stepped into the shower, where a sudden thought grabbed her. It was the very same thought that grabbed her each and every time—no lie—she stepped into a shower.

In almost every great horror or mystery, the shower was the very place where someone, mostly the poor innocent female, *bit it*. She certainly didn't want to end up like poor ole Janet in *Psycho*.

As Amelia hurried through her shower, keeping her eyes glued to the shower curtain, she wondered briefly how her thoughts could meander from sexy Ethan Munro to poor doomed Janet in such a short time. ZuZu would have called her a Weir-Doe, as her best friend had a habit of doing. Amelia preferred the word *quirky*.

Accomplishing the fastest leg-shaving in the history of womankind, she rinsed, dried off, applied her lotion, then pulled on her undies and bra. Wrapping the towel turban-style around her hair, Amelia wiped the moisture from the mirror, bent down to grab her makeup bag from its place in the corner, and then rose.

A woman's translucent face stared at her from the reflection.

Amelia gasped and turned around. Nothing—no one—was there. When she turned back, the reflection had disappeared. Her heart thumped wildly, and she had to take a few deep breaths to calm herself. A few words to self couldn't hurt, either.

"Okay, get a grip, girl. You like haunted, remember? Ghosties and stuff? Aren't you the one who begged the staff of Spirit Hunters to let you accompany them on an investigation? Isn't Halloween your favorite holiday? You asked for it, you got it. Now buck up and take it." She nodded to herself for reassurance. After several moments of deep breathing and staring at her own reflection, she nodded once more.

Dangit, she'd seen a ghost-face in the mirror.

Although hesitant at first, she smiled.

Cool.

One thing, though, that Amelia was certainly *not* was an impostor. Nor was she a liar. She'd be the first to admit that she'd been scared. Who wouldn't be freaked out by that? She was one of the world's biggest scaredy-cats. The only difference was, she liked it. *A lot.* Oh, boy, she could hardly wait to tell Ethan and the guys.

Who she'd be meeting—*in the flesh*—as soon as twilight, rather, the *gloaming* came upon them. And though she had no window to speak of, to give her a view of the outside, she knew she had a relatively short amount of time to finish getting ready. She wasn't a primper by any means, but she didn't want her hair all poking up and the hem of her dress stuck in her panties, either. So after drying her hair and brushing her teeth, she as-fast-as-she-dared applied her scant makeup and lip gloss, deodorized and perfumed her body, then slipped on the sundress ZuZu had picked out, which, in all honesty, was quite lovely, with an empire waist and a slim ribbon tie to the back. Thankfully, the scooped neckline wasn't overly scooped—not that her Victorian-era boobs, kindly termed such by ZuZu, needed any encouragement at all to show themselves. She found her white strappy sandals, pushed her feet into them, grabbed her iPod, tucked her hair behind her ears, and stepped out into the passageway.

Jack was still sitting, just over the threshold.

Amelia scowled at him. "You naughty cat. You *knew* about the ghost lady, didn't you? That's why you won't come in the room."

Jack flicked his tail and closed his eyes.

"Hmm. See ya later, chicken boy," Amelia said, and started off down the corridor.

In just a few minutes, she'd be shaking hands with six medieval men. Warriors.

They'd all hacked off at least one head in their day.

Excitement hummed through her veins as Amelia hurried along, the grain of a story about six enchanted sword-wielding Scotsmen and an American girl haunted by their castle's resident ghost growing by the minute.

It wasn't until she'd nearly made it to the staircase that another thought crossed her mind.

She'd felt absolutely no threat whatsoever from the ghost-face in the mirror.

Which, to her calculations, meant she'd been visited by a different spirit altogether.

Chapter 11

By the blood of Christ, never, in all the centuries passed, had the gloaming hour seemed so scarce. Puny. It was bluidy puny, that's what it was.

Ethan, eager to get back to the keep and spend as much of what little time remained in Amelia's presence, instead had to listen to the squabbling fools who made up his kinsmen. All wanted to sit beside Amelia at supper. All wanted to be the first to aid her in lifting a blade for the first time. All wanted to have a listen at her music box—iPod, she'd called it.

All, including his own pitiful self.

He, though, was not a squabbler. He was laird, and by the saints, he wouldn't act as idiotic as his men. He'd fairly choose who would be first today, then tomorrow, and the next, and so on. Eventually, he'd take a turn.

Although he damn well wanted that turn this day.

Worse still, he wanted all that time with Amelia *alone*. Something he not only couldna have, but had insisted his kin not to *allow* him to have.

By Christ, he wanted to kiss her. Fiercely. He wasn't exactly sure when that particular want had overcome him, but damn his soul, it had. Not only that, it'd interrupted his sleep, his entire wakefulness.

A bigger fool than Ethan Munro couldna be found, and he damn well knew it to be true. He no more could be alone with her, and by the devil he couldna kiss her, than he could live a normal mortal life. He knew not who enchanted him and his men, but whoever it was had done so out of hatred for not only himself, but for any woman he showed the least bit of favor to. 'Twas seemingly the curse of it before he'd become trapped in the bluidy enchantment, and could damn well be the way of it now.

And he'd not risk anything happening to Amelia Landry.

All at once, Ethan noticed his kin had stopped arguing, and were downright quiet. He paused in his walk toward the keep and turned to look over his shoulder. "Aiden, you willna—"

Ethan closed his mouth. The men had stopped several paces back, dead in their tracks, and were staring straight ahead, past Ethan. Gilchrist had his mouth open. Aiden, well, to see him with such a stunned look upon his face was frightening, by the by.

Slowly, Ethan turned to see just what had halted the five warriors.

No more than a handful of steps away stood Amelia, just outside the keep's front doorway.

The air left his lungs, leaving him feeling just like he had when Rob had knocked him from the scaffold whilst building the tower. His knees felt gummy and frail, as though he had no bones within, and he could do nothing but pray to God that none of the weaknesses showed, and that his stupid self wouldna fall over his big feet once he started moving again.

Damnation, the lass was beautiful. He could do little more than stare. Aye, she'd jest him good once he was finished, but for now, he'd do it.

Modern maids, he concluded, did not mind showing their bare person. Which, he also concluded, was fine indeed with him. Amelia's skin, a golden color flecked with sun speckles, stood stark against the white gown she wore, which, he might add, came to her knees. It pulled snug beneath her breasts, which, he might add once again, with that low neck left plenty to the imagination. A simple plain white gown, and she looked like a goddess. Amazing.

No jewels. No baubles. No high-coiffed hair.

Amelia Landry didna need any of it.

It was then Ethan realized he'd taken a wee bit too long with his ogling.

Not near enough for him, for he'd enjoy nothing more than another hour or two of naught *but* ogling. Well, mayhap he could think of something more, but not at the present. But for Amelia, aye. She'd started to squirm, right where she stood in her white little slippers, or whatever those modern things on her feet were called.

"Stop standing there ogling me, you big perv, and come here"—she held up her music box and wagged it—"that is, if you want to have a listen before the guys beat you to it."

Ethan moved then, and just as well. The pounding behind him came not from a herd of horses, but from his big-footed kinsmen. Blessedly, he reached Amelia first, before the herd stampeded them down. He didna think he'd rushed too fast, for he'd no' wanted to look like a green little lad, but damnation, he had only a scant hour. And he'd spent ten minutes of that bathing.

Amelia's eyes locked with Ethan's just as he reached her. They softened, widened, and then moved shamelessly over his entire body, from the toe of his boots to the top of his head. When they settled on his gaze once more, she licked her lips, a smile lifted one corner, and she stuck out her hand. The one not holding the iPod.

"Hello, Laird Munro."

Ethan left his gaze in place, looking square into those lovely eyes of hers. He reached blindly for her hand, wishing he was pulling her against him instead. "Aye, Amelia Landry, *hallo*," he said, just before he lifted her hand to brush a kiss across her verra soft knuckles. Soft hands, yet strong, well formed—

"Move out the way, lad. You're takin' too long," said Aiden with a mighty shove.

Thus ending his almost-encounter with Amelia's hand.

Indeed, he'd moved too slow. Had he no' taken so much ogling time . . .

Aiden pushed his big stupid self in front of Ethan, gave him one more shove for good measure, and then proceded to grab Amelia by both shoulders, pull her close, and plant his mouth right against hers, and then kissed her with a big, loud smacking sound.

Damn him.

Worse, each of his own kin—the verra ones who'd be dead before the gloaming ended if Ethan had anything to do about it—pushed their stupid selves in the same place, and each gave Amelia a kiss on the mouth. On the damned bluidy mouth.

He'd gotten a handshake.

She had the nerve to giggle. Mayhap even squeal a time or two, in that way lasses do whenst showered with male attention. He'd know. He'd showered plenty of maids in his day.

Most had turned up dead, dunna forget.

Ethan took a step back. Aye, most had turned up dead, including his own wife, and he wasna about to provoke any misgivings about his fondness for Amelia.

Besides, 'twas only fondness, by the by.

Naught more.

Should've worn a bib, she told herself. *At least then the slobber wouldn't have run down the front of my new sundress.*

The slobber, Amelia noted, came not from the five—count 'em, five—medieval guys who'd just pulled her into bear hugs and planted big sloppy kisses right on her lips. *Nooo*, not from that.

The slobber came from her own saliva glands, the ones that had suddenly activated into hypermode the second she'd laid eyes on a very live-in-the-flesh Ethan Munro.

She'd hidden the slobber well, she thought.

After flying down the stairs, Amelia had found the great hall empty. So what did she do? Tore out of the hall like some rabid bat, and as soon as she'd flung open the door and stepped out into the waning Highland twilight, she'd seen them.

Rather, seen *him*.

Ethan Munro, the enchanted one, standing right next to you is a pretty powerful experience.

Ethan Munro, in the flesh, climbing out of an inland loch, wrapping a fresh length of plaid around himself with deft hands, water dripping from his soaked hair . . .

Wow.

Then, for that soaking wet warrior to clap eyes on you, and for you to actually *see* the desire and determination burn there? Double wow. No words could come close to defining what Amelia had felt in that split second, when Ethan had first seen her, *knowing* he could walk right up to her and touch her. And that there was only a limited amount of time to do it.

She was mentally adding it to her list of things never to forget. *Ever*.

Peeking through the wide shoulders of the Munros, she spied Ethan, now standing back and letting his kinsmen have their time with her. He seemed patient. In control.

A mental image of her scooting through their kilted legs, grabbing Ethan by the hand, and dragging him off, came to mind. It made her smile.

She almost did it.

Instead, she pulled herself together and gave the nearest bulk of muscle, which happened to be Torloch, a gentle shove. "Okay, okay, you guys have had quite enough hovering." She returned the wicked grin Torloch gave her. "Sheesh. You fellas act like you haven't been around a girl in—"

"Centuries, lass," Aiden finished, the glint in his eyes as wicked as Torloch's grin. "Bleedin', bloomin' centuries."

"Well, be that as it may, buster, I'm not your next chicken nugget. Now shoo." She gave them each a push in the direction of the door. "We've got things to accomplish, supper to eat, and music to listen to. So move it!"

Rob, Ethan's younger brother by nearly nine years and almost the spitting image of him, stopped beside her and gave her a winsome smile. "You remind me quite a lot of my sister, you do. No' in looks, mind you. Just your boldness." He gave her another quick peck on the cheek, then stepped inside.

Sorely, tall, a bit lankier than the rest, with dark hair and blue eyes, came next. "You dunna remind me o' my sister at all." He kissed her again on the mouth, but ducked her swat and scrambled into the hall with a chuckle.

Amelia was beginning to wonder if she should have done a little research on Scottish customs. Even though the kisses she'd received from the Munros had been more of the family type, they'd still been kisses by guys other than her own family. A kiss was a kiss, darn it. ZuZu would absolutely die if she knew.

And would kill to trade places with her.

Finally, the Hadrian's Wall of Muscles dissipated, and only one big, giant stone remained. Ethan. She almost laughed at the solemn look on his face. Standing there with his arms crossed over his chest, he waited patiently for her.

There was a lot to be said about a guy who had patience.

So she'd heard.

Amelia closed the few steps between them, crossed her own arms over her chest, and grinned. "Stop your pouting, Mr. Munro, and let's go eat."

"My kinsmen are naught but *geintleach*." He glanced at her. "Heathens."

"They're okay. Besides, I gave them the iPod." She inclined her head. "Come on."

Together they walked, side by side, Ethan with his hands clasped tightly behind his back. His presence was almost overwhelming. He smelled like fresh air and . . . Zest? She leaned in and took a whiff. Yep, Zest.

"Guthrie buys it for us in bulk. 'Tis a pleasing scent, aye?" He lifted his forearm and sniffed it.

Amelia chuckled. "Yeah. It really is."

They walked a bit more, and all at once, Ethan grabbed her by the arm and pulled her to a stop. "Amelia?"

With her heart in her throat, she swallowed and met his gaze. "Yes?"

Ethan's eyes searched her face, lingered on her lips, and then lifted again to stare at her. "You look . . . fetching in that gown."

Amelia gulped. "Thanks."

Still staring, his voice deep, he said, "I'll walk you to the table now."

With a nod, and feeling like the village idiot, Amelia agreed. "Okay."

Being from South Carolina, where fireworks are still very much legal and to prove it, you can drive a few miles on any given day and find a fireworks warehouse, Amelia had plenty of experience with all sorts of explosives. Black Cats and M-80s had always been her poison of choice as a kid. Not a weekend went by that she and her brothers and sisters didn't set off a sack full in the backyard.

That's what Ethan reminded her of. A lit M-80, full of tightly wound power, ready to explode as soon as the fuse ignited, then *kaboom!* She had to wonder, as he placed her hand in the crook of his arm, just how long his fuse was—no pun intended.

And when, if at all, he'd explode.

"Why do you have such a naughty look upon your lovely face?" Ethan asked as they neared the table.

As Amelia sat at the long wooden table, surrounded by six hungry medieval warriors, she really could do little but laugh. "I'll tell you later. I promise."

Exactly ten minutes later, and supper, which consisted of meat pie and potatoes, was over. Amelia glanced at her watch, and then at Ethan. "Is it just an hour, or does the time vary?"

He stood, grasping her by the elbow and pulling her up. "It varies, aye, but not by much. Come. Leave these dolts with your music box and what few crumbs remain on the table." He looked at her. "I'll take a turn with it later. For now, I'd rather walk. With you, if you've a mind to?" He lifted a brow. "Jell-O-Butt, remember? You said 'twas your way of staying fit after a hearty meal."

Amelia smiled. "Are you accusing me of eating a lot for supper?"

"Methinks you ate nearly as much as Rob did."

She laughed. "And you're the gentleman who'll offer to help me walk off those extra calories, huh? Well, then, it's not every day a fourteenth-century warrior offers that up. I'm game."

They headed outside and started across the meadow, and Amelia immediately noticed they had a trailer. A follower. Several yards behind, but still a follower. She looked over her shoulder, then back to Ethan. "Why is Sorely behind us?"

Ethan kept his gaze trained straight ahead. "Because, Amelia. I asked him to."

"Why?"

It was several seconds before he glanced down at her, and when he did, the fading twilight caught in his pewter gray eyes, the intensity turning them a shade darker. "I fear for your safety, that's why. Any woman I've grown close to has found her death."

Amelia's heart fluttered. The fact that the cause of such fluttering came in the form of a seven-hundred-year-old guy who had substance for about one hour a day was certainly a perplexing thing. She smiled. "Not only do you barely know me, Munro, but all those mysterious deaths happened centuries ago."

He stopped then, and looked out across the loch. "He's also there to make sure I keep me hands off you."

Gulp.

Amelia stared at Ethan's profile as he continued to look out over the water. A good, strong profile, to her notion, and sexier than any man she'd ever met or seen. The thought of kissing him made her knees turn mushy. But in the real world, she had *rules*.

She had a mind to put him at ease, so they could at least enjoy their first walk in the flesh, for crying out loud.

"Listen, Ethan," she said. "A., I have rules. Lots of them. One of them in particular involves no kissing or touching on the first date. Call me old-fashioned, but that's me in a nutshell. And just so you know ahead of time, since you are about the *sexiest* thang

I've ever laid eyes on, and there might *eventually* be some sort of a minor issue that arises, I don't sleep around. Savvy? Yes, I see it in your eyes, the big question, and I'll answer it. Of *course* I've had sex before, but it was a long time ago, when I *thought* I was about to be married, and since all of that was a big fat mistake, I've taken a solemn vow to withhold sex until the One, aka my husband, *begs* me for it on my wedding night. And B., even if I couldn't control myself and my nearing-thirty abstinent self full of sexual urges and just . . . threw you down in the heather and had my way with you, I think ole Sorely back there"—she jerked a thumb in that direction— "wouldn't stand a chance in hell of getting here in time to stop me." She gave him her most devilish grin. "I'm quick that way."

He turned to her then, eyes glinting. Body shaking. Mouth turned up at the corners. Then that wicked, wicked grin burst into a loud, echoing bellow of a laugh. Ethan laughed so hard, tears came to his eyes, and he scrubbed them with the heels of his hands. After a moment, when he could look at her and *not* laugh, he shook his head. "By the blood of Christ, woman," he said, smiling. "By the sacred blood of Christ, you are unlike any lass I've ever known."

Amelia grinned, waved at Sorely, who'd stopped and had his hands up in a *what's going on?* gesture, linked her arm through Ethan's, gave him a tug, and inclined her head to the loch. "Come on, stud. Let's get going before we run out of twilight. Besides," she said, falling into stride beside him, "I haven't told you about the brand-new ghost who showed up in my bathroom mirror."

Chapter 12

Ethan stopped and stared at Amelia. "You what?"

"Saw another ghost." She scratched her chin. "Well, I suppose I didn't *see* the other one, but I'm pretty sure this spirit was a different one." She shook her head. "I didn't feel any malevolence at all. No threat."

Part of him, the sane part, wished a *normal* mortal had come upon the Munros to give them aid, one with just as much reception, mind you, yet . . . normal. One who would be afeared, mayhap, of a bluidy ghost in the mirror.

"I think it was a woman's face, but it was so translucent, I can't be sure. But I got the feeling it was a woman. I stayed and stared into the mirror for a while, but I didn't see it again."

Aye. One who mayhap didna insist on remaining in the verra room where ghosties did things to gain her attention.

Ethan shook his head. "Saint's, woman, why didna you tell me sooner?"

A naughty grin pulled at Amelia's mouth, making her eyes tip upward, as well. "Because. I'd just gotten out of the shower. Standing there, with nothing on but my understuff." She wiggled her brows. "I leaned down to grab something off the floor, and poof! Just like in the movies, when I rose, there she was, staring back at me in the mirror." She lifted one shoulder in a shrug. "Besides. Like I said, I felt no threat—none whatsoever." She shivered. "Not like that other night, when the room turned freezing cold. Now, that was freaky."

"Next time, lass," he said, "call out. One of us, me in particular, will be there straightaway." He looked at her hard, akin to the look he gave his kinsmen when their mirth distracted them from their duties.

"Don't give me that lairdly glare, mister." She grinned and pulled him onward. "Besides, you were busy being nekkid in the loch."

Damn, he couldna help it. He grinned. "So I was." They walked a bit more, and Ethan turned in the direction of the knoll.

"Does it bother you?" Amelia asked. "Being here, seeing that"—she pointed at the place where Devina had been found hanging—"and not knowing, all this time, what really and truly happened?" She shook her head. "That would drive me nuts."

Staring at the very spot where that damned gibbet had stood erected, his wife's dead body on the ground beside it, Ethan considered. Aye, it had nearly driven him mad, he'd pondered so hard and so long—for years he'd done the like. "Over seven hundred years, lass, will ease the insanity a wee bit. No' much, but some." He shrugged. "Didna matter how long I pored over what facts I could recall, 'twould always end with me no' knowing what the bluidy hell happened that day." He glanced at her.

And again his knees nearly gave out from beneath him.

The faded light of the midsummer's gloam made her sun-touched skin appear darker, and her long, straight, fair hair a bit lighter. Those unusual eyes, which dipped down at the inner corners, toward her nose, and swept upward at the outer corners, toward her temples, were rimmed by long, feathery lashes. He noticed now how it was streaked with various shades of nearly white, to a deeper gold. And before he could stop himself, he pulled her to a stop and reached for it. As he rubbed the strands between his fingers, he stared, fascinated by its softness, the way it felt thick and healthy, yet soft as down feathers. It looked rather fetching, he thought, tucked neatly behind her ears.

He looked at her. "Why is it you broke your legendary rule with my kin?" he asked. "But not with me?"

With the toe of her shoe, she kicked at a clump of heather and gave a half grin. "I thought we'd already settled the kissing issue, Munro." With boldness, she stared right up at him. "Hmmm. Legendary rule, huh?" She shook her head. "Their kisses were of the familial type. You know—like giving your sister a kiss."

"I know what familial means, Amelia."

She reached up and patted him on the shoulder. "Well good, then. You now understand fully the reason they were allowed to kiss me and you're not." She grinned and began the ascent up the knoll, and then glanced over her shoulder. "Yet." She waved him closer. "Come on, slowpoke, before you turn into smoke."

Well, Ethan thought as he scrambled up the incline behind her. What could he say to that?

At the crest, Amelia found a smooth rock, brushed it off with her hand, tucked the hem of her gown beneath her, and sat. "Wow. What a gorgeous view."

Ethan squatted down beside her, resting his forearm on his knee.

He'd rather it be crooked around the back of her neck, pulling her head close to his . . .

"What is that? I saw tons of them on my drive here."

He looked and followed her pointing finger. "A rowan bush."

"Are they all small like that?" she asked.

Ethan shook his head. "Most grow rather large, and can last for centuries." He inclined his head toward the forest. "There are some there, in the ravine, hundreds of years old."

She nodded, and gazed out, where the sun had already dipped below the crags, leaving the sky various shades of purple and red and orange. "How is it you learned to speak English?"

Ethan chuckled. "We picked up small bits here and there throughout the centuries, but no' much at all. 'Twasn't until Guthrie came along that we learned it in full." He shook his head. "That man is no' a patient teacher, and had he been able to clobber us, he'd have done so many a time."

She turned to him and smiled. "Well, you and the guys must be wonderful pupils. You jockey the English language pretty darn good. Even the American version."

He gave her a nod. "There are some things you say that baffle me, but I can usually figure it."

And then she surprised him. She reached over and lifted one of his braids, pulled it close, rubbed her fingers over it. "Your hair fascinates me. Most guys these days wear it really short. Why do you braid it?"

That Amelia found anything about his person fascinating was a good thing. And, Ethan found, that while their banter edged around jests and plants and hair and language learning, the banter was passing comfortable. Easy. He felt he could sit upon the craggy knoll and have speech with the lass until the wee hours of the morn, and that she'd find interest in his speech, and he in hers.

"Hello?" Amelia said, waving a hand before his eyes. "Earth to Ethan." She grinned. "That's what we say when the person you're speaking to zones out."

"Ah," Ethan said. " 'Twas thoughts of you that zoned me out, by the by."

"Oh, really?" she said, jutting her chin a bit higher. "Like what?"

He shrugged. "In my day, the only time men and women had a score of minutes in speech was in bed." He grinned at her. "No' your average speech, I'd warrant, and more noises, really, than actual words." He winked. "You're passing tolerable to talk to, Amelia."

One fair brow lifted. "Passing tolerable? That's it?" She brushed off her skirt and feigned irritation. "And if you spent your time in bed with women talking instead of, well, you know, then, I wouldn't tell the guys about it." A smile pulled at her mouth. "Just some friendly advice."

Ethan chuckled. "Well-taken, then." He looked at her. "In truth, I thought about the ease in which we have speech, and how much I find pleasure in it, by the by."

Her smile widened, her already-white teeth nigh unto glowing in the gloom's light. "Somehow I bet that just isn't the norm for a medieval guy, huh? Taking pleasure in talking with a woman?"

"Modern lads are different, then?"

Stretching out her long legs, she tucked the material of her gown snuggly about them and crossed her feet at the ankles. "Hmmm. You got me there, laird. Some guys, I imagine, like to talk to their women. My dad likes to talk to my mom."

"And what about the man you nearly wed?" He threw a stone and watched it bounce into a clump of heather. "Did he take pleasure in having speech with you?"

"He seemed to at first," she answered. "But most people always act a certain way when they first meet. You know? Put their best face on? Polite, manners, act interested in all that you do?" She snorted. "Later, wooo-boy, you really find out what people are like."

A hawk screamed from the pines, and the sound echoed across the meadow. The sounds of the night grew louder, and Ethan knew he had but a handful of moments left of twilight.

Tomorrow, he'd plan his time with Amelia a bit wiser.

Amelia stood and peered out over the loch. "Did you hear that? How cool." She smiled down at him. "It was a hawk, right?"

"Aye," Ethan answered, and stood up beside her. "So what sort of person are you, Amelia Landry?" He looked at her. "What would I find after time passed?"

She turned to face him full-on, and her features

were cast in shadow. The glassiness in her eyes remained, though, shining and full of mischief. "You'd find the same me you see today." She held her hands out. "This is what you get. All except this sundress, of course. ZuZu suggested I buy it, you know. To set a more professional example. I guess she thought my ratty robe, which she cut into shreds before I came here, and my bikini top weren't cutting the mustard." She grinned. "Seriously. I live at the beach, so you'll usually find me in very casual clothes. I eat Cheez Whiz straight from the can. I love fast food, sugar, and I really like to talk. A lot of times to myself. Out loud. I love to read, especially Bram Stoker, H. P. Lovecraft, and Stephen King. He's the master of horror, you know."

"I see."

"Anyway, I love scary stuff—books, movies, you name it. Could be, though, because I was born on Halloween." She clapped her hands together once. "That's about it. Now, your turn."

"You were born on All Hallow's Eve?" he asked.

She nodded. "October thirty-first, at eleven fifty-four p.m. How's that for a *woo-woo* effect? Almost at the midnight hour."

"We've a connection, then. Although I know not the hour, I was born on that same day. 'Tis why so many feared me, I suppose. By a superstitious means, you ken?"

"I sure do ken. Now, what else?"

He held his hands up. " 'Tis no' that much to tell, lass. My day was vastly different than the times you live in now."

"Bad answer, chief. Spill the beans. Let it all hang

out." She smiled. "Come on, no secrets. What sort of things do you like?"

"Swordplay. Fisticuffs. Fighting. Hunting was rather enjoyable. Eating." He grinned. "I remember being rather fond of a good tumble."

"What man isn't?"

He shrugged. "Medieval?"

She laughed and stuck out her hand again, this time grasping his. She shook it. "Absolutely medieval. Ethan Munro, it has been a great pleasure sitting with you on this knoll and learning all sorts of fantastic stuff—*oops!*"

Suddenly, Amelia was against him, had actually fallen against him. Ethan grabbed her by the waist, and for a moment, they did naught more than stare and breathe. Her very nearness, the feel of her hips beneath his hands, her hands flat against his chest, the scent of her hair, and, by the blood of Christ, those lush breasts verra close made Ethan all but growl. "I'm no' carin' overmuch for your rules about now, lass," he said. He dropped his gaze to her lips, which looked powerfully soft and inviting, and frowned. "That blasted first date rule in particular."

"Phew," she said, her voice hoarse, barely above a whisper. She fanned herself. "It's hot out here, don't you think?" She licked her lips, her eyes wide, unblinking. "Don't you?" Still, she remained pressed against him.

"Beg pardon, lass," Ethan said, lowering his head, bringing his mouth closer to hers. "But forgive me for ignorin' your bluidy rule."

"But—"

All at once, Ethan's substance faded with the remaining shards of twilight. Amelia stumbled straight through him as though he wasna even there.

'Twas the way of it, his enchantment. There, yet no' there at all.

Behind him, he heard a very naughty word escape Amelia's mouth, and he chuckled. When he turned around, she'd regained her posture and was smoothing out the front of her gown. In the faded twilight's glow, her arms and legs and face took on a dark, mahogany glow against the white of material and fairness of her hair. She scowled at him.

"I couldna help myself, lass," he said. "You stumbled—"

"I didn't stumble against you before, Ethan," she said. Slowly, a grin replaced the frown. "I didn't stumble at all."

Ethan blinked. "Then what happened?"

With a slow glance, she looked around the knoll.

An eerie feeling settled in the pit of Ethan's stomach. And with good reason.

Her grin widened. "I was pushed."

Chapter 13

Amelia stopped at her door and turned. After a huge debate with Sorely, who'd met them at the foot of the knoll, and then a continuation of that debate with the rest of the Munros as to the hows and whys she'd been *pushed* into the big laird she presently stood in front of, she was literally tired. Tuckered. Pooped out.

None of them wanted her to stay in her room, and all of them wanted to stay with her. The laird included.

"Ethan, stop pouting. Honestly, no matter where I go here, whoever's trying to reach us will do it through me." She inclined her head to the far wall, indicating the direction of the loch. "The knoll, my bathroom, the bedroom—I could change rooms a dozen times and it won't matter. They'll just follow." She crossed her arms and ducked her head to look into his very irritated downcast eyes. "That's a good thing. Don't you see?"

He looked up. "I dunna see, nay." He crossed his own arms over his chest and leaned back against the wall. "And I'm no' pouting. I just dunna like it when—"

"You're not in control?" she finished.

"Aye. That."

"Well, Mr. Enchantment," she said, and was rewarded a darker frown for it. "You've no substance for twenty-three of the twenty-four hours that are in a day, and you've been that way for centuries." She smiled. "It might be high time you turned a little of that control loose and trust me."

Ethan glanced back down. " 'Tisna that I dunna trust you, lass." When he lifted his head, his eyes locked on to hers. "I couldna live with myself if something happened to you. You ken?"

Amelia found she liked hearing the phrase *you ken?* quite a lot. "I really do understand. Ken-ing as we speak, actually."

He smiled, and to her, that was something.

"Ethan, the presence that pushed me into you wasn't a threatening one." She considered. "It might have been the same entity that I saw in the mirror."

"Amelia, if one ghost can gather enough force to push your body into mine, then so can another." He shook his dark head, both braids dragging across his shoulders. "I dunna like it." He heaved a hearty sigh. "But your head is thicker than a mule's, by the by." He looked at her. "I'll be just here, and if you need me for anything, just call out me name." He lowered himself to the floor and sat, legs bent, forearms on knees, head back, plaid hanging just so. Gargantuan sword now lying on the floor beside him.

Amelia leaned against the door frame and stared at him for a moment. She was getting more and more used to him and the others, and pretty soon she wouldn't think it too big of a deal at all to be speaking to an enchanted medieval man.

But for now, it still totally fascinated her.

"Thanks for a great evening," she said, resting her head against the old wood. "You were nearly the perfect gentleman."

Ethan narrowed his eyes. " 'Twas no' easy, I can assure you."

She laughed. "No doubt. But you know something?"

"Aye?"

Pushing off the door frame, she smoothed her dress and stepped just inside her room. "Tomorrow will be our *second* date."

A grin started at one corner of his very sexy mouth, and spread into a full-blown, teeth-showing smile. "I know that."

She waved. "Good night."

"Aye, and to you, Amelia."

She quickly shut the door before she crossed the passageway and made an attempt to make out with an enchanted guy.

Tomorrow's twilight wouldn't happen soon enough.

Clear their names . . .

Sitting straight up in bed, Amelia realized it wasn't a dream. She'd just been whispered to. Again. Fumbling for the lamp switch, she turned it on and grabbed her watch from the bedside table. 1:22 a.m. She'd been asleep for three and a half hours.

She jumped out of bed, nearly knocking Jack from the foot, ran over to the door, and threw it open.

"Ethan! Wake up!"

Ethan sat exactly where she'd left him earlier. He jumped straight up, looking as alert as he had before. "What in bluidy hell, Amelia?" he said. "Is something amiss?"

"No, no, nothing amiss. Just listen. I've got an idea."

Just then, all five Munros came up the corridor.

"What is it, girl?" Torloch said.

"Aye," said Sorely. "Did the ghost wake you up?"

She waved her hand. "No. Well, yes, sort of. Just listen. I've got a great idea, I think, and I *really* want you guys to agree to it. So listen with ears wide-open. Okay?"

Rob poked a forefinger into each ear and scrubbed. "Aye."

Moving her gaze to Ethan's, she started. "There's a couple of parts to this idea, so just pay attention closely—that means my eyes are up here, *Aiden*," she said, snapping her fingers and directing the big warrior's stare from her chest, which—oops, had very little covering on it—to her face.

"Sorry, lass, I canna help it." Aiden had the good grace to blush. "Truly."

With a groan, Amelia ducked back into her room, dug through the chest, and pulled on her big sweatshirt with the silhouette of Alfred Hitchcock's profile on the front. Served her right, she supposed, for jumping up and running out with just her ideas and a tank top and drawstring bottoms on. But dangit, she was used to living alone, *not* with six big medieval oglers.

"Now," she continued, stepping out of the room. She noticed Ethan was glaring at Aiden, who didn't seem to be bothered by it one little bit. She'd worry about that later. For now, on with her plan. Crowded into the narrow passageway, the Munros listened.

"I propose two things here," she said, making eye contact with each man. "First, I'll try to make contact with the specter that's been whispering in my ear and appearing in my bathroom mirror. Oh. And shoving me."

Ethan's face grew tense. "What did you hear, lass?" He moved closer. So close, they were nearly touching.

If only they could.

" 'Clear their name,' " she said.

"That is it?" asked Gilchrist, who thoughtfully rubbed his chin. "No' thing else?"

"That was it." She met Ethan's gaze. "But if I *tried* to purposefully talk to this ghost, maybe I could get a few answers." She smiled. "About *you*."

The men glanced at one another.

"You know? *Clear their name?* It seems obvious the spirit means the Munro name." She smiled. "Whoever's presence is speaking to me knows you're innocent of murder, Ethan, and is trying to get me to help."

Ethan's penetrating pewter gaze didn't falter from Amelia's—not once. "What's the second part of the proposal, Amelia?"

With a deep breath, she told them. "I want to write your story, Ethan. The whole story. All of this." She waved her hand between all of them, herself included. "The murder, enchantment, you, me, the ghosts—all of it."

Ethan scrubbed a hand over his jaw. "What of our names?"

"Fictional." She saw the confused look in his eyes.

"I'll use a different clan name. We'll make it up together, if you like." She walked over to him and tilted her head back to look him in the eyes. The very sexy, *unsure* eyes. She could feel it in her soul, how much Ethan hated feeling that way, out of control, uncertain—especially being laird of the men who'd been cast into the enchantment just for being a Munro knight. Just for following their leader.

He felt a responsibility to them even after seven hundred years.

Amelia ducked her head to the side to gain Ethan's attention. When he looked at her, she smiled. "I really, really want to write this story, Ethan. But not if you don't want me to." She glanced at the others. "Not if any of you prefer me not to." She turned back to the Munro laird. "But I promise to do a phenomenal job."

"Methinks to say her aye," said Rob.

A murmur of *ayes* sounded through all the men. All but one.

Ethan's watchful gaze continued directly, and Amelia knew he was running a hundred things over in his mind. True, she wouldn't write the story if he didn't want her to. But man, she sincerely hoped he wanted her to.

"You seem eager about this," he finally said.

She smiled. "I haven't been excited about a project in more than a year."

"Will you read it to us as you go?" Torloch asked. "Methinks that'd be a fine idea, wouldna you agree, Ethan?"

"Our verra own bard," Sorely said.

"And such fine subjects," Aiden said with a grin.

Ethan met her gaze and he gave a nod. "If anyone

could do our tale fairness, 'twould no doubt be you, Amelia Landry." He grinned. "I say aye."

"Woo-hoo!" Amelia yelled. *"Yes!"*

The guys cheered with her.

Without thinking, she threw her arms around Ethan's neck. Of course, they went right through him.

"Oops," she said, and the men roared. She gave Ethan a deep, long look. "Guess I'll save that for the second date."

Someone whistled.

It wasn't Ethan.

His stare was so smoldering, Amelia thought her Hitchcock sweatshirt would burst into flames.

Boy, she was in big trouble.

"Enough, by the Bruce's sword, enough! What's wrong with ye young folk?" Guthrie hollered up the stairs. "Go to bed, and stop all that carrying on!"

With much bustling and grumbles, the Munros all trudged off to their chambers. All except Ethan, of course. He stood beneath the low-light torch lamp in the passageway, a feral look in his silver eyes.

Amelia backed into her room. " 'Night."

He cocked his head. "I vow I see something in you that wasna there before."

She grinned. "And what is that? Excitement? Mischief?"

He studied her for several seconds, and the energy between the two of them all but snapped in the air.

Rubbing his chin, he smiled. "Contentment."

When Amelia climbed into bed, she did so with a big smile on her face. Ethan was right. She was content, especially with her work. For the first time in months, she felt exuberantly anxious to start on a project. The fact that the subject matter within had everything to do with Ethan Munro was certainly no secret—not to her, anyway. The man simply *wowed* her. Of course, his looks went beyond those of fantasy. But Dillon-the-ex-fiancé-turned-jackass had been a fantastic-looking guy, too. Not an Ethan Munro, by any means, but still quite sexy. One major, simple difference stood out, though: real versus not real. Eventually Dillon's real self came out, thank God, and in Amelia's eyes, no matter how fantastic the eye candy, the *real* greatness came from within. That, to her, defined the wow factor.

She snuggled down into her covers and grinned. She rather liked the great stuff she saw inside Ethan. Confident. Strong. Loyal. Funny. *Very* determined. Trustworthy. And whether he would admit it or not, a kind, soft heart. Sure, he'd hacked off more than one enemy's head—that was the way of his day. But she could tell, just by the way he handled his men, that he took great care of his loved ones, and whoever *was* a loved one could count on his steady, devoted presence. In her mind, they were probably the luckiest people in the world.

A fleeting thought caused her to pause, and it filled her mind as she drifted off to sleep. It wasn't of ghosts, or malevolent entities, or best-selling novels, or drastic deadlines, or publishers who might drop her due to lack of quality work. Or, in her case, lack of work, period.

Instead, it was of enchantment. Of six men trapped, existing yet not living life. Of trying to cram some sort of normalcy into a single hour every day. Of having a rare few souls even be able to see them, much less interact with them.

Amelia closed her eyes, listened to the creaks and groans of the fourteenth-century tower house, and as sleep overcame her, she thought of one more thing.

How on *earth* she'd handle falling in love with a seven-hundred-year-old warrior, trapped in an enchanted window in time . . .

Chapter 14

The morning came, and Amelia sprang out of bed at just a few minutes past six a.m. She stretched, grabbed the pen and pad of paper from the desk, then fluffed her pillows and settled her back against them. Jotting a few notes, a few names, and then a rough outline of the story, she read it over, squealed, and jumped back out of bed.

Raising her arms in the air she did a little *Dirty Dancing* kind of boogie.

Woo-hoo! She was *back*!

"Ahem."

Amelia squeaked and nearly tripped over her own victory dance. Turning, she found Ethan, propped against her closed bedroom door, booted ankles crossed, and a glint in his eye.

A very merry glint in his eye.

She put a hand to her fluttering heart. "Ethan! What are you doing in here?"

A slow grin crossed his face. "I heard you moving about in here and thought to see why you were squealing so early in the morn." The grin widened, his eyes moving over her. "I'm verra glad that I did, too. But I want a solemn vow from your lips, woman, that you will never venture to do such frolicking in front of the men." His eyes smoldered. "Particularly garbed in *that*."

Crossing her arms over her chest, because, good grief, she was still in her pj's, she gave a casual shrug. "And to think I was going to throw that little routine into the daily pre tae kwon do exercises as a warm-up."

Ethan said something in Gaelic under his breath.

Amelia laughed. "Okay, shoo! I've got to get dressed, take my morning walk, and *git bizzy*." She walked over to where she'd left her watch, checked the time, and grinned at Ethan over her shoulder. "I have to do this walk alone this morning so I can talk to myself about the book. You know? Oh, and don't forget about our second date tonight." She batted her eyes. "Just as soon as your pumpkin turns into a coach, I'll be ready."

Even though she was pretty sure he had no idea what she meant by the pumpkin/coach thing, he pinned her with a deep, dark stare. The kind that lasts so long it makes you squirm. The muscles in his jaws flexed and even being an enchanted, nonsubstantial ghostlike entity, M-80-type energy radiated off of him in waves.

"I willna forget." Then he slipped through the wall.

Just the feral look in those silvery eyes, and the deep, rich brogue that tinged his words made breathing a little difficult. Made it *a lot* difficult, actually.

Boy, she could really use a can of Cheez Whiz.

She'd think about that later—the craving of the Whiz and the way Ethan Munro made her knees wobble. She had a busy day of planning ahead, notes to take, research to begin, along with a beginner's tae kwon do class to teach.

Not to mention date number two with a seven-hundred-year-old fighting machine.

Maybe thinking of the second date as a research venture would keep those darn butterflies from beating the crap out of the inside of her stomach. She doubted it. Besides, the anticipation of the second date was supposed to be fun, right? She'd think *fun, fun, fun* for the rest of the day.

Grabbing her shorts and hoodie, she dropped her pj's, got dressed, and brushed her teeth. After a quickie glance at the mirror, which proved empty of any sort of ghost or spirit, Amelia pulled her hair into a ponytail and set off. No iPod today, she thought. No outside interruptions. She was in high-octane writer's mode for the first time in over a year. Only the sounds of Highland nature and the feel of the mist against her skin to start her day, yessiree.

Tonight she'd try to make contact with the friendly ghost who had graciously pushed her into the hard chest of Ethan Munro. And thank her. Or him. *Profusely.*

Drawing in a big lungful of air, she smiled. She could hardly wait.

Slipping into the passageway, Amelia tiptoed downstairs, across the great hall, which was empty anyway, out the front door, and into the splendor of the Scottish Highland midsummer morning.

Ethan watched from the ramparts at the top of the tower as Amelia happily trotted across the meadow and toward the wood. 'Twas a fine Highland morn, with the sun just creeping over the top of the crags, and a light mist hovering over the ground.

Finally, she slowed to a walk, and every few steps or so she'd bend over and inspect, touch, pluck, or bring to her nose and sniff whatever clump of some bit of plant or bush or tree she'd come across. At the old yew tree, she stopped, squatted near its thick, gnarled trunk, rubbed the bark with her fingers, and then turned upward and peered through the limbs.

"You should tell her that we used to climb to the verra top o' that same yew and throw sticks by the handfuls at unsuspecting victims," said Aiden. "Remember that winter when the vicar came to visit? We were no' quite a score, aye?"

Ethan chuckled. "Aye, fool, and me arse still aches with the memory of the blisterin' Da gave us, no thanks to you." He looked at his cousin. "You were a verra bad influence."

Aiden shrugged. "I did me best."

"What is she doin'?" asked Rob, pointing.

Torloch edged up to stand on the other side of Ethan. He peered out. "Looks like she's sniffin' the bark." He shook his head. "Modern maids are baffling."

"Why are you no' with her, Ethan?" asked Gilchrist.

Ethan shrugged. "She's busy with her bard's work." He glanced sideways at Torloch, then Gil. "Inspecting and sniffing and such. Research."

"She told you to stay here, aye?" asked Sorely, who leaned on the hilt of his sword.

Ethan frowned. "Aye."

Being the idiots they were, his kin roared with laughter.

Ethan's frown deepened. Aiden slapped him on the back. " 'Tis all right, cousin. Give the girl a bit of solitary sniffin' time, and then go into the wood after her."

"Aye, Ethan," said Rob. "She's already mentioned not knowing anything about the plant life." He grinned. "You can name them all for her."

Ethan considered. Aye, 'twould be a fine afternoon to amble through the forest, and mayhap they'd see a bit of animal life along the way.

Sorely wiped his brow. "Why do you think the spirits are interested in Amelia, Ethan? Why no' just contact us?"

"Aye," said Gil. "We've been here plenty long for the ghosties to have a word wi' us."

Ethan shook his head. "I vow, I don't know. Mayhap 'tis simply that Amelia is mortal and can physically help?"

Torloch rubbed his chin. "Guthrie is mortal."

"Aye," said Rob. "But he's no' experienced any other beings, save us."

Ethan watched as Amelia turned, threw up a hand and waved, and then disappeared through the mist into the dense copse of pine, elm, and rowan, her hair swinging off the back of her head like a horse's tail. Ethan waved in return. "I dunna ken myself, Rob," he said. "But if anyone is brave—and daft— enough to help us, 'tis Amelia."

Every man said his aye. Ethan knew they'd already grown fond of the lass, and how could they not have? But their fondness was passing different than his.

Amelia, to him, had become necessary.

Never before had a woman seized his thoughts as

she, and by Christ, even whence he was in slumber, he dreamed of her. Fetching, aye. She was that, indeed. Engaging in conversation, true of heart, brutally honest—all traits he admired in anyone, but to find them all bound into the form of the most captivating of women? And by the sword, she made him laugh. He couldna recall when the last time his tears had leaked from laughter. A bluidy miracle, Amelia Landry.

"Look ye, lads, at our laird's face," said Aiden. "What think you?"

"Besotted," said Torloch.

"Aye," Sorely, Rob, and Gilchrist all agreed at once. "Most definitely besotted."

Ethan stepped away from the rampart's wall and glared at each of his kin. "I am no' besotted."

"No? Are you the verra same lad who at any moment plans to go chasing the lass into the wood to pick flowers?" said Sorely. "That seems verra besotted to me."

"No one asked you, fool. Besides. I wasna going to pick bluidy flowers," said Ethan. He stopped and rubbed his chin. He gave his best gnarly smile. "A round with the blades with you dolts would better suit this fine morn instead of a womanly turn through the forest, methinks." He met each man's eye. "What say you?"

That indeed brought grins to the warriors' faces, and they each reached for their sword.

Of course, 'twas a rather hefty tale on Ethan's part. He'd much rather take said womanly stroll through the wood with Amelia than knock swords with his foul-mouthed kinsmen.

Not that he'd ever admit the like.

He'd forgo the stroll with Amelia. He'd go tomorrow. Mayhap he'd go every day, henceforth.

Besides, he thought, unsheathing his broadsword, a bit of frustration taken out on his irritating family would suit him just fine. Mayhap, even, 'twould settle his innards.

He had a second date with Amelia to prepare for, after all.

With his left hand, he grabbed his sword, once again grateful that, although enchanted and ghostlike to the mortal world, he moved like flesh and blood with his like-enchanted kinsmen.

He hoped he could manage not losing a limb before the morn was over.

Holding the big blade with both hands now, he pointed it at his cousin. "You first, little lad," Ethan said to Aiden.

Aiden grinned and began to move. "My pleasure."

Amelia stretched out the muscles in her back, rubbed her eyes, and glanced at her watch: 6:20 p.m. Dragging the pointer to the File tab, she clicked it, then Save, and then closed her laptop. She smiled. Not a bad day's work for someone who'd just found her groove.

One thing was for sure, though. Once she started really getting into the writing, she was definitely going to have to find a really great spot outside to work. While her bedroom was spacious and quite cool, she couldn't work clammed up in a windowless room. She wanted the Highlands, the outdoors—maybe somewhere with a nice view of the loch. Definitely a place where she could sniff that clover . . .

Reaching down, she gave Jack a quick pat, then moved to the clothes chest and opened the lid.

What on earth to wear on a second date with Ethan?

Amelia dug. Dug like a teenager going out on Friday night. The Bram Stoker T found its way into her hands, and she smiled. "Not tonight, Bram ole boy, but definitely tomorrow."

Jeans? Capris? Another sundress? Finally, her fingers brushed across something soft and silky, and she grabbed, pulling up a dark blue rayon sundress with tiny white flowers. Baby-doll cut, just to her knees, with an empire waist. Another ZuZu special. *Perfect*.

Besides, she thought, laying the dress across her bed to ready it for a good wrinkle releasing. It wasn't every day she had a date with a handsome warlord. Why not look her best?

After picking out a pair of dark blue wedgie heels, Amelia hurried through a shower, the whole getting-ready routine girls go through, including leg shaving, lotioning, hair drying, makeup application, teeth brushing, and, once finished, applied a little vanilla-sugar-flavored lip gloss (*Thanks, ZuZu!*), a single squirt of perfume, and all without the first interruption by a ghost—friendly or unfriendly.

She was slightly disappointed about the no-ghost thing, once she thought about it. Sexy-fun-medieval guy on one hand, friendly ghost on the other. *Hmmm*. Definitely Ethan.

Once again grabbing the iPod, Amelia hurried from the room. Twilight grew near, and she didn't want to waste one single second of it.

Taking off down the corridor, Amelia scooted

around corners as fast as she could without tripping, and finally, blessedly, to the stairway leading to the great hall. She'd made it nearly to the bottom when the door flew open.

Ethan stepped inside, dropped a stack of plaids, and made his very determined, persistent way toward her.

Chapter 15

Amelia blinked, stared at Ethan's face, and continued down the stairs. He moved toward her with long strides, eyes locked on hers, as if he'd known the exact spot she'd be in once he'd walked through the great hall door. She could have been anywhere. But as soon as he'd entered the castle, he'd come directly toward her. He had the look of a man with an intention—of what exactly, Amelia wasn't sure. At present, he looked as though he'd just plow her over. With brows pulled into a slight frown, mouth drawn tight, and eyes somewhat narrowed, he almost seemed angry. No, not angry . . .

Where on earth had he gotten that shiner? And what was that stack of plaid material for?

She held her ground, smiled, even though she was pretty sure it looked dopey, and kept right on walking. He grew closer, closer still, and Amelia stopped and fought the urge to step out of his way. "Ethan, what's—"

Ethan Munro walked right up to her, and with no hesitation, no fumbling—nothing but sheer resolve, took Amelia's face between his big hands, tilted her head back and just to the side, then took the briefest of moments to linger, stare into her eyes before he lowered his head and settled his mouth over hers.

The world stopped all around her.

Ethan's mouth was gentle as he situated it over hers, and Amelia could feel the restraint he used with his fingers, holding her head, her jaw fiercely, as if using that bit of pressure would keep him from consuming her in one big breath.

She sincerely hoped it didn't.

Then Ethan let out a long sigh against her mouth, slid his thumbs along her jaw, and tugged, urging her to open, and she did. Just the sensation of the calluses on both hands chafing the skin of her face made her shudder. Her lips trembled against his, and when he tasted her with a slow, gentle swipe of his tongue, Amelia sighed at the sensations that crashed over her, and she reached with her free hand and brushed her fingers over his stubbled cheek.

As if her acceptance of his kiss set off a switch inside him, a low growl sounded from deep in Ethan's throat, and his kiss deepened. No longer gentle, or slow, it was the kiss of a desperate man, one who'd found something he'd been searching for and he was not letting go. Amelia felt it with every fiber within her, by the hunger of his mouth, his tongue searching hers.

Without warning, his hand found the iPod, pried it from Amelia's fingers, and tucked it somewhere on his belt. She hardly cared. He could have thrown it into the hearth for all it mattered.

As long as he did not stop kissing her.

The hand that had released her of the iPod found its way to the small of her back, and the other kept a firm grasp on the back of her neck. Ethan pulled her closer, and Amelia used both free hands to wind her fingers through his damp hair. He groaned against her mouth, and excitement fluttered through her as they both satisfied a hunger, a desire so strong that it left Amelia's knees weakened, her heart hammering out of control.

Ethan's hand, the one at the small of her back, slowly and with just the right amount of pressure, caressed the swell of her bottom, and God help her, Amelia groaned and leaned in to him . . .

Then, all at once, Ethan stopped, grabbed her by the shoulders, and pushed her backward. Both gasped for air and stared.

"What's the matter?" Amelia asked, her breathing sounding very much like that of a teenager who'd been making out for far too long in the back of someone's car.

Not that she'd ever done that before. Okay, maybe just once.

Ethan only stared at her, his gaze moving over her face, settling on her mouth, then down her body and back up again. Desire flashed in those silvery depths, and it made Amelia's insides quiver, made her skin warm.

Made her want his mouth back against hers.

"Why'd you stop?" she asked. She'd be mortified at herself later. For now, dangit, she wanted to know why.

Ethan dropped his hands and backed away from her a bit more. "Because, Amelia," he said, his breath harsh, his accent much stronger, deeper than usual, "your rule, aye? 'Twas either cease, or take you right here." He scrubbed a hand over his jaw and studied her for several seconds. "Christ, woman," he muttered, then put his hands on his hips, tilted his head back, and stared at the rafters. "Bleeding Christ."

And then he said a harsh, one-worder. It sounded like Gaelic. Probably a curse, she imagined.

She had to firmly agree.

Lifting a hand, she fingered the skin by her mouth, made tender by the abrasion of Ethan's stubbled cheeks.

A shiver ran through her.

When she looked up, Ethan's stare was fixed on her again. She did indeed have rules, damn every one of them, but she'd sworn by them and for now, raging hormones or not, she'd stick to them. Better to just move along, she figured.

For now, anyway.

"What happened to your eye?" she asked.

He shrugged. "Naught but a friendly tussle with Aiden."

Amelia quirked a brow. "I didn't know you could get injured while enchanted. Not that I know many enchanted persons."

"Only betwixt us Munros—"

A deep, loud, rowdy rumble of words Amelia didn't understand sounded from just outside the great hall, interrupting Ethan's sentence. She recognized the voice, she thought. "Is that Aiden?"

"Aye, 'tis." He turned and walked toward the door, then bent down and picked up the stack of plaid cloth he'd tossed down on his way in.

Then it dawned on her.

Ethan was indeed a devil. And he probably deserved that big black shiner he sported.

Amelia smothered a snort. "Are those guys out there *naked*?"

Ethan grinned over his shoulder. "Naked and mad."

Amelia laughed. "You want me to open the door?" She imagined five big nekkid medieval trick-or-treaters. "Seriously. I'll do it."

"Nay, you willna," he said, and then stared hard at her. "You're more fetchin' than you were yestereve, methinks." With a grin, he opened the door, threw out the plaids, and then slammed the door shut.

More shouts—probably Gaelic curses, of which she'd love to learn a few—and then after a few minutes of quieter grumbles, Aiden's distinct booming voice shouted once more. "Open the bluidy door, cousin!"

Ethan did, and his five kinsmen piled inside, their plaids barely in place as they cinched, brooched, and belted. All carried their swords in their hands, and they leaned them against the wall.

Sorely was still barefoot.

"Damn you, Ethan," Gilchrist said. "You didna have to take our clothes."

Aiden, who sported a similar black eye as his cousin and a cut on his cheekbone to go with it, walked past Ethan and straight to Amelia. He looked her over, head to foot. "You dunna look overwrought."

Amelia smiled. "And why would I?"

Aiden's eyes, a silvery blue, sparked mischief. "I know my cousin." He cocked his head, steadfast in his perception. "Damn lucky horse's arse, he is. Damn lucky."

"Come, Amelia," said Ethan, at her elbow and tugging. "I've a place to show you and we've no' much time."

Amelia smiled and waved at Aiden. "See ya later."

Aiden grunted.

"Teach me some of those naughty Gaelic words later, okay?" No telling when she could use them.

Aiden threw back his head and laughed, and then hollered at his kin. "Come, lads, now that we're all properly clothed, and let us see what Guthrie has cooked for us this eve." He glanced around. "Who has the bluidy iPod?"

Ethan slipped it from his belt and tossed it to Aiden, who caught it with ease.

Amelia laughed, and then as she hurried with the determined Highlander, reveled in the feel of her hand engulfed in Ethan's big, rough one. He pulled her right outside and slammed the door. Overhead, she noticed the swirling clouds of dark purples were mixed with those of gray. A storm approached. Oh, boy, how she loved a good storm, although she wasn't too sure she wanted to stand out in one.

"Who's going to be our guard tonight?" she asked.

"No guard," he answered, and continued in the same direction that she'd taken into the forest earlier that morning.

"I'm surprised," she said. "Especially after you left them nekkid in the loch."

Slowing his pace somewhat, he glanced down at her. "They trust you more than they trust me."

"Do they know I'm almost thirty and have been celibate for over a year?"

Ethan laughed. "Do you know I'm nigh unto seven centuries old and celibate?"

Amelia whistled low as they slowed even more. "Yikes. You got me there, laird."

Ethan grunted.

Amelia glanced over her shoulder at the keep, and the view made her stop in her tracks. The tall, gray ominous tower house reached toward the dramatic swirl of a thunderhead. Everything had turned that eerie dimness, void of color except the purple heather in the meadow. The loch appeared to be ink instead of water. "Wow. Look at that."

Ethan did, and he paused.

Amelia wasn't quite sure she'd seen anything so beautiful. "It's breathtaking."

"Aye, impossibly so."

She turned to find Ethan staring dead at her.

Quite a bit more breathtaking, she thought, than any scenery she could recall. Their shared kiss not a handful of moments before rushed back, made her shiver, and by the craved look in Ethan's eyes, he just might be remembering, too. In many a novel, she'd read of men looking at women with such deep desire and hunger, they all but turned to mush. Amelia couldn't quite determine what *mush* was, but she indeed did now know what that feeling must be like, because that's *exactly* how Ethan was looking at her. *Starved.*

She tilted her head back and gave a smile that probably came off as weak. "Are you taking me deep into the forest to make out with me?"

With one of those big, calloused hands, Ethan used the pad of his thumb and ran it lightly over her lips. "If that means kiss you senseless, then aye. I am."

Breathe? Was she supposed to be *breathing*? Good Lord, how could a primal man, a warrior who hacked away at his enemy's very necessary body parts, walked around and tore meat from bones with his teeth, dressed in one giant piece of cloth (what *was* under there, anyway?), continuously carried, and probably slept with, a sword nearly as tall as she, be so gentle and passionate? Where'd he learn to kiss like that, anyway?

The thought alone made her tremble.

Linking his fingers through hers, Ethan gave a tug. "Come, lass, so we can find shelter before the rain begins."

As they began walking again, Amelia sighed. "I think next time—"

"Tomorrow."

She smiled. "Yes, tomorrow, I'll find some rubber boots to wear. These wedgies aren't exactly made for hill walking."

Ethan stroked her hand with his thumb. "That will be quite a sight whilst you wear a gown."

"I'll reserve the gowns for when we, I don't know, dine in." She glanced at their interlocked hands. Big veins fanned out over the back of Ethan's hand and roped up his forearm, over his bicep, and disappeared beneath the silver band he wore. With her free hand, she traced the vein closest to his wrist, pushed on it with her fingertip a few times, and he glanced down.

"What are you about, lass?"

"You must swing that big sword around a lot," she said. "You've got spongy veins."

He nodded. " 'Tis a fine sport, swordplay. I'll teach it to you, mayhap starting tomorrow."

"Sounds good to me." They walked into the forest, a canopy of pines and various other trees native to Scotland that she'd ask Ethan about later. Earlier, the trees had made it shady, blocking the sun's view. Now it was rather dark and shadowy. Still, it was breathtaking, and the heavy scent of pine and clover filled the cool air.

Ethan led her down a different path, one that disappeared into another part of the forest—one she'd missed earlier. In the distance, the sound of rushing water hummed. Something else she'd missed.

The woods grew dense, the path little more than a footpath but obviously well traveled. Birds chirped overhead, and Amelia pulled closer to Ethan's side.

Somehow, the ridiculous urge to holler, *Lions, and tigers, and bears, oh my!* came over her, but she held it in.

"You're no' frightened, are you, storyteller?" Ethan asked, a chuckle in his voice. "Ye who purposefully beds with spirits?"

"Well, it is kind of dark in here," Amelia said. "Where are we going, anyway?"

With a gentle tug, Ethan maneuvered her in front of him, and their bodies brushed close in the exchange. Once in front, he placed his hands on her hips, crowding in behind her, and whispered against her ear, "Close your eyes and walk."

Amelia sighed and did so, and moved her hands to rest on his. His warm breath against the sensitive part below her ear made her want to just fall against him, but he had a purpose, and she was quite determined to find out what it was. They walked, and she picked her footing with care.

Ethan's mouth again was at her ear. "Now stop, Amelia, but keep your eyes closed. And listen."

He slid her hair to one side, and his lips settled against her neck. "What do you hear, lass?"

Chapter 16

"U m," Amelia said, her voice cracking just a wee bit. "I, uh, can't hear anything with your mouth on my neck."

Ethan smiled. Damn, he did a lot of that lately. How could he help it? Amelia Landry was by far the most charming lass he'd ever known.

No' to mention the most beguiling. He used full restraint, just to keep from pawing her like some starved creature.

Mayhap, he was one.

Ethan scraped his chin against the verra soft skin of Amelia's neck, and then pulled back, just a bit, else he'd no' be able to control himself.

That kiss earlier had seared him to the very bone. It'd left him wanting more. He knew, though, he couldna have more. Mayhap more kisses, aye. He'd beg for those if he had to. But nothing else. Amelia deserved more than that. Better than him. Her company, and access to her lovely mouth would have to be enough for now.

"Keep quiet and listen, girl," he said. "Closely."

"Okay."

She did, and the only noise besides their breathing

were the pine martins and insects, and if she strained her ears—

"Oh!" she said in a loud whisper. "I hear it! Only . . . what do I hear?"

Ethan chuckled, wrapped his arms around her waist, and pulled her against him. The feel of her warm body, the slight shudder of her breath, the roar of her voice vibrating through her back and to his chest made him want to tighten his hold on her and never let her go. Keep her there forever.

Impossible, he knew, and instead settled for having her here now, in the gloaming, snuggled easily, and he brushed his mouth once more against the soft shell of her ear. He felt her shiver, and he knew he'd treasure the sensation for the rest of his days. " 'Tis fairies singing."

Amelia sat still—a miraculous event in itself, he thought—and tilted her head toward the sound. Then she turned to him, that cocksure grin that he found completely endearing, with one corner of her mouth lifting higher than the other, crossing her face. Had they no' been so close, he'd have never seen it, so cast in shadows were the wood.

"You're full of it, Munro. There's no such thing as fairies."

He kissed her jaw, and she squirmed. "You're being savored by an enchanted fouteenth-century man and you say there are no fairies, aye?"

She made some sort of sighing noise, and Ethan smiled. "Come, lass, I'll show you."

They walked through the thicket, up a slight rocky incline, where the sound of water grew louder. The wood cleared, allowing a bit of light within, and Amelia gasped.

"Oh, wow." She stared a moment, then turned back to him. "How beautiful."

Pride leaped up from within at Amelia's pleasure of his home. " 'Tis a *bhùirn*." He glanced at her. "Fresh water, moving fast."

"Burn," she said, repeating the Gaelic word. He rather liked the way his language sounded on her tongue. "What is that sound? You know, it actually *does* sound like high-pitched singing."

Moving her over to the flat rock, near the edge, he held her elbow whilst she found her balance, sat, and he climbed down beside her. " 'Tis the water slipping fast over the reeds and grass." He smiled. "My mother used to bring me and my brothers and sister here, and we sat upon this verra rock and listened to the fairies." She turned her face, partially cast in shadow, toward him as he continued. "Being the little devil that she was, she'd also bring a handful of rowan berries, or stones. When we werena lookin', she'd toss them into the burn and yell in a hushed whisper, 'See you there, children! 'Tis the fairies after all.' "

Amelia smiled at him. "I can't believe I'm sitting on a rock that you sat on when you were a little boy." She shook her head and looked out across the water, and the first raindrops began to fall. "Your mother sounds great. I bet you miss them all." She lifted his hand and held it.

"Aye, to the point of ache, at times. To have lived so many years." He looked at her then. "Lifetimes, Amelia. I've lived scores of lifetimes, but 'tis only been one for me. A big, long, never-ending lifetime. An unfulfilled one at that." He looked at her. "Until you."

The waning glow from the gloaming shone in her upturned eyes, and they looked like two jewels. Glancing down, she traced the hard calluses of his palm, across the curve in his hand. She picked the other one up and did the same. "From your sword?"

He stared at her, thinking just how soft her fingers felt sliding across his roughened hands. "Aye."

"Funny. I never thought of both hands being used."

He grinned. "Big sword."

She looked up at him, the usual mirth gone. "I didn't expect any of this, you know?" Her gaze lowered. "*Definitely* didn't expect you, that's for sure."

Ethan grasped her by the chin and lifted, forcing her gaze back to his. "Nor I, Amelia. And I've thanked God and the saints over and over for sending you here." He wanted to say *to him*, but didna feel he could claim that right.

And he had no bluidy idea how long he'd get to keep her, either. *I'll take what I can get . . .*

"You've missed your supper, you know," Amelia said, threading her fingers through his. "You're gonna be hungry."

He tucked her hair behind her ear. "Some hungers can be ignored, in truth." He leaned closer, inhaling the scent of her hair. "Others canna be ignored at all." He let his gaze move over her, the gown with wee white flowers, the womanly shape of her throat, and by the blood of—

"You're ogling again," she said. Her voice was naught but a hoarse whisper. "I think I like it."

He grinned at her.

"But time's almost up, and frankly, I'd rather make out—"

Ethan leaned over and covered her mouth with his, and she sighed against him. Her lips moved with his, gentle at first, tasting with her tongue. Her hand crept up to his face, found the scar beneath his eye, traced it, then lowered her fingers to the junction where their mouths met, and Ethan thought his heart would burst from its cage. He cupped her cheek and tilted her head just so, and he was lost in the sensation of her kiss, of the stirring she caused that had been dormant for centuries, and it was then that the rain began to fall heavy upon them, splattering against their faces, soaking their hair, yet they didn't stop. Amelia moved closer, leaned in to him, and the groan she made low in her throat all but drove Ethan over the edge.

And just that fast, the twilight hour ended.

Amelia pitched forward as he lost substance, but she caught herself with both hands on the flat rock.

She cursed under her breath, and then gave a charming, apologetic smile. "Sorry."

He laughed, but it wasna a true laugh. "Trust me, lass." He stood to move out of her way, although she'd be able to pass right through him, as it were. "You're no sorrier than I, I'll warrant. Although 'tis vastly amusing to hear someone so beautiful speak in such a foul manner."

She scooted her feet beneath her bottom and stood, brushing off the seat of her gown. In the waning light, he saw the whites of her teeth as she smiled. "Keep calling me beautiful and I'll swear all you like."

This time, he did laugh. "Come, you witty bard, let's get out of the gloom before you canna see two paces before you."

Back under the canopy of trees, where the rain couldna reach Amelia, they started a slow return out of the forest. Whilst he and Amelia walked close, they each kept their hands engaged; he clasped his tightly behind his back, she wrapped hers about her own waist.

He sorely wished it could be different.

And mayhap, if Amelia was awarded an audience by the spirits in his hall, things could be different.

If only.

"Please tell me where a medieval guy learns to kiss like that," Amelia asked in her usual bold way. "Is there a School of Toe-Curling you attended?"

He grinned. "If I did, you must have found the same school in the twenty-first century."

Amelia laughed at that. "Hardly." She looked at him. "You must have brought it out of me."

Ethan shook his head. "Indeed, lass, you are a jester." He looked at her. "I rather like that about you."

With a gusty sigh, she picked her way through the dense wood.

Earlier, he'd physically helped her manage. Now he was little more than a bluidy ghost . . .

"Stop it, Ethan," she said. "I can look at your face and tell you're thinking pouty thoughts."

He shifted his sword. "I'm no' thinking pouty thoughts."

"Yes, you are," she said, stopping at the junction of the footpath. "We've tomorrow at twilight, right?"

He smiled. How could he not? "Aye."

"Good. I think we both need some toe-curling experience." She grinned at him. "You know? To get good at it?"

He laughed, and the sound carried through the trees. "I wholeheartedly agree, although the lads will begin to get a wee bit jealous, methinks."

"Pah," she said, staring down the north path. "Lads, schmads. They'll get over it." She smiled. "Especially once I carry out my surprise." She pointed. "What's down there?"

Ethan looked. "Eventually, the border to Munro land. Otherwise, just more trees and such, along with the aged yew. I'll take you to see it tomorrow, lass. Now, what surprise?"

"Oh, you'll see," she said, lifting her brows in that jesting way that let Ethan know she was up to no good. "It's a secret, buddy, and I can keep a secret longer than anyone. I perfected the craft as a kid."

"Why do I have verra little trouble believing that?"

Amelia laughed. Ethan rather liked the sound.

They continued to walk until the keep came into view. The rain had slowed, but by the overhead still lingering, the gist of the storm hadna hit yet. They'd made it to the meadow before the rain picked up.

"You know something," she said, seemingly uncaring whether the rain pelted her or not. "It might be a good thing, your substance lasting only an hour."

Ethan glanced down. "And why is that?"

The rain began to fall heavier, and Ethan noticed that Amelia looked even more fetching soaked by a Highland storm than she did perfectly dry.

She laughed and tucked her wet hair behind both ears, exposing the fine cut of her jaw and smooth skin of her damp face. "Because there's no way I'd ever get any work done if I had you in the flesh all day long."

Ethan gave her a grin. "Toe-curling?"

"Aye," she said, mocking his accent and doing a fine job of it. "Definitely toe-curling."

Together they laughed, and only later would Ethan tuck away the moment as one of the most cherished of his entire life—live or enchanted.

Because deep down he knew what they'd found could never last, and that the summer would eventually draw to an end.

And Amelia Landry would return to her bard's life . . . elsewhere.

Chapter 17

A week went by before any more *woo-woo* stuff happened. And, as always, it happened when Amelia was alone.

Funny, too, that. Every night before she'd gone to bed she'd made a routine of calling out to the spirits. Sure, she sounded like a dork, but hey, she'd been visited by the ghost lady *and* Mr. Freeze. They'd come to her willingly. So why not give a shout-out?

First, she'd stood in the bathroom, staring into the mirror. She'd even reenacted the old pick-up-the-thing-from-the-floor just to see if, when she rose, the face would be staring at her again. Not once did it happen. It frustrated Amelia to no end, because she hadn't asked for it to happen in the first place, and then when she'd *wanted* it to happen, nothing. Nada. Zip. No wispy smoke, no apparition, no spine tingles.

Not even a good hair raising.

Dangit.

Next, she'd brought a few extra candles from the kitchen to her bedroom and had sort of a little mini séance on her floor. She wasn't a medium by any means, but she'd watched her fair share of *Ghost*

Hunters, so she sort of got the gist of it. Or so she thought.

Nothing but a few chuckles had she stirred from the other side, and she didn't mean the *Other Side*. She meant from the *other side* . . . of the *wall*, and the chuckles had come from six big, medieval warriors who thought she and her antics highly amusing. But again, nothing happened.

Until now.

The one morning she decided to take another walk in the forest alone, it happened. Ethan had already taken her down the north path a few times, toward the border of Munro land, and had shown her the old yew tree. She stood in front of it now. Older even than the one he'd shown her before—the one at the end of the meadow where he'd gotten his butt whipped by his dad for chucking sticks at the vicar.

Now, *that* tree had to be close to a thousand years old if Ethan and Aiden had climbed in it as boys. They'd thought of it as old *then*.

This yew, though. Sheesh. It was older than *Jesus*, and when she'd said that out loud, Ethan had bent over at the waist and laughed. Reputed to be nearly two thousand years old, it actually sat only partially on the Munro border, with the biggest, thickest, gnarliest trunk, probably at least twelve feet around.

And it was whispering to her.

Only, the words were garbled and so low Amelia had a difficult time understanding. She stood at the base of the tree and looked up, wondering if, for a second, the whispering could be the sound of the leaves rustling. She cocked an ear, and when that didn't help, she leaned over and pressed an ear to the trunk. Finally the unintelligible whispering stopped, and the words became clear.

"Break the ssspell," she heard. "They must go back . . ."

Amelia stood there with her ear pressed to the ancient bark for what seemed like forever. Not another word followed. Even when she knocked on the trunk and said, "Hello? Excuse me? Are you still there?" Nothing happened.

She'd been given a message, and that was that.

All at once, the forest grew darker, as if what small amount of light filtering through the thick canopy of trees disappeared behind thick black clouds. The whispers grew in numbers, low voiced at first, then getting louder, but at the same time, hushed, as though twenty people were speaking all at once, fighting for airtime and all wanting to be heard—but not by *her*. Amelia understood none of it.

And this time, it wasn't coming from the old yew tree. It was coming from all around.

There went those darn hairs on her neck again.

As she hurried fast from the forest, not so much scared, but freaked out, the whispering grew angry, but luckily, stayed behind her. And once she cleared the wood and stepped out into the meadow, the sounds altogether stopped.

All except for a single ominous laugh.

Amelia stopped and looked back. While she saw nothing out of the ordinary, she *felt* a chill, in the dead of a midsummer morning, that reached clear to her bones. The same kind of coldness she'd experienced in her bedroom that one night.

So she definitely had two different spirits at work

here. A nice one, and a not-so-nice one. Good cop, bad cop. One trying to tell her something, the other trying to keep her from it.

She continued to stare at the primeval forest, the very one where little Ethan Munro and his bratty cousin Aiden used to play and pull their shenanigans, where the lady Munro had taken her children to hear the singing fairies.

Looking at it now, not one thing seemed out of the ordinary.

But Amelia knew better.

She turned and made her way back to the keep. Her stomach had started growling nearly an hour before, so she was more than ready to grab some breakfast, find Ethan, tell him about the whispers, and then continue where they'd left off the day before with the character charts.

So far, she'd learned a great deal about Ethan Munro.

Not to mention it gave her plenty of opportunity to just sit and stare at him, talk to him, and wait with high anticipation for the fall of each night's twilight.

Amelia grew fonder of the warrior as each day passed. All of them, actually—they really were great guys. But Ethan in particular.

It scared her a little.

Actually, more than a little. If she allowed her mind to wander and worry, all sorts of reasons *not* to become so attached to Ethan would crowd her mind. Some of those reasons were born of pure insecurities on her part—insecurities of the regular sort, like, What if Ethan just stopped liking her, after she'd already fallen for him? Or the more sensible big red flag, How would a relationship ever work out between a mortal and an enchanted soul—one who never dies . . . ?

Or maybe he *could* die? He could certainly get a big black eye. She hadn't thought of that before.

Good Lord, she didn't have a clue. With so much going on, the guys, the enchantment, the ghosts, her deadline—who had time to seriously ponder the what ifs? Not her, nosiree, and no way.

Just as she grew closer to the great hall door, sounds from behind the keep rose in the air. Loud sounds. Mean sounds. Grunts. Cursing. *Cheering.*

And the *clang clang* of steel hitting steel.

Hungry or not, *this* she had to see for herself.

Highland mist, Amelia decided, needed no schedule. At any and all times of the morning, day, or night, it could swirl and sift throughout the trees, over the meadow, the loch, and through the surrounding hills. She found she liked it. It gave the landscape a moody, eerie look and feel, which was right up her alley, of course.

The mist had slipped over and around the keep, wafting sheets of near-translucent white drifting like a live thing, and as Amelia eased around the corner of the tower house, to investigate the noises, which sounded a lot like a medieval battle, she froze in her tracks and held her breath. She wanted to stay undetected, lest they stopped doing the very cool stuff they were doing.

A swordfight, between Sorely and Torloch. Not a choreographed sword fight, although those interested her, too. Hardly anything was better than watching two sexy guys duke it out with a pair of swords, even if they were just acting.

Tor and Sorely weren't actors. They were real, honest-to-goodness medieval warriors, ones who'd not only dueled with swords for fun in their time, but had done it for pure, raw survival.

Big difference between medieval guys and actors.

She'd checked all their hands. Calloused, every one of them, from the grip of their two-handed broadswords. And it amazed her.

Tor and Sorely were in the thick of it, and they looked dead serious on killing each other. One would thrust, the other deflect. The sheer force in which the blades crashed together proved these guys meant business. Their biceps, cut and muscular, flexed with each swing of the sword, and with each swing came a rather naughty-sounding Gaelic word.

Actually, they were all shouting and speaking in Gaelic. Amelia couldn't understand a single word, but she could tell the naughty ones from the regular ones.

The naughty ones were followed by rowdy laughter.

Finally, Sorely and Tor's swords came together, then up, and they were face-to-face. Tor planted his elbow in Sorely's eye, who in turn swore and did the same back to Tor.

Aiden stepped forward and shoved the two stalemates apart. He hollered something in Gaelic, the rest of the guys cheered and replied, and then Ethan came forward, unsheathing his sword.

Gulp.

With an excited flutter in her stomach, Amelia watched as Ethan and Aiden made a slow circle around each other. All fun and laughter had completely disappeared from Aiden's face. Both had the same stance: bent at the knee, careful, predatory, slow steps, eyes fixed on each other, sword double fisted above their heads.

Truly a sight to behold.

Definitely adding it to that running list of things to remember forever.

Aiden took the first swing, and Ethan easily deflected. At six foot seven, Ethan moved like a panther slinking through the forest for prey. With those silver bands encircling each bicep, his roughened length of plaid draped casually, yet perfectly, over his chiseled body, he looked every bit the ancient Celtic warrior he was.

With a few encouraging shouts from the sideline Munros, the cousins began their swordplay, each taking bone-crunching swings at the other's head. Amelia caught herself ducking a few times, as if the blade swung at her own *encapitus melonus*. Once she almost squealed out loud, and she clamped her lips shut and put a hand over her mouth to keep the noise in.

Finally, just like Torloch and Sorely had done, Ethan and Aiden locked up with their swords, face-to-face. But with a strength that made Amelia's mouth go dry, Ethan shoved his hilt forward and knocked Aiden in the chin.

Someone shouted and the next thing she knew, Ethan and Aiden threw down their swords and withdrew knives from somewhere within their plaids. They circled, crouched, and the mist slinked through their legs and bodies.

Had Amelia not known any better, she'd swear the cousins were preparing to kill each other. Their faces were drawn tight, their mouths pulled into deter-

mined frowns, and already each sported faded re-
minders of the last time they'd duked it out.

Were they really going to knife fight in that thick
mist? How on earth could they see each other? And
it seemed the thicker the mist, the more the peanut
gallery, aka the Munros, cheered them on.

Amelia watched, stomach in knots. While Mel had
done, in her opinion, a fabulous job portraying William Wallace, and the battle scenes had been grue-
somely impressive (one of her favorite scenes had
been when the battle line of Highlanders mooned the
English), she thought nothing could compare to
seeing very real—even in their enchanted states—
warriors fight hand-to-hand combat with a short pair
of sharp pointy knives.

Amelia wondered briefly if Ethan and his clan had
fought with Wallace. She'd make it a point to ask
him about it.

Just as that astounding thought passed, something
caught Amelia's eye. Faint, barely there—so much so
she wondered if she had really seen it. *She had.*

Through the heavy mist, and moving about Ethan
and Aiden, a figure wearing a dark cloak emerged.
Although no face could be seen in the shadows of
the cowl, it appeared to be watching Ethan's every
move. Amelia blinked, unsure of her eyes. Could it
be the same figure from her dream?

Ethan took a swipe at Aiden and his arm passed
right through the cloaked form.

Amelia gasped, and then the figure turned and
looked straight at her.

And then it threw its shroud-covered head back
and laughed and started to drift toward the keep.

With her heart beating fast, Amelia moved from her spot near the corner and called to the figure. "Hey! Wait a minute! Come back here!"

When it turned, it lifted a long arm, beckoned, and hurried away. Amelia did the only thing she thought to do at the time.

She followed it.

Chapter 18

Just as Amelia hollered, Ethan jerked. Aiden's blade tip caught the side of his chin, but Ethan ignored it. Instead he watched Amelia hurry toward the rear of the keep from where she'd been watching their swordplay. Aye, he'd seen her, but hadn't let on.

"What's she doin'?" Aiden asked. "Pardon for the nick, there, old man."

"Who is she yellin' at?" Sorely, followed by Tor, Rob, and Gil, stopped to watch her.

As if she heard, Amelia shouted over her shoulder, "Can't you guys see it?"

"See what?" Ethan returned, glancing around.

"I dunna see a bluidy thing," said Aiden.

"Och, damn, that hardheaded girl," said Ethan, and stuffed his knife in his belt. He picked up his sword and sheathed it as he ran after her. What was she up to now?

His men followed, which was just as well. Not that any of them could help, but he wasna about to let Amelia go trailing after a spirit without him.

As she entered the rear of the keep, beside the larder entrance, she disappeared. Ethan hurried, and once inside, he paused.

"There," said Torloch. "She's gone up the larder steps."

"Even Guthrie doesna go up those," said Rob. "What's she doin'?"

Ethan let his kin muse out loud. He sifted through the wall and headed up the once-used back steps, which wound in a tight coil the length of the tower, clear to the ramparts. "Amelia!" he called.

"I'm here," she said, way above, and her voice sounded muffled. "Hurry!"

Ethan did, as much as his big self could, by the by. Unable to take more than two steps at a time, he wished he could fly. But he was enchanted, no' a bird. He hurried as best he could.

His men all managed the steps below him, cursing and, he imagined, elbowing one another as they clambered to reach the top. 'Twas a long bluidy climb.

Eee-than!

With his heart in his throat, Ethan ran as fast as he could up the remaining steps. The old wood door to the ramparts swung open at the top, and he hurried toward it.

Rushing out onto the landing, he searched for Amelia. Then he froze.

The daft girl stood on the narrow wall of the bulwark, her face white, and her eyes wide. Bare arms stretched out for balance, she trembled. Her lips were blue and she looked half frozen.

His men filed out the door, crowded behind him, and cursed, and Ethan held up a hand to warn them to stay steady. Their unease filled the air, and with good reason. His woman was teetering on the bluidy wall.

Ethan met Amelia's frightened gaze, which scared the hell out of him. She wasna the type to be afraid of anything. He prayed that when he spoke, his voice sounded steady and not crackin' with fear for her safety. "Step down, Amelia. Easy."

"I," she started, then cleared her throat. "Can't."

Ethan kept his eyes on her. "Yes, you can."

Amelia closed her eyes tight, and her footing faltered.

"Open your eyes, Amelia," Ethan said evenly. "Do it now, lass, and step down."

Without moving her arm, she pointed downward with her finger. "Can't." Her voice was barely above a whisper, and she didna open her eyes. "Rats."

"Where?" whispered Gilchrist in a like voice from behind. "I hate rats."

Ethan scanned the walkway, then looked at Amelia. "There are no rats, love. Come down."

She wouldna, though. Amelia stayed frozen to the spot.

With a deep breath, Ethan eased toward her, to where he was standing directly beside her. He spoke calmly. "Amelia, there are no rats. 'Tis only a vision. Now, step down." *Christ, if she fell . . .*

Still keeping her eyes squeezed shut, Amelia blew out a few gusty breaths, lowered one leg verra slowly, and muttered curse after curse—most of which Ethan didna understand—until her foot touched the walk. The other leg followed, and she stood as still as death, eyes closed.

Ethan let out a sigh of relief. "Open your eyes, girl."

She did, slowly, and one at a time. Glancing

around and behind her, to the other side of Ethan and the men, she looked up at him, her expression befuddled. "There are no rats."

"Nay, there's none."

She breathed out a long breath and leaned her rear against the bulwark wall.

The men all edged forward and gasped.

"Lass," Ethan said, "move away from the wall."

She did, and started to pace. "But there *were* rats, Ethan. Hundreds of them, all over here." She indicated with her index finger.

"Are you sure they're gone now?" asked Gilchrist. "I hate the bluidy things."

One thing Ethan loved about his brother Gil, he was brutally honest. Even when it came to admitting fear of a rodent.

Amelia continued to search. "They're gone." She turned and looked at Ethan. "But they were here." She shook her head and glanced around a bit more. "I'm a big chicken, admittedly, but there are some things I'm not afraid of—like heights—and some things I'm *petrified* of, like rats. I'm horrified of them." She waved her hand. "And that shrouded specter made hundreds of them attack me, which is why I jumped up onto the wall." She returned her gaze to his. "You didn't see it, did you?"

Ethan couldn't take his eyes off Amelia. He wanted to pull her to him tightly and kiss her senseless, and at the same time he wanted to strangle her. Slowly. "You could have fallen to your death, woman," he said. "I dunna care if you were following Christ Almighty himself, dunna do it again alone."

She flinched at his sharpness, but nodded. "Okay."

She glanced at his men. "Thanks, guys. Sorry to be such a pain in the—"

"Amelia," Ethan said. He could tell she was angry now, and probably still afraid and didna want to admit it. "I—we couldna bear to see something happen to you."

She smiled, heaved another sigh, and walked toward the ramparts door. "I know, and I appreciate it." Pushing the door open, she stepped inside. "I think I need a break"—she waved her hand—"from all of this."

Ethan exchanged a look with his kin, they shrugged, and then followed Amelia back down the back larder steps.

Amelia muttered the whole way down.

For Ethan, he was just glad to see her down. Muttering, mad—it didna matter to him, as long as she was safe.

That, he noted, had become quite important to him of late. Mayhap since he'd first clapped eyes on her.

When they reached the bottom, Amelia and Guthrie, who'd just returned from the market, conversed about department stores, rentals, and *deeveedees*—all of which left Ethan clueless. From the looks of his kin, they were just as stupefied as he.

"Lass," Ethan said. "Dunna be angry."

She turned from Guthrie, who'd merely shaken his head and began taking out various foodstuffs from the brown sacks he'd brought in, and gave Ethan a wide, glorious smile. "You silly boy, I'm not mad. I am, though, in need of a serious ghostless break for a day. Enchanted guys I can handle." She shuddered. "But that thing I followed to the top of the castle freaked me out, and I need to shake it off the best way I know how."

"Why'd you follow it, lass?" asked Aiden. "None of us saw it."

"Aye, could you tell it was wicked?" Rob asked. "And how did it persuade you into going clear to the top of the keep?"

Lifting an apple from the bowl on the table, Amelia buffed it against the thigh of her trews—shorts, rather—and looked right at Ethan. "I first watched it watching you, when you and Aiden were fighting. It was so weird, how it followed you with its eyes. Then it walked right through you." She shrugged. "I was surprised, and must have sucked in some air, because the thing looked dead at me."

"What then?" Ethan asked.

"It beckoned to me," she continued. "No words, just waving me on with a long, robed arm. So I did, and once I made it to the top of the keep, it was there waiting on me."

Ethan did no' like the way this tale was going. "Did you see a face? Or get any sort of a bad feeling about its presence?" he asked.

Amelia shook her head. "I only heard more whispering."

Ethan cocked his head. "More?"

She nodded. "This morning, in the forest—"

"Och, lass," he said, rubbing his jaw. "What happened in the wood?"

"Simmer down, sport," she said.

Someone, more than likely that fool Aiden, snorted. Ethan ignored it and met Amelia's gaze. "Go on."

"On my walk, I visited the old yew near the border

of your land." She pulled herself up onto the counter and sat, took a bite of apple, chewed it, and continued. "I heard whispers coming from it. Actually, I thought from *behind* it." Another bite, chew, swallow. "But I put my ear to it and realized it came from within—or so it seemed."

"So this wasna a threatening whisper?" Sorely asked.

Amelia shook her head, the ball of hair wobbling to and fro. "I felt no threat this time," she said. "The whisper said, 'Break the ssspell,' making the S sound like a snake, and then, 'They must go back.'"

Ethan nodded. "Is that all?"

She looked at him. "No. More whispers started up, and they sounded everywhere at once, and I couldn't understand anything." She shrugged. "When I left the forest, a very maniacal laugh sounded from deep in the woods. Now, *that* was creepy."

Ethan moved closer, and wished mightily he could touch her. Grab and shake her, more likely, but hold her safe. The lass had more nerve than most lads he'd grown up with, and it made him fear for her life. He had the feeling, though, if he told her as much, she'd make it a point to do the verra thing he didna want her to do. "I'll go with you from now on." He cleared his throat. "In case I might can hear the whisperings, as well."

"Aye," said Aiden. "We canna miss out on so much sport as that, lass."

"All except the rats, o' course," said Gil.

Amelia slowly munched on her apple, eyeing each man over the stem of it. Once finished, she tossed it into the waste pail and grinned. "You may have fooled plenty a maid back in the day, but not this ole girl. I know what you're up to." She looked directly at Ethan. "Especially you. Don't worry. I won't go into the forest alone anymore. Promise."

Ethan stared at her, and she batted her long lashes at him in a flurry. His kin laughed out loud, and Ethan fought hard to keep it in, but he chuckled at his Amelia.

His Amelia?

Damn. He was bluidy doomed.

While she laughed and jested with his kin, Ethan watched her, and wished mightily that twilight would come early and stay late. Whilst he appreciated her loveliness in the eve, when she'd don a gown and heeled slippers and stuff she'd roll on her lips from a little tube that tasted verra grand, indeed, he rather liked the way she looked now, as well. Her hair in that amusing, floppy ball, a sleeveless tunic that bore the face of a rather formidable-looking man with fangs and a black cloak, and a pair of hacked-off trews that showed enough of her legs to have gotten her lovely neck stretched as a witch back in his day. Her footwear—*sneakers*, she'd told them—were things to be had in the twenty-first century by one and all. Rather comfortable-looking, he thought. Comely, as well.

On Amelia.

With a clap of her hands, Amelia jumped down from her spot upon the counter. "Okay. Remember that surprise I told you guys about? Well, tonight's just as good a night as any. I need a break from the *woo-woo*, and this will be just the thing."

Aiden, always one for surprises, grinned at her. "And what be *woo-woo*, lass? A musical troupe, mayhap? Tricks?"

"Are you going to read to us?" asked Rob.

Amelia laughed, and she turned those eyes on Ethan. "You'll see. Tonight. After the gloaming has passed."

Ethan didna know what a *woo-woo* was, but it sounded amusing enough to him. As long as Amelia was involved, how could it no' be?

Chapter 19

Driving back from the village after gathering everything she'd need to entertain six big medieval guys, she smiled and gave herself a mental pat on the back. Not only had she succeeded in *not* scraping half of Scotland's sod with the front bumper of her rental car, but she'd even managed to keep her eyes open when she'd passed not one, but three lorry trucks. You know, the ones traveling toward her on the very narrow road that was flanked by a wall of rocky earth on one side, and an ancient wall on the other? Had it not been for some serious wanting to have a girl's night in, she'd have never left the Munro Keep. Luckily, though, Hewitt and his wife gave her a helping hand with the things she needed, since she was out in the Scottish countryside where TV and appliance stores weren't in huge demand at every corner.

Hewitt the storekeeper, she decided, was a lifesaver. An angel in plaid. Rather, tweed. When she'd gone into his store to ask where she could acquire a big-screen TV, DVD player, and movie rentals, at first he'd chuckled. Then he'd shown her to the back of the store, where he rented the latest and most classic of DVDs. Amelia had picked out the ones she wanted; then Hewitt had called his wife, closed the store, and accompanied Amelia to his home, where his lovely little wife, Mary, also in tweed, had the DVD player already packed in a box. Hewitt then loaded the TV—not a big-screen, but plenty big enough—into the boot of Amelia's rental and sent her on her way, refusing to accept the first penny for the use of their electronics.

Hewitt and Mary. Nicest folks on earth.

Of course, ZuZu would croak if she knew Amelia had set up a mini movie theater at the castle. But ZuZu wasn't going to find out.

Amelia turned down the lane that led to the tower house. The book would be finished well before deadline. Finally, she had material that excited her, and the self-experiences she'd weave into it absolutely fascinated her. Even without knowing what *really* happened to Ethan and his guys, the story was fantastic. Never in a million years would she have thought the fourteenth century would pique her interest so much. Of course, having Ethan Munro in the center of it helped quite a lot. Maybe that was the reason behind her enthusiasm.

No maybe about it, sista.

Wouldn't it be something, though, if she could actually *solve* Ethan's mystery? The spirits of Munro Keep were trying to tell her something—the good one and the bad one. Maybe she'd eventually figure it all out.

After spending weeks on research, taking notes, and hair-raising experiences, she couldn't wait to get started.

Of course, she'd have to make sure her writing was wrapped up by twilight each night.

She had a date with a fourteenth-century warrior, you know.

Multiple dates, at that.

As she crested the hill on the one-lane track leading to the keep, she stopped and stared out over Munro land. As it did that very first day, it took her breath away. One would think that having weird experiences with specters and ghouls and whispering old trees would be enough to dim the beauty of the dark, imposing tower house, but somehow, it didn't. Not for her, anyway. To Amelia, it was beautiful.

For tonight, though, she was going to put all of the mystery and ghosties and murder behind. She was, after all, from the South. Charleston, South Carolina, was known far and wide for well-bred young ladies. The epitome of genteel upbringing, manners, and etiquette.

She wasn't one of them. Not exactly, anyway.

She, Amelia thought with a snort, just knew how to have a damn fine time.

If only she had a few Black Cats and M-80s . . .

As it edged closer to the gloaming hour, Amelia rushed around the kitchen to make sure everything was ready.

"Excuse me," she said cheerfully.

Ethan stepped back, then bent over and stared into the bowl. Again. "What did you say that was?"

"Salsa."

Sorely rubbed his jaw and stared, too. "What's it made of?"

Amelia grinned. "Stuff. Hot stuff. Tomatoes, onions, peppers—I promise, you'll love it." She picked up a corn chip. "You take one of these and scoop it up"—she showed them how—"and eat it." She showed them how to do that, too.

Rob and Gilchrist were both inspecting the contents of the oven. "What did you say this was again?" asked Rob.

"Pizza."

"It all looks good to me," said Torloch.

Aiden chuckled. "That coming from a lad who has eaten a score of hedgehogs."

Torloch grinned.

"Okay, lass," Guthrie called from the great hall. "The tele is all set."

Amelia gave the warriors a grin and wiped her mouth on a napkin. "Oh boy. You're going to love this."

As she hurried out of the kitchen, six heavy sets of footsteps followed her out.

Guthrie stood by the hearth and the large wooden table in front of it. On top of that, Hewitt's TV. On top of *that*, the DVD player. He handed her the remote.

"All set, lass," he repeated. "All you need to do is this"—he showed her a few things, with, Amelia noticed, all six Highlanders looking over their shoulders—"and you can watch all the movies you fancy." He shook his head. "Canna get any local channels, though. No reception."

Amelia grinned. "That's okay. We won't need any." She leaned over and kissed his ruddy cheek. "Thanks, Guthrie. You're the best."

Guthrie turned red and waved her away. "Daft American. Get on with ye."

"Where are you off to tonight, old man?" asked Ethan. "Another eve of gaming?" Guthrie grinned and scratched a place under his old cap. "Hardly. The widow's made me supper." The twinkle in his watery blue eyes nearly made Amelia laugh out loud. "Dunna wait up on me, aye?"

The guys all laughed.

"Okay," Amelia said, once Guthrie left. "Let's all be ready tonight, okay? I'm going up now to shower and change." She looked at Ethan, who'd been staring at her with that sexy stare all afternoon. "You boys be ready to jump in the lake—"

"*Loch*," corrected Sorely.

"Right, loch," she said. "No stealing each other's plaids, either, or dunking each other under water. No time for that tonight, okay? Now, chop-chop!" She clapped her hands. "Move it, lads!"

With rowdy laughter, the Munros did in fact chop-chop, right out the door. All but Ethan, who lingered behind.

Amelia had just grabbed two of the bowls of chips and was about to take them into the great hall when she heard his voice.

"Hold there, lass."

She stopped. Ethan stood right behind her, and he leaned close to her ear. "I vow 'tis been more than twenty-three hours since I last kissed you," he said.

She turned and looked at him over her shoulder, not a few inches away.

His eyes smoldered, the color of ash. "I canna do anything else this eve until I've done that."

Amelia's legs wobbled, but she grinned. "Then you'd better hurry up, huh, laird?"

Ethan didn't say a word. His eyes said it all.

He turned and left the larder.

Amelia smiled.

With the speed of a woman who had a date with a Scottish knight, Amelia finished setting the junk food up on the long table in the great hall. Guthrie had put out the drinks—soda to start out with, because the last thing she wanted was six big inebriated medieval guys whose swords were part of their daily wardrobe. Pizza was warming in the oven.

And the Munros, the ones born in the thirteenth century, for crying out loud, were going to eat junk, drink sugar, and have their very first meeting with Count Dracula.

Satisfied that everything was in order, Amelia, excited and eager, ran up the stairs to get ready.

Just the look on Aiden's face made Ethan laugh out loud.

"Damn me, but 'tis scorchin' me mouth," Aiden said. He chewed, his eyes watered, and then he belched. "Bluidy hell, once you get past the burn, 'tis wondrous." He dipped another chip into Amelia's *salsa*. "What say you, Ethan?"

Ethan's own eyes watered. "Aye. Methinks the pizza was passing fine, as well." He glanced at Amelia. "You eat this all the time?"

She was sitting cross-legged on the floor in front of them, and she laughed. "You could say it's my main staple of nutrition. Along with this." She held up a small metal can of sorts and wiggled it. "I can eat this all day long."

"What is it?" asked Rob, shoving another piece of pizza in his mouth.

Amelia grinned. "Cheese."

"Bluidy hell," said Torloch. "How is it they shove hard cheese into such a small opening, yet when it comes out, 'tis like honey?"

Ethan watched his kin with mirth. So amazed by Amelia's *junk*—at least, 'twas what she called it—that their bellies were nigh unto popping.

He, on the other hand, had not been quite so gluttonous. He'd reserved that sin for Amelia.

For now, he had little time remaining of the hour and he wanted to spend it with her. And by the look she'd just sent him, thank the saints, she thought the verra same.

Standing, she gave her hands a clap. "Okay, fellas, finish up what you like, and in just a bit I'll introduce you to the count." She weaved between Aiden and Tor, and both let out a whistle.

"Och, Ethan," Aiden said. "We get pizza, and you get Amelia?"

Amelia smacked him on the back of the head as she walked by.

The men roared.

"If you have room in those cast-iron pots you call stomachs, in the freezer you'll find ice cream," she said. "Make sure you eat it really, really fast, though."

Rob was already halfway to the larder.

As Ethan and Amelia stepped out into the cool evening of twilight, he threaded his fingers through hers and they walked along to the edge of the loch. "Why did you tell them to eat it fast? 'Tis a custom of yours, aye?"

Amelia burst out laughing. "Sort of. I just gave them all a case of brain freeze." She smiled up at him. "They deserved it for all the hassle they've given me and you."

Damn if he'd ever heard of brain freeze, but he was fair certain he didna want it. "Doesna sound verra pleasant, the brain freeze."

"It is, and it's not," she said, and handed him a small white disk of sorts. "Here, have this instead. You suck on it. I promise nothing will turn to ice except your breath."

Ethan watched her put one in her own mouth, thought it safe enough, and did the same. Inhaling, his breath did indeed turn cool. "What is it?"

Amelia edged him over to a wide square of plaid stretched out on the grass beside the loch and pulled him down atop it. They sat facing each other.

"It's a mint," she said. "It's to make your breath fresh."

Ethan sucked on his and quirked a brow.

She laughed. "Trust me; you wouldn't want to kiss someone who's been eating chips and salsa."

He grinned. "And pizza, and cheese from a can, no' to mention—"

"Okay! I get it," she said, and kicked off her white slippers. *Sandals*, she'd called them. He rather liked the way they showed her painted little bare toes.

Then she looked up at him and scooted closer. "Wanna test out the mints?" she asked, and batted her lashes.

Looking down into those odd yet beautiful eyes, Ethan felt a rush of exhilaration, and he traced with his forefinger first her jaw, then the bridge of her nose, and then across her bottom lip. Her sweet mouth opened, just a fraction, and her eyes turned glassy.

And as Ethan slid his hand around the back of her neck and lowered his lips to hers, he realized the twilight hour would never satisfy him. 'Twas no' nearly enough time to savor the treasure who had stormed into his life and seized it with as little as a laugh, a quirked brow, a quick wit, and a great amount of courage. No' to mention her kisses made his heart sing. Nay, one hour a day wasna nearly enough.

But when Amelia's soft hand grabbed his and lifted it to her throat, he forgot about his despair over his enchantment and kissed her.

And by the blood of Christ, she kissed him back.

Chapter 20

Sensations surrounded Amelia, and she reveled in them with a zest and enthusiasm she had never thought possible. All of them. The lap of the loch against the shoreline, the tweetings of night birds, the gentle breeze that swept through the glen and rustled the leaves, carrying with it that fresh, tangy scent of clover, the stiff heather and meadow grass— all of those things combined around her, made her feel a sense of home, a sense of rightness.

Then there was Ethan.

He left her with those same senses, along with the sense of never wanting to leave. *Ever.*

Especially when he touched her the way he presently was doing.

One thing Amelia noticed about Ethan Munro— subconsciously, mind you, because there was no way could she form intelligent thought while he touched her—was that the man could kiss. Not just kiss, you know, with tongue and teeth and the occasional nip of the lip. He *kissed*. No, scratch that.

He made love with his mouth.

She felt as if with every inhalation, every small gasp of air, she breathed a little bit of him in.

Those big, calloused hands always touched some part of her while kissing. No sexual parts, or anything naughty, because that would *definitely* cross the line and lead her to break her rule of no sex before marriage. Not just cross the line, mind you, but leap across it with gusto. Throw herself over it, even. Already, she was toeing that line . . .

Ethan held her hand while his mouth moved slowly over hers, and the two sensations at once made her see stars behind her eyelids. With his thumb, he traced the length of each finger, the soft, tender spot between them, her inner wrist, and she could feel the hard knobs of skin on his thumb, one at the first bend, then another in the cradle, where those big, fourteenth-century hands gripped a sword every day of his life. And while he was caressing her hand, his mouth was caressing hers, with a gentle sucking of each corner of her lips, a slow drag of his tongue across hers, and with each erotic movement, even when his mouth left hers to kiss the area below her ear and down her neck, came an invitation for more.

Amelia sighed, and while Ethan settled his warm lips against the skin of her neck, she trailed his arm with her fingertips, over the ever-present band of metal encircling his bicep, and over his chest, until she found the opening in his plaid, where she marveled at his Adam's apple, the strong cords in his throat, and then his stubbled jaw, where he seemed to have a perpetual five o'clock shadow.

"Amelia," he said on a sigh against her ear.

It came out *Ah-meh-lay-ah*, and she thought she'd never heard her name pronounced so beautifully.

With both hands, Amelia pushed through that

long, thick mane of glorious hair and grasped the back of Ethan's neck, pulling his mouth to hers, and with nothing but instinct of motion, lay back on the blanket she'd spread out, and Ethan wrapped both arms around her, encircled her completely, and followed her down.

For a brief moment, he stopped and stared down at her. With the faded light, his features were dark, but she could still make out the silver in his eyes, the crescent-shaped white scar beneath the one, the slash of another scar that all but separated one dark brow, as well as the intense, firm set to his jaw. He said nothing, just stared, and then he lowered his mouth again, where he tasted first her top lip, then her lower, where he lingered, suckled, and deepened the kiss, and when one of his large hands skimmed her side, then across her ribs, over her hip, Amelia wriggled beneath his weight, trying to get just a little closer . . .

And then, with a quick suddenness that left a void so large she gasped, Ethan's body turned to nothingness. He simply turned to air. Somehow, he'd moved, though, and now stood above her. She didn't move for a second, just lay there, breathing.

Ethan turned, walked to the edge of the loch, looked toward the faded sky, and cursed. In Gaelic. Loudly.

Amelia sat up, pulled her knees to her chest, and wrapped her arms around them. "Ethan, come here." When he didn't move, she patted the spot next to her. "Please?"

At first, he just stared across the loch, his broad back to her, that impossibly large sword, the same one he'd rested in the grass, now secured in its place in the leather sheath. After a few more muttered curses, he turned and came back, throwing himself down in a totally casual guy way, beside her, one knee bent, one forearm resting atop it. He stared straight ahead.

"Ethan—what's your middle name? Or second name?"

At first he didn't answer. Then, "Arimus."

Wow. That R rolling made her swoon. Amelia smiled. "Ethan Arimus Munro. Now, *that's* sexy. *Dang* sexy. Like, phew!" She feigned a swipe of a sweaty brow. "Hot sexy. Burn-me-where-I-sit sexy." She leaned forward and ducked her head to see around the curtain of hair that had fallen over his shoulder. "Just . . . damn sexy."

He looked at her, shook his head, and then chuckled. "I vow, woman," he said. "You leave me truly bewildered."

"Good. That's my aim in life." She smiled, and then looked at him hard. "You really are amazing, Ethan Arimus Munro. It's not just any ole fourteenth-century guy who could manage to come along and sweep me off my feet."

First he looked at her feet and then met her stare, and it penetrated her straight to the bone. Because it was midsummer, the light never completely faded, and the slice of moon hanging just over the loch made it just a bit brighter. She noticed the small sun lines, or laugh lines, that fanned out from his eyes, and the tinier lines in his lips. The muscle in his jaw, which was forever flinching, flinched now.

Ethan drew a deep breath. "I fear verra little, Amelia." His profound gaze pinned her to the spot. "But I fear you." He glanced away. "So much, it chokes me."

A knot tightened in Amelia's stomach, and her mouth went dry. "I'm not all that scary, am I?" she asked, knowing the smile she pasted on her face looked dopey.

Several seconds passed without Ethan saying a word. He just stared straight ahead, as if something beyond the loch's shoreline interested him, with both knees pulled up now and both forearms resting atop them. That long dark hair draped over his arms, down his back, and the bands at his biceps pulled tight against the flexed muscles they encircled. Amelia thought he'd never look at her again. Then suddenly, he did.

Again, he stared at her, long and hard, as though whatever it was he wanted to say sat just there, on the tip of his tongue, desperate to form words but relentless to stay put.

"I fear the emptiness I'll feel, here"—he passed his hand over his heart—"when you take your leave."

Amelia blinked, and her smile felt even weaker than before. "I'm not going anywhere—"

"Aye, lass, you are," Ethan interrupted. "Your life is elsewhere, Amelia. Your family, your home—'tis far from this place." His stare bore into hers. "You will leave. You've no choice."

The air left Amelia's lungs in a slow *whoosh* as reality smacked her upside the head. God, he was right. Already, she'd been gone a month. She had eight weeks before her book was due. Eight weeks before she boarded another jet and flew back home to her family, her life, her job, her little cottage on the beach.

The one she lived in alone.

How was she supposed to know she'd meet and

fall head over heels for a seven-hundred-year-old warrior? *Didn't see that one coming, did ya, big shot?*

Amelia looked at Ethan. Stoic, he hid whatever thoughts of emptiness he feared, for his face revealed nothing. It only held that tense expression.

What was she doing? Spending every single day with a guy, necking with him for one hour of each day, and . . .

. . . growing closer to him by the second.

God, she was an idiot.

"Amelia, I'm sorry," he said. "I didna mean to cause such a troubled look upon your lovely face." He ducked his head and peered at her. "Truly, I should have remained silent." He chuckled. "We medievals are a sensitive lot, you know."

Amelia took that very moment to lighten the mood. Why spend the rest of her time with Ethan sulking? They had eight weeks together, and by God, she'd not waste it pouting. She gave a big grin, one that felt more real this time. "Sensitive? You *hack* people's heads off," she said, pulling her forefinger across her throat in a cutting-off motion.

Ethan shrugged. "Mayhap a few."

They stared at each other, unspoken words passing through the air. They'd stay there, those words, floating around on a gentle Highland breeze, there, but not aloud. For now she wanted to enjoy Ethan's company for as long as possible. "Wanna lie here and watch the stars for a little while?" she said, lying back and patting the spot beside her. "Come on."

Ethan glanced skyward. " 'Tis a rather weak display this time of eve," he said. "But far be it from me to play the fool and no' lie beside a fetchin' lass in the heather when invited." He stretched out by her, keeping enough distance apart so he didn't slip through her, linked his fingers together and placed them behind his head. He crossed his booted feet at the ankle and sighed.

Both were silent for a moment.

"Good thing you didna wear a gown this eve."

A second of silence; then Amelia burst into laughter. Ethan started to chuckle, but then joined her in a full-fledged laughing fit.

But deep within her heart, Amelia ached, for she knew that it would all come to an end far sooner than she'd like. Only later would she realize that she'd passed the solitary chance to tell Ethan Munro her innermost thoughts.

That she loved him.

Chapter 21

Two weeks went by before another ghost made contact.

Amelia had wondered if it would even happen again.

Lying on her belly, stretched out on her bed, she worked on her outline with pen and paper. The story was proving to be a tad bit difficult.

The clock on the bedside table read 11:00 p.m. in neon green numbers. Laying aside her pad and paper, Amelia stretched, bringing one knee up and turning at the waist. Her back cracked, she repeated the opposite side, and then she rolled off the bed, ready to go downstairs to get a drink before sleep.

As soon as her feet hit the floor, she froze.

And immediately knew she no longer stood in the room alone.

Scanning the chamber, she didn't see anything out of the ordinary. Open-beamed rafters overhead, the clothes chest, her desk, the bedside table, a corner lamp, and the bathroom. Nothing seemed out of place. It was more of a feeling than anything else. And that feeling grew stronger.

"Hello?" she said in a whisper. She knew Ethan

would be on the other side of her door, sitting against the wall, *guarding*. He did so every night. And if he heard her making a ruckus, he'd pop in and investigate.

And possibly scare off the spirit.

Amelia waited, breath held.

Then the slightest of breezes brushed her neck, lifted a hank of her hair, and a whisper slipped into her ear.

"Break the sspell . . ."

Amelia heaved a sigh. "You've already told me that," she whispered. "*How* do I break the spell?"

"They must go back . . ."

Great, Amelia thought, a ghost with dementia.

Looking around the room and still seeing nothing, not a wisp of mist, nor a face, she took a deep breath and blew it back out slowly. "Tell me how to break the spell. Please?"

Silence—not a whisper, not a hair lifting. Nothing.

"Please?" she said a little louder.

"Youuu . . ."

What did that mean? *You?* Only the word had stretched out.

"Follow . . ."

Amelia's eyes darted around. Follow? How the heck could she follow if she didn't see anything?

"Wood . . ."

She smiled. After dark, and the good ghost wanted her to go traipsing in the woods? *Fantastic.* Slipping on her sneakers, she pulled her hair into a ponytail, grabbed her mini flashlight and tucked it into her yoga pants, and moved to the door.

As soon as she opened it, Ethan stood. Before he could say a word, though, Amelia placed a finger over her lips, he nodded, and then she motioned for him to follow. Silently, he fell in behind her and they eased down the passageway.

Once in the great hall, Ethan leaned close to Amelia's ear. "Where are we going?"

Even at a precarious time such as being led through a fourteenth-century castle by a whispering specter, hearing Ethan's deep, rich voice, tinged with that incredible, medieval Scottish brogue, made Amelia shiver. She must have actually done it, the shiver, and Ethan must have noticed, because he gave a soft chuckle—which was just as rich as his voice.

"To the wood," she said. "So says the good ghost."

"Why?" he asked, still whispering.

"I don't know," she replied. "Hush, and just follow, before you scare it off."

They walked in silence thereafter, and Amelia noticed only her feet made a soft *swooshing* noise in the grass. Ethan didn't make a sound at all.

A thought struck Amelia, and she did everything in her power not to laugh out loud at the absurdity of it. But Ethan, ever so conscious of her every move, noticed. They'd just passed the old yew tree in the meadow when he spoke.

"What's so funny, lass?" he asked.

Amelia shook her head. "It's just so bizarre. Here I am, following an unseen specter's voice, accompanied by a seven-hundred-year-old enchanted laird." She looked at him over her shoulder. "To me, it's pretty darn hilarious."

"Hurry, youuu . . ."

Again, Amelia shushed Ethan and they did hurry. Drawing close to the dark wood line, Amelia slowed.

"Man, it's dark in there," she said. She clicked on her mini flashlight and stared at the tiny, narrow stream of light. She shook her head and peered into the shadows. "I can't see a thing."

"Alone . . ."

Amelia froze.

"Without him. By youuu . . ."

"What is it?" Ethan said, his face drawn tight, brows furrowed. "I dunna like that look on your face, lass."

She stared up at him. "It's telling me to go into the woods alone. Without you."

Ethan had no hesitation. "Nay."

"But, Ethan—"

"Nay, Amelia," he said, and not in a whisper. "Good spirit, bad spirit, it doesna matter to me. You've already been placed in danger once. You could have fallen to your death, or do you no' recall that?" He leaned forward, his voice edged and low. "Nay."

Amelia glanced at the shadowy forest. "I guess you're right." She looked back at him. "But I've got to go in there at some point, Ethan. A ghost from the past is trying to tell me something, and I can only assume it has something to do with you." She shoved her hands into her warm-up jacket pockets. "Maybe even the death of your wife, or your enchantment. So you better believe I'm going to find out what's in there." She inclined her head. "I'll have a bigger flashlight ready next time."

A slight curve touched Ethan's sexy mouth. "Quite a fierce lass, aye?"

Amelia feigned a scowl. *Double* aye."

They turned and walked back to the keep, the Highland moon throwing a silvery light across the misty ground.

"In the morn we'll go to the wood. Together."

Amelia was quite satisfied with that. For now.

The next morn Ethan was actually surprised to find Amelia still in her chamber. With that hardheaded look about her from the eve before, he'd thought she would have tried to sneak out.

He'd been ready for her, too.

Rather, his kin had.

One could never be too careful when dealing with a determined twenty-first-century lass.

The chamber door opened, Jack scooted out first, followed by Amelia. Ethan stared in appreciation.

How could he no'?

In truth, he'd done his best to keep his distance from the lass. They'd continued their trysts each eve during the gloaming hour, but he'd not allowed himself the dangerous pleasure he'd had that one night, when he'd lain atop her, felt every soft curve beneath him, and had nearly taken far too much from her. He'd wanted her so fiercely that night; it pained him still to think on it.

Which he did oft enough.

He'd almost done another foolish thing that night, as well. By the blood of Christ, he'd nearly told her the depth of his feelings for her. He hadn't, though. Somehow the words had stayed firmly within his stupid self.

And that's where they'd stay.

Although each time he looked at her, like he did thusly, he found his tongue wanted to spew forth all manner of soft and mushy words. The sort of words that, if heard by his kin, he'd be tormented mercilessly for the rest of his bluidy days.

Instead, they'd spent their solitary hour together, with Amelia sharing the twenty-first century with him, and he the fourteenth with her. He finally had his turn at the iPod, and by the saints, 'twas a wondrous thing, indeed. The music sounded clear, soft at times, loud at others, and seemingly right in his head. How his mother would have loved it.

Aye, they kissed. He'd cut his own stupid head off before giving that luxury up. 'Twas torture, though, for each time he tasted, he wanted more. But he always ended it before the ending of it could not be helped. He'd look upon her, like he presently did, more likely than not with the same daft look on his face.

By Christ's saints, she was lovely.

Garbed in a gown with two separate parts—a top and bottom—the bottom, which reached to her calves, was the same shade of green as her eyes. The top was white, sleeveless, and had small buttons from the neck to the waist.

Just then, Amelia lifted her arms above her head and pulled her hair into that adorable floppy ball, and the hem of her top rose, exposing her flat stomach, and, dear God, her navel. Tanned skin, taut with womanly muscles, it all but made his mouth go dry . . .

"Ogling?"

He blinked, for indeed he had been ogling, and enjoying every moment of it, and smiled. "For a certainty. Are you ready?"

She reached down, patted Jack on the head, and nodded. "Let's go."

Halfway across the meadow, she glanced up at him. "Did you know William Wallace?"

Ethan nodded. "Indeed. A big lad, taller than me, he was. Powerfully fierce about his homeland." He looked down, and her mouth was slightly ajar.

"You *knew* him?"

Ethan nodded. "Of course. No' many a healthy lad didna back then. 'Twas a driven man, that one, and had a knack for raisin' spirits during battle." He nodded. "A fine leader, Wallace. No' a finer one since him, by the by. He gave that bleedin' murderer Edward a run, for a certainty."

Amelia stopped in her tracks. "Wait. You *fought* with William Wallace?"

Ethan blinked. "Aye. We all did."

"Wow." She winced. "Do you know what happened to him?"

Ethan nodded and they began to walk once more. "Aye, Guthrie told us. Captured and turned over to English soldiers by a Scottish knight just a pair of years after our enchantment. Tragic death, his." He nodded. "A damn good man."

"Unbelievable," Amelia said in a hushed voice.

Ethan guessed it truly was.

They walked on in comfortable silence and entered the wood. For no reason at all, they headed down the path to the old yew. Once the old gnarled tree came in sight, they stood before it and stared.

Ethan inclined his head. "Did the ghostie tell you to come here?"

"No," she said, and rubbed her fingers over the bark. "But I feel drawn to it somehow. It fascinates me."

Ethan knew the feeling well.

"You know," she said, looking at him. "Some people who are in lo—er—are really crazy about each other carve their names into the bark of a tree." She used her finger against the aged wood. "Sometimes just initials, for instance, EAM plus AFL. Other times"—she grinned—"the whole name, like, John loves Lucy, or John and Lucy forever." She shrugged. "An American custom, I think."

He moved closer. "And if our names were forever engraved in such a tradition"—his sexy mouth lifted into a sexier grin—"what would it say?"

Amelia's eyes glazed over, as if in deep thought. Then she smiled. "Ethan and Amelia. By the by."

He gave a wistful smile. "Indeed." He cleared his throat. "Er, do you hear anything else this morn, Amelia? No whisperings at all?"

She cocked her ear to the wind, listened, then shook her head. "Nope. Not a thing. I'm starting to think these specters are ornery and slight control freaks."

He couldn't be too sure what a *control freak* was, but he got the gist of it.

They'd contact Amelia when good and ready.

"Come on," she said. "Tae kwon do first, then more research for the book."

And with that, they left the wood, leaving the ghosties and whispering yews behind.

At least, until they decided to show themselves again.

Chapter 22

"What is all this, lass?"

Amelia looked at Torloch and grinned. "This is my time line." She hollered over her shoulder. "You guys come here for a second. I need your help."

Ethan leaned a hip against what Amelia liked to refer to as the makeshift Mission Control office. Guthrie had helped her set it up the day before, and it was perfect. Long and wide, it was made of smooth wood and had plenty of room for her roll of white art paper, sticky notes, and scene cards. He leaned over and looked hard at her scribblings.

"Lass, we've only learned modern English two scores ago," Ethan said.

"Aye, and whilst we are fast-learning lads, Guthrie was our teacher," said Sorely, who braced himself with both hands and peered at the table's contents. "We dunno know what half of this means."

Amelia chuckled. "That's okay. I really just want to go over the time line of events and then do a little filling in. There are a number of holes here."

The men grunted.

Picking up her pack of multicolored Sharpies,

Amelia uncapped a red and started at one end of the table. "Okay. Here"—she made an asterisk—"is the proposal for the marriage between you, Ethan, and Devina of Clan MacEwan."

Ethan watched in silence.

Amelia drew a small line and made another asterisk. "Here's the wedding day, and here"—she drew one more—"is the day after. Now, Ethan, you were sleeping and awoke to the hollering of Daegus Mac-Ewan, right?"

He nodded.

"Okay." She drew a big circle and wrote *DAEGUS MAD* in the center. "Then Rob rushed in and affirmed that her kin had backtracked and returned after leaving the day before, correct?"

"Aye," Ethan said.

"All right." She stared at the long white sheet of paper covering the table. She capped her pen and pointed with it. "Ethan, you found your sword missing, Rob ran out ahead of you to alert Aiden and the guys, you dressed, left, met Aiden in the passageway, where he handed you another sword, and you all left for the knoll." She looked at everyone. "Am I right so far?"

Six medieval *aye*s sounded at once.

"Okay." Amelia studied the line. "You Munros approached the knoll, saw the gibbet, Devina's body on the ground covered in a MacEwan plaid, and on the gibbet was your plaid and sword jammed into the wood, right, Ethan?"

He nodded, his face drawn tight.

Apparently, even seven hundred years or so doesn't help erase such a bad memory.

"Ethan, you *did* actually see her, right?" she asked.

He looked at her. "I did."

Amelia nodded. "So a fight ensued, Rob there killed Daegus as he was about to poke you with his blade." She inclined her head toward Ethan. "And then the other MacEwans showed up, ready for a slaughter."

Rob nodded. "Aye."

Amelia leaned over the table and met Ethan's gaze. "Then what happened?"

Ethan started to pace. "Just as the MacEwans started to rush down the knoll, a mist gathered. 'Twas thick and blanketing, and we could no' see a hand before us."

The guys nodded in agreement.

"Just before everything went dark, I heard a voice." He stopped and looked at her. "A whispering voice, low, mayhap a woman, but no' saying anything I could understand."

Amelia glanced at the others. "Did any of you hear it?"

They all shook their heads.

"Only Ethan," said Aiden.

"It sounded like a chant," Ethan said, rubbing his chin.

"Or an *enchantment*," added Amelia. She stared at her time line, made a few more notes with her pen, then turned and leaned against the table. "You've mentioned before that Devina spent all of her time in the chapel. Why?"

Rob answered. "Because of the accusations surrounding Ethan."

"Aye," said Aiden. "She was more likely than no' prayin' for her soul's safety from the devil she'd just wed."

Ethan nodded. " 'Tis so."

Amelia scratched her forehead with the tip of the pen cap. "Forgive me for asking this, but didn't you two consummate the marriage?"

Ethan glanced at his kin, then at Amelia. "Nay. She wouldna come near me, and I wasna going to force her."

Amelia looked at Ethan with even more respect than she had before. "Coming from a medieval guy, that says a lot about your character."

Ethan grunted.

"Who else, besides Devina, and apparently her uncle Daegus, wasn't too happy about your marriage?"

Ethan stroked his chin, then rubbed the back of his neck. "No one. I canna think of a single soul who would have cared enough to murder."

"Had other women come to the wedding?" Amelia asked.

"Aye," Aiden said. "Scores of them."

"None of them murderers, though," Ethan said. "And there were eight, no' scores."

Amelia cocked her head. "How on earth do you know none of them were murderers?"

"No motive," said Gilchrist.

"Okay, so let's make a list," Amelia said, "of the women, not including Ethan's mom and sister, who came to the wedding. Not that the female enchantment caster was someone invited to the wedding, but now that we have a time line and it's visual to me, it makes sense to at least eliminate who we can as possible suspects."

"Are you sure you're no' a constable?" Rob asked.

The men roared.

So did Amelia. "Okay, smarty-pants, I do write mysteries for a living, don't forget."

Rob nodded with a grin. "I yield, then."

"As you should," said Amelia, and everyone laughed. "Okay, let's get started on that list."

It didn't take them long.

Amelia stared at the women's names. Each had their own mini bio, which was pretty impressive seeing how over seven hundred years had passed since the wedding took place.

Only one on the list caught Amelia's eye. "What happened to"—she peered at the name—"Marynth's husband?"

Ethan crossed his arms over his chest. "He'd died earlier that year."

"Aye, fell off his horse and broke his neck," said Sorely.

"She was Devina's cousin?" Amelia asked.

"Aye. Daegus' own daughter."

Amelia tapped the pen to her lip. "Were they close? Marynth and Devina?"

Ethan nodded. "Verra. Like sisters."

Amelia blew out a gusty breath. "Well, so much for the list. It looks like the enchantress could have been anyone. Maybe even a guy."

"Aye, anyone with scorn for Ethan," said Aiden.

Amelia considered. "Or someone who had the *hots* for him."

The confused looks on the Highlanders' faces made Amelia chuckle. "That means they like you a great deal."

"Och," Rob said. "You mean fancy."

Amelia winked. "Exactly." Tossing her pen on the

table, she stretched. "Good job, fellas. I've got to let this stew in my brain for a while." She smiled at Ethan. "I think I'm going to go for a walk. Wanna come along?"

Ethan met her gaze. "Absolutely."

As they left the hall, whistles and suggestive hollers followed them out.

"Ethan's got the hots for Amelia, methinks," said Torloch.

The Munro warriors all roared.

Amelia didn't care.

She had a handsome laird for a walking buddy.

As they walked out, Amelia held up her right hand, and slowly lowered all fingers but the middle one.

The men behind her roared even louder.

A few hours later and Amelia and Ethan found themselves along a frothy rushing stream at the far side of the Munro estate. They'd covered quite a lot of ground, and along the way found out more and more about each other, their families, about growing up. The scenery was beyond breathtaking. Hilly countryside covered in green grass, clumps of heather, and scattered rock made up the Munro land, and Ethan had already pointed out several grouse, a red fox, and a pheasant or two. No mist to speak of, but a light rain had started to fall, making everything crisp and alive. Walking beside Ethan changed the way Amelia saw the land. Before, she could easily see in her mind's eye the warriors running about, dirty, bloody, carrying swords and fighting. But with Ethan, she saw another vision, one of a man whose family came first, a hunter and provider, a lover of nature, a loving son, aggravating brother, protector of his little sister—a prankster hiding in a tree throwing sticks at a vicar.

Time flew by, and before Amelia knew it, the twilight hour grew near. Standing at the water's edge on a large, flat rock, she picked up a stone and tossed it into the burn. "We'll never make it back to the keep before the gloaming." She glanced at him. "Even if we ran the whole way, we wouldn't make it." She smiled an apology. "I guess I talk a lot, huh?"

Ethan rubbed his chin. "Aye, there is that, in truth."

Amelia gave him a mock frown. "I just like to know stuff, that's all."

He laughed quietly. "I find it vastly endearing, Amelia."

She cocked her head. "I'm sorry I've broken your routine for the day." She shrugged. "No bath, no food—"

"Hmm," he said, tapping his temple with a forefinger. "Let me think. Bath and food, or the company of a fetching lass with verra soft lips who fancies me?"

Reaching up and patting her lips with her fingertips, Amelia shook her head. "Feel like regular ole lips to me."

"I'll be the judge of that, lass."

She smiled, although her stomach had butterflies. "I've a mind to let you, too."

And then, he did just that.

And just that fast, the rain picked up, a fast, steady fall of water that would have them both soaked in no time.

Not that Amelia cared.

"Let's go there," Ethan said, grabbing her hand and pulling her as he said it. " 'Tis naught more than a craggy hillock, but 'twill give us a bit of shield from the rain."

Across the heathery meadow they ran; rather, Ethan dragged her, and she happily let him. By the time they made it to the front face of the hillock, the rain had picked up even more. When they stopped, Ethan grasped her by the shoulders, placed her back to the hillock, and then he moved in front of her.

He looked down. "Does that help?" he asked.

Amelia lifted her gaze. Ethan's long hair hung in rain-soaked hanks, water dripping off the ends of the braids, his nose, his chin. His arms were wet and slick, the cut of the muscles pronounced by the odd lighting of the gloaming and the downpour.

"Yeah," she finally replied, and it came out barely more than a whisper. She looked up, rain dripping down her own face.

Ethan lifted a hand, and with the back of his knuckles grazed her wet cheek, pushed her soaked hair back from her face, rubbed it between his fingers, lifted it to his nose, and inhaled. His eyes drifted shut as he smelled her hair, then dragged it across his lips. When he opened his eyes, the silvery ash color had turned as stormy as the clouds above them.

Amelia couldn't find her voice, so she concentrated on breathing instead. She could do little more than stand upright, and had it not been for the rocky earth at her back, and Ethan's big frame at her front, she would have slid to the ground.

Ethan seemed fascinated by her wet hair; he

stroked it, tucked it behind her ears, and then fixed his gaze on her feet, then slowly took in the rest of her. A slow perusal that made Amelia's breath catch.

And then he set his gaze on hers.

And Amelia's heart slammed against her ribs as he lowered his head.

Chapter 23

Ethan felt like a bumbling whelp of a score and three, kissing a lass for the verra first time. His insides ached, his heart pounded fast and hard, and he knew if he spoke, his voice would be high-pitched and cracking.

All that from a lass whom he'd kissed scores of times before. This time was different, though. Vastly. And he knew *why*.

The vision of Amelia soaked through and through by a Highland rain during the glow of twilight was indeed a sight he'd remember forever. With her soaked skin burnished from the wetness, it looked like the smooth surface of a jewel, and his hands itched to touch it. Her drenched gown, white with the smallest of blue spots and already pulled snug by the strings beneath her breast and tied at her back, clung to her body, the flat of her stomach, the shape of her thighs. Each breath, which grew faster, deeper, made her chest rise and fall, and her throat moved with each small swallowing motion. Those luminous green eyes watched his every move, wide lashes spiked with rain, and Ethan knew he'd bank every small detail to memory.

Including the way Amelia stood there, motionless all but for her rapid breathing, allowing him to drink his fill.

Now, his patience exhausted, he touched.

Starting at her hands, he slipped his fingers through her long, slender ones, their skin sliding easy from the rain. Grazing her knuckles, he encircled her small wrists, then moved up the length of her arms, marveling at the delicate bones of her shoulders beneath the rough palms of his hands. Amelia's breathing grew faster as he brushed her collarbone with the back of one knuckle, tracing the length of it from shoulder to shoulder. She shivered, a small gasp escaping her throat, and she looked straight ahead, staring not at his eyes but at his chest. He lifted her chin with his thumb, and their gazes met.

And Ethan all but lost feeling in his knees.

Desire shone in Amelia's eyes, and grasping both her hands, he slipped them around his neck. Then he angled her head just so, slipped one hand behind her head, and lowered his until their lips touched.

Ethan tasted Highland rainwater and Amelia, and he drank thirstily, as though he'd never sampled either. Her mouth moved beneath his, trembling, and when he met her tongue with his, and they tasted each other, she made a soft moan low in her throat. Ethan deepened the kiss, frantic at first and discovering every minute detail of her lips, and then he pulled back and settled his mouth over her throat, then her bare shoulder, slowed his breathing, his pumping heart, before he lost all control.

Then Amelia's slight fingers left his throat and tangled in his hair, and she tugged him back to her mouth. They locked gazes first, the rain falling fast between them, and they came together once more, a slow tasting and discovering, and as their kiss deepened, Ethan wrapped one arm around her waist and pulled her against him, and with his free hand skimmed down her soaked gown, over her ribs, then hip, the feel of her warmth beneath the cloth making him yearn to touch her bare skin.

Christ help him, he tried to control himself, he did. But more than lust drove him to want to do all but crawl inside Amelia's skin. Much more.

Ashamed yet driven by such desire that he truly couldn't stop himself, Ethan ran his hand down her hip, grasped the wet cloth of her gown, and pulled until the hem rose high enough for him to feel the skin of her thigh, her bare hip, and when Amelia pressed into him as he skimmed the soft flesh, his hand rose higher, to the taut skin of her buttock. He groaned and kissed her hungrily, there in the rain, soaked to the bone. And she kissed him back with just as much fervor, her hands grazing his throat, his cheek, his chest.

Ethan moved his mouth over her shoulder. "Christ, Amelia," he said, trying to control his own breathing. "You're so beautiful." He tugged at her sleeve, exposing more shoulder. "I'll never get enough of you." He tasted her skin there with his tongue and thought he'd die right there. *"Grú mo chroí."*

As soon as the Gaelic words left his mouth, a fierce wind kicked up, the rain hardened and turned to hail. Large jagged stones of ice pelted them, and Ethan shoved Amelia against the hillock and shielded her with his body.

"Ethan!" she yelled over the wind, her arms tucked in against his chest. "What's happening?"

The hail felt as though they'd been volleyed by a seize engine, so hard they hit his back. " 'Twill be fine, lass," he yelled back. "Just keep still!"

Amidst the unnatural wind and hail, an eerie whisper rose to his ear, making his skin prickle, his belly ache. Ethan froze, glanced down at Amelia, whose head rested snugly against his chest.

He recognized the pitch of the whispering voice.

'Twas the same one he'd heard the day Devina had died.

Fiercely, it spoke again, whispering fast and harsh in his ear, seeping deep into his head for no one to hear but him. And this time, he understood the words. They made him sick inside.

Amelia glanced up at him then, her eyes questioning. "What's wrong?" she asked, and when he didna answer, "Ethan?"

He didna answer the whispering voice at first, either, and it grew louder in his head, enraged, and so forceful he thought the pain and harshness of it would bring tears to his eyes.

Nay! he shouted in his mind. *Go to hell!*

The wind turned, a fierce gale, sending sharp, hard clumps of hail around his body and directly into Amelia's. She ducked, but several struck her on the side, the face, and the head. She screamed, and the sound was more than Ethan could bear. He moved to cover her, but the wind changed again, the balls of ice pelting her from the opposite side.

Cease! He screamed silently at the spirit. *Do it now!*

"Ethan! What's going on?" Amelia yelled over the whipping wind. "Answer me! Please!"

He didna, though. But inside his head, where that

damned whispering voice of the unseen specter all but consumed him, he relented when it shouted its command once more. Against his bluidy will, he relented.

Aye! Aye, damn you! he screamed from within.

Silent to Amelia's ears.

Ethan took one final glance at the woman huddled against him, eyes wide with fear. He wanted desperately to kiss her once more, to hold her head steady and ease that look of dread from her face with his lips.

She'd never know the words he'd spoken to her in his native tongue. Ever.

'Tis done, he said silently to the malevolent phantom in his head.

The verra one that had the power to kill.

I said, 'tis done, he repeated.

With that, the wind and hail ceased, everything calmed, leaving a soft Highland mist in its wake.

Amelia's hands were all over him at once, running her fingers over the reddened marks left by the hail.

Ethan backed away from her. "Are you all right?" he asked.

She looked him in the eye and nodded. "Yes, but you took the brunt of it." She glanced skyward. "What on earth was that?"

"Highland weather," he said. "Unpredictable at best."

"I'll say."

He inclined his head in the direction of the keep. "We'd better hurry before it grows too dark to see our way back."

Amelia studied him, straightening her gown where

moments before he'd lifted the hem and caressed the softest skin he'd ever touched in his life. "Okay. Let's go."

With a nod, he led them out of the glen. Amelia tried more than once to entwine her fingers with his, and each time he pulled away. She noticed because the tension in the air all but stood his hair up. But she kept silent. 'Twas the first time since meeting her that he wished mightily for the gloaming hour to end.

Then suddenly, it did.

The connection between them, Ethan decided, reached a depth far greater than even he could imagine. Without a single word, Amelia knew something bad had happened. She might no' realize the whole of it, and by the bluidy saints in heaven, he'd no' tell her. He couldna.

Her verra life depended on it.

They walked in silence back to the keep. Once there, Amelia declined the offer by his kin to watch another movie, and went to bed without a single glance or word to him.

He stood there and watched her climb the stairs.

Inside, deep within his chest, Ethan died.

Amelia figured that she knew a little bit about a lot of things. She'd done tons of research over the years for her books, ranging from archaeology, to forensics, to physics, to biology.

The one thing she knew a lot about without any research whatsoever was rejection. And it'd just happened.

Again.

Aiming for a certain knot in the wood rafter above

her bed, she threw her thinking ball and hit it dead center. It dropped back down and she caught it.

That'd been at least the gazillionth repetition since leaving Ethan at the foot of the stairs.

She tossed up the ball and caught it.

Gazillion and one.

Ethan's rejection hadn't been like Dillon's, though. That much she knew. Dillon had simply been a putz. A schmuck. A big fat pecker head to the nth degree.

A *dipshit*, her granny had proudly added over tea one afternoon. A fond memory, that one. Sort of a discombobulated scene from *Steel Magnolias*, ZuZu, Amelia, her younger twin sisters, Maggie and Erin, her mom, and her granny had all gathered on the shady front porch of her grandparents' old Charleston plantation house, sipping iced tea and eating wide wedges of key lime pie while under a hurricane watch, sharing naughty names for the man—er, *one-eyed asshole* (that had come from her mom)—who'd broken Amelia's heart. Quite a scene they'd made, she thought, all cute and proper Southern ladies on the outside—her granny had always worn sweet gingham dresses in a variety of colors—potty-mouthed little name callers on the inside. That day she'd done a lot of crying, but thanks to her wacky womenfolk, whom she fondly termed the Sisterhood, she'd ended up laughing.

Amelia seriously doubted the situation with Ethan would end up in laughter.

Something more frightening drove Ethan's rejection, and while Amelia knew it, the pain of it still came—in waves. What hurt worse was that Ethan wouldn't share it with her. Apparently, modern man and medieval man were pretty much alike in some areas, and after being raised by her father and living with a set of older twin brothers, she knew when a man shut down mentally, that was it. Finite. And Ethan Munro had indeed shut down.

And dammit, it hurt.

Once more she tossed her thinking ball to the bull's-eye on the rafter, nailed it, and caught it. Staring at the old, worn tennis ball and tracing the letters she'd penned with a permanent marker, Amelia did exactly what the ball was made for.

She thought.

It dawned on her, not so suddenly, that she had a certain flaw in her character. Well, probably more than one, but this one stood out in her mind more than, say, drinking milk straight from the gallon jug, or using the three-second rule when dropping something edible onto the floor.

Amelia had a tenacious bone in her body. She could admit it, true enough. And that bone grew when it came to helping those she loved. More than once it'd gotten her into trouble. More than once, the person on the receiving end of her tenacity-fueled help didn't want it to begin with.

More than once, she'd not given a horse's patootey.

And by God, she didn't give one now.

"Lass?"

Amelia jumped, thinking it first to be Ethan. In a flash, she recognized Aiden. Rolling off the bed, she headed for the door, thought better of it, grabbed a pillow, and held it to her chest before opening the door.

Aiden stood on the other side, a somber look upon his handsome face. He gave a weak smile and inclined his head to the pillow.

"Och, you're a wily one," he said.

She smiled. "So I've been told."

He looked her in the eye. "Are you well this eve?"

Quirking a brow, she rubbed her chin. "Has he told you anything?"

With a hefty sigh, Aiden shook his dark head. "Nay. He told us to guard your door and no' to follow him."

Amelia nodded. "Where'd he go?"

"He didna say."

"Somehow, that doesn't surprise me." She looked at him then, Ethan's cousin who'd conned him into doing so many naughty things as boys. "Something happened tonight, Aiden. I don't know what, but I can't just let him shut me out."

He smiled. "If anyone can reach him, 'twill be you."

Amelia prayed he was right.

Chapter 24

Two weeks passed, and Amelia realized rather quickly that only one other time in her life rivaled the intense misery she was experiencing at present: the Landry family's RVing vacation to the Grand Canyon. Her twin brothers, Seth and Sean, had been eighteen, she'd been sixteen, her twin sisters, Maggie and Erin, fourteen, and ZuZu, who'd accompanied the Landrys on nearly every vacation, also sixteen. Her granny had gone, too. And don't forget Firecracker, the half beagle, half *something*.

All within a day of leaving, she, ZuZu, Maggie, and Erin had *started*. That's right. *That* time of the month. For all of them. Oh, and her mom and granny were both on hormone supplements.

It had been like some warped version of *National Lampoon's Vacation*. The only thing missing was a recently deceased Aunt Edna bagged and bungee corded to her rocker on top of the Griswold family station wagon.

Horrible trip. Girls against girls. Girls against guys. It was a sheer wonder any of them survived it.

Yet it seemed like a Cleaver family picnic outing compared to the tenseness of the Munro Keep ever since Ethan had withdrawn. At first he'd stayed around his kin, but every time Amelia would try and engage in conversation, he'd give short, terse answers and then *poof!* he'd be gone. She persisted, though, and would nonchalantly try and edge closer to him during a movie, and he'd not so nonchalantly find another place to sit. His mood had grown dark, and he'd started snapping at everyone. Finally, he'd all but disappeared.

Another hurt. And Amelia was getting frustrated.

And at first she'd given him plenty of space. She needed time to try and figure out just what the heck had happened anyway. He'd not even opened up to the guys, and they'd all sported black eyes at one time or another.

Probably the worst was during the twilight hour, when the guys would solidify. Ethan would disappear into the wood and not return until long after Amelia had gone to bed. Finally, she'd stopped pushing.

So every day Amelia did her daily routine. She went through tae kwon do forms with the guys. All were present, of course, except Ethan. Sorely, Aiden, Rob, Tor, Gil—they were all very quick learners, mindful students and, as big as they were, quite nimble. Although once Amelia started teaching them their kicks, she had to turn her head more than once.

Not easy, though, to turn your head from a line of sexy medieval Scottish warriors wearing kilts, kicking their legs up high with limber ferocity. No sirree.

So they'd complete their morning forms; then Amelia would work on her story table and time line, scratch notes and scenes on note cards, and the guys would stay with her all day in case she needed some small bit of information, or description, or display of how to properly grip a broadsword.

Which is what brought about the tenseness.

Sort of.

In all the two weeks without Ethan, not once had an entity of any sort contacted her. Not even so much as a flick on the ear. And she'd tried, she truly had, to get some sort of response from *either* ghost—the bad one or the not-so-bad one. Nothing had happened, though. Everything remained quiet.

And then, an epiphany. A slap to the back of the head, a V8 moment. The oldest darn trick in the book. She'd watched ZuZu perfect it in high school. It was a wonder Amelia recalled it now, since she'd never even used the method. *How to make a guy jealous.*

Perfect.

The only difference was that she was dealing with seven-hundred-year-old guys in their prime. Virile, young—minus the seven-hundred-year-old thing, which really didn't count anyways, because they'd been enchanted all those years—and each with an ego the size of Texas.

Still, if they couldn't draw Ethan Arimus Munro (she loved saying that sexy name) out of hiding by way of temptation, i.e.: coaxing, asking nicely, begging, or in the fellas' cases, threatening, they'd flush him out with Amelia's last weapon: *Amelia.*

And Aiden Munro would prove to be the most perfect bait.

At the next twilight hour, Amelia and Aiden walked out to the meadow, in plain view of just about anywhere from the keep. Ethan had once again disappeared.

She narrowed her eyes at Ethan's cousin. "All

right, Munro. Let's get one thing straight here. I want you to repeat back to me the words *This is all for show and for Ethan's benefit, and I'll not cop a feel or get fresh in any way, shape, or form.*" She deepened her frown. "Say it."

The big Highlander threw back his head and laughed.

"Aiden, say it."

With his thumb and forefinger, Aiden pinched the tear ducts of his eyes and shook his head. "I cannot."

Amelia bit back a smile. "Come on. You're wasting twilight." She poked him in the chest. "Just remember that I am far more advanced than you in martial arts. I've had to actually register these"—she held up a foot—"as lethal weapons." She scowled. "Don't make me use them."

Aiden held up a hand. "Aye, okay, lass." He shook his head. "You're killin' me. You know that, right?"

Amelia smiled and patted him on the shoulder. "No, I'm not. Now, come on. And as a final warning, my reflexes are lightning fast. No accidental boob brushes allowed, or you may end up flat on your back."

One dark brow lifted over an eye with a wicked gleam. "I may take ye up on that."

"Aiden."

He smiled, and it looked so much like Ethan's it almost hurt to look at it. He held up a hand in surrender. "Verra well, no accidental brushes of any sort if I can help it." He glanced at her clothes. "No gown this eve?"

Amelia rolled her eyes. "How on earth do you expect me to try and swing that sword around in a sundress?"

Aiden wiggled his brows.

"Let's get to work. Do you have any idea where Ethan goes?"

"Aye," Aiden said, unsheathing his broadsword from a leather scabbard on his back. "Not only did we spend our childhood here together, but our enchanted life here, as well. There's probably no place on Munro land that I couldna find him."

Amelia looked at him. "So if he's watching, he could be anywhere, right?"

"Aye."

She shook her head. "I can't believe I'm about to do this. Okay," she said, looking him dead in the eye. "Don't you dare act weird on me after this, do you hear?"

"Yes ma'am."

"Fine. Let's use lots of laughing, and when you get behind me to help me heft the blade, *pretend* to nuzzle my neck. And when you do the other . . . just don't enjoy it so much."

Aiden quirked a brow. "How on bluidy earth do I pretend to do that? You either do it or you dunna."

"Ugh," Amelia grunted. "Let's just do this." She looked at him. "I hope it works. It's kind of childish, though, and I feel like an idiot."

Aiden only grinned.

"By the way," she said, and by God, she meant it, "thank you. You're a good cousin and a brave warrior for doing this."

"For you only, Amelia," he said with a solemn smile.

So they began. Amelia knew the other warriors were probably all glued to a peephole somewhere in the keep, or they'd each tagged their own arrow slit for their surveillance, or all piled up at the back kitchen doorway like the gang from *Scooby-Doo*, watching the show. She didn't mind really.

She had a feeling Aiden just might need their help.

So with Aiden crowding very close from behind, with his big arms overtop hers as he helped her lift the sword, and an occasional nuzzling of the neck, which was really Aiden whispering in her ear "methinks this is fine sport, indeed," the gloaming hour passed with no signs of Ethan. Aiden, being the prankster that he was, made the entire hour a lot of fun. They laughed—true laughs, because Aiden was a total clown. He in fact, did show her several trueto-life sword-wielding moves.

The Munro laird remained a recluse.

By the fourth day of their dopey little charade, still void of the raging mad and jealous Ethan they'd hoped to flush out, storming across the meadow and grabbing Aiden by the scruff, Amelia had all but lost hope. And patience.

Aiden was enjoying himself a bit too much.

And Amelia was getting desperate. She'd even gone into the wood to look for Ethan, to tell him enough was enough. But she'd found no sign of him. Even the Munros had searched, and after they'd returned looking worse for the wear, sporting new split lips and shiners, Amelia changed course.

Drastic measures were in order.

When she met Aiden on the fifth twilight, Amelia linked her arm through his, stifled a laugh after seeing the stunned look of surprise on his face, and whispered, "No swordplay this time. Let's just go sit by the loch, and follow my lead."

"I'm already likin' the sound of that, lass," he said with a grin.

Together they walked over the meadow and to the loch's edge, sat down, and started up idle chitchat. She told Aiden about the trouble she and her brother got into with the Black Cats at school, and she laughed when he thought she meant real live black cats. Then she told him about the Dillon voodoo doll ZuZu had made for her, and how they'd poked it repeatedly with sharp pins. He clapped his hands together and laughed, and actually, it was really nice company.

Then Amelia leaned her head against Aiden's shoulder and whispered, "Take down my hair."

"What?" he asked.

Amelia decided she should have discussed this with him beforehand. Too late now. "Pinch the clip together by the handles and take down my hair."

"Ah," Aiden said. Then he did it.

"Good," Amelia continued, and leaned up and looked at him.

Aiden's comical look nearly made her burst out laughing. She held it in, though, because she hoped and prayed their little scheme would work. Even though Aiden looked a lot like Ethan, and was in his own right a very handsome and sexy man, the chemistry between them was familial.

In other words, she felt like Audrey Griswold about to kiss her brother, Russ. *Bleah.*

Then, before she lost her nerve, or snorted out loud, or burst into a giggle fit over the look on Aiden's face, Amelia grabbed him by the hair, yanked his head down, and pressed her closed mouth against his. Hard.

At first, he froze. Shocked, no doubt, that Amelia had been so bold. And then she felt him relax, which should have sent off warning bells in her head, but he, being the fiend he was, acted just too fast.

A cunning warrior, Aiden Munro.

Amelia felt Aiden smile against her mouth, and then the devil threaded his fingers through her hair, and laid a big, wet kiss on her.

Just before he was snatched to his feet.

All at once, Amelia was alone on the loch shore, and a stampede of booted feet sounded behind her. Before she even turned around, the sound of fist to face met her ears. She looked.

Ethan stood over Aiden, who was laid out, unconscious, flat on the ground. Slowly, Ethan looked up, turned his gaze on her, and it left her so cold, she almost shivered. Never would she have thought he could look so infuriated. And hurt. A muscle jumped in his jaw, and his brows were dark slashes over his eyes.

"Ethan—"

"Dunna," he said, and started to walk past her.

By now the rest of the Munros had reached them. Aiden had come to, shaking his head, and was leaning on Sorely, rubbing his jaw.

"No, *you dunna*," said Amelia. "This was all a setup, Ethan. To get you to come out of hiding. To work things out."

He kept on walking. "There is nothing to work out."

Amelia grabbed his arm. "Stop it, Ethan, and look at me! You can't just keep ignoring me, or all of us, and stay holed up in the forest, or wherever it is you go!"

He jerked his arm free and headed back toward the wood.

"Dammit, Ethan, stop!" she hollered.

He didn't even slow down.

Quickly, she thought of something and prayed it would work, prayed she'd remember how to pronounce the words, and with a big, deep breath, she hollered, *"Grú mo chroí!"* It echoed through the glen.

That stopped him.

The other warriors all gasped. A manly sort of gasp, but a gasp still. Then silence.

Slowly, Ethan turned.

Amelia held her breath. She had no idea what the Gaelic phrase meant, but by the look on Ethan's face, it must've been pretty darn important.

He'd said it to her while kissing the boots off her, that day in the rain.

As he made his way back to her, face drawn, brow furrowed, she prayed she'd done the right thing.

Chapter 25

Ethan's insides stormed the closer he got to Amelia. Anger boiled inside of him, a fury he'd not felt in over seven centuries. The sod ripped beneath his boots as he stormed toward her, and she stood still, unyielding, until he grabbed her by the shoulders and pulled her close. Her eyes widened, and it sickened him inside to see the look of dread upon her face. It couldna be helped, though.

"Dunna *ever* say that aloud again! Do you hear me?" He gave her a shake. "Answer me!"

She just stared at him, those odd-shaped eyes glassy and unblinking.

He gave her another shake. "Dunna say it!"

He felt his body leave the ground for a moment, Amelia's arms were suddenly out of his grasp, and a big fist had been planted against his jaw. His head snapped back, but he didna fall. Holding his chin, Ethan stared at Torloch, who gave him a vicious glare—one he hadn't seen since battle.

Torloch pointed at him. "I dunna know what's gotten into you, Ethan, but you'll no' touch Amelia that way again."

Ethan glanced at her then, and her face had the look of someone who'd just lost a loved one.

Christ, he wanted to wipe that look from her face and replace it with the one she'd had that day in the rain, before—"

"What do those words mean?" she asked, boldly moving toward him. "Tell me!"

The wounded look was gone, and just that fast, replaced by one of pure fury.

Ethan preferred that.

She marched right up to him and poked him in the chest. "Dammit, Ethan, you tell me what those words mean!"

He started to turn away again, but the lass was relentless. She grabbed his arm. "Don't you walk away!"

He shrugged her hand off, and recalled rather fast that Torloch had a penchant for fisticuffs.

This time, Tor struck his eye. The swelling began immediately. He didna care. For the last time, he turned to walk away.

Amelia ran in front of him and blocked his path. "Tell me!" she shouted. "I'll just follow you wherever you go until you do!"

Ethan stepped around her, but she jumped in his path once more. "Tell me!"

"Dammit, woman, move!" he yelled.

Torloch grabbed him, locked his arms behind him, and held him tight. "Tell her, laird. Before we run out o' twilight."

Ethan stared at Amelia, her chest rising and falling with angered breaths, her hands balled into fists by her side, her face pinched in anger.

Christ, mayhap if he told her, she'd leave him alone.

Torloch, damn his arse, gave Ethan a shake. "Tell her!"

"Love of my heart!" Ethan shouted. The resolve ran out of him. He quieted. "It means love of my heart."

Amelia took a step forward, lifted her hands, and when the soft skin of her palms cradled his cheeks, he let out a hefty sigh.

"Look at me, Ethan Arimus Munro," she said, her voice softer now, yet hoarse from shouting. "Please."

Ethan did. Damnation, he couldna help it. Even knowing it placed her life in danger, he couldna look into those green eyes, so wide and trusting, and keep his feelings from her any longer. 'Twas selfish, and beyond dangerous, he knew, but he couldna deny it any more than his own next breath. *"Táim I ngrá leat,* Amelia Landry. By the blood of Christ"—he shrugged loose from Torloch's grip and slid his hands over hers—"I'm in love wi' you."

Amelia's eyes closed on an exhale, and a tear leaked through her lashes. Finally she looked at him. "That kiss with Aiden wasn't real. It was only to—"

Ethan stopped her words with his mouth, and behind him, his kinsmen cheered. Amelia fell into him, wrapped her arms around his waist, and kissed him with such fervor, he all but wished his kin would leave them.

"I love you, Ethan Arimus Munro," she said against his lips. "Forever."

Ethan smiled, although worry gnawed at his gut. He'd discuss what had happened later, after the gloaming. For now he wanted his woman no other place but against him. *"Go síoraí,"* he said.

"What's that mean?" Amelia asked, her lips softly dragging against his.

"Forever," he told her.

And he prayed it would be true.

And with his men chortling and whistling around them, Ethan stood there by the loch until the last second of twilight, kissing his beloved.

Right then, he cast a fervent request to God and the stars above that she'd never be taken from him, that her life would be spared.

Even if his was not.

When the last of the twilight was swallowed up by the summer's eve, Ethan walked beside Amelia, back to the keep. As he neared Aiden, he stopped. "I didna mean to hit you so hard, cousin."

Aiden grinned and wiggled his jaw. " 'Twas worth it."

Ethan knew it, too.

Amelia sat as close to Ethan as she could on the sofa without slipping through him. Still, that wasn't close enough by far.

He loved her, you know. *Táim I ngrá leat* is what he'd said to her. In front of his kin, even. Gaelic words of endearment. The medieval L word, so to speak, but in a much more romantic way. Not just *I love you*, but *I'm in love wi' you*. It'd sounded beautiful, exotic, perfectly medieval.

It had struck the core of her soul.

Ethan had quietly sat next to her and explained everything that had happened that day in the rain, leaving out their very, very passionate kiss. The whispered voice, the harsh wind and biting hail.

The threat to kill her if Ethan didn't leave her alone.

"So that whole hail storm and wind had kicked up once you'd voiced your love for Amelia aloud?" asked Rob.

"Aye, and the more I argued with the voice, the more violent it became." He shook his head. "Passing odd, to hear something so strong inside myself, and even more odd to answer it back."

"You're positive 'twas the same voice from before?" asked Gilchrist. " 'Twas a long time ago, Ethan."

He looked at his kin. "I'm sure of it."

Amelia rubbed her brow. "I feel we're nowhere with all of this," she said. "I'd thought for sure once the ghosts started speaking to me that we'd get a clue. Now they've both clammed up."

"Aye, but we want the bad one to stay that way," said Gilchrist. "It doesna like you, Amelia."

"I wonder why the malevolent spirit doesna just cast another enchantment," said Aiden. "What stops it?"

"Probably being dead," replied Amelia. "Maybe once the enchanter died they lost their powers, or whatever they're called."

Ethan nodded. "I think Amelia has it aright." He looked at all of his men, and then at Amelia. He drew a deep breath. "Mayhap you should go—"

"I'm not leaving." Amelia frowned. "Running away is not the answer, Ethan."

"Neither is putting your life in danger," he said, his voice low. "I'll not have it."

"I'll stay inside," she said.

"You're verra first experience was inside," answered Ethan. He rubbed the back of his neck. "By the blood of the saints, 'tis frustrating."

All the warriors grumbled in agreement.

Amelia stood and stretched. "Well, we've really no choice but to continue on as before. Even if we knew who the enchanter was, not to mention the murderer, who may be one and the same, it wouldn't help us break the spell."

She stopped and blinked.

"What is it, Amelia?" asked Ethan.

She started to pace, arms crossed over her chest. With one finger, she tapped her jaw. "The gentle spirit has more than once urged me to 'break the ssspell,' along with the message 'they must go back.'" She glanced at the men. "I think that means *you* must go back, in—"

"Time?" finished Aiden.

"You mean back to the day of Devina's death?" asked Sorely.

Ethan remained quiet, but he'd leaned forward and now rested his forearms against his knees. He stared at the space between his feet.

"Mayhap Amelia can pen a time enchantment?" said Rob. He looked at her. "Can you?"

"I'm a writer, not a witch," Amelia said.

"That's a fact to be pondered," said Aiden. He rubbed his jaw.

Amelia grinned at her coconspirator. "Don't pout, Aiden. You're a wonderful kisser, by the by."

The men chuckled.

"Anyway," she continued. "I'm guessing here, since my field of expertise usually doesn't include magic, but when an enchantment is cast, wouldn't there be a backup somewhere? I mean"—she snapped her fingers—"maybe whoever enchanted you did so with the plan to *unenchant* you at some point, but the enchanter was killed before that could happen."

"Which is why we've been stuck in this place for seven centuries," said Gilchrist.

Amelia smiled. "Exactly."

"I rather fancy the twenty-first century," said Rob. "Well, if I'd be able to leave our borders and see more of it, that is. I do like the tele."

"What would sending us back there do?" said Ethan. His gaze bore into hers, as though he'd been thinking hard on the same question for several minutes. "What outcome could it have?"

Amelia thought about it. "I don't know. Unless you went back before Devina's murder." She looked at him. "Maybe you're supposed to go back and prevent her death?"

Ethan worried his brow with his thumb and forefinger. He thought, and then with those mesmerizing silver eyes, he locked gazes with Amelia. "Even if we did all of this, lass, and we were able to go back to our time and right Devina's murder. Then what?"

So caught up in trying to find a solution and solve the crazy mystery of the Munro resident spirits and Ethan and his kin's out-of-this-world enchantment, she hadn't bothered to think of just what the outcome would finally be.

All at once, Amelia knew it. Knew it clear to her bones. The thought hit her square in the gut and nearly knocked her breathless.

"We'd have to stay there, back in our time. Isna that right?" asked Torloch.

Amelia turned and stared into the empty hearth. "I don't know," she said. "I really just don't know."

So many thoughts crashed over her at once, so forceful and so plentiful, they made her brain ache. How could something as simple as leasing an old creepy tower house for the summer for a little bit of writing solitude have turned into such a life-altering quandary?

One thing she did know.

No matter the outcome, Amelia would lose Ethan.

Chapter 26

During the week that followed, everything remained quiet. For the most part, that is. Every morning, Amelia trained the warrior-knights in their newfound love of martial arts. Fast learners, all of them. They'd become quite good, too, and had even started sparring with one another—quite a sight to behold, watching fourteenth-century warriors spar in the arts. Fast of hand and foot, paired with their honed skills of sword fighting, and the guys had indeed become lethal weapons.

During the afternoon hours, Ethan remained by her side. Whether she was busy writing scenes on her note cards, or filling in the fictional portion of her time line, he stood close, unable to physically touch her, yet Amelia had never felt more caressed than during those hours. With his eyes alone, Ethan had the power to make her skin burn with a single look, and the way he'd lean close to her, mere inches apart— good grief, she was sure the keep would experience a major power outage.

And all the while, Ethan kept a close guard on Amelia. As did all of the Munros.

At twilight, for that magical gap in time between

daylight and darkness, she and Ethan were insepara-
ble. Both were careful not to say the L word anymore; it had somehow seemed to trigger the ugly
response from the malevolent ghost, which, they'd
all come to believe to be a woman. Ethan had racked
his brain but could find no good candidate as to who
that woman might be.

Ethan, Amelia realized rather fast, needed no words
to express his feelings. Although careful not to stray
too far from the keep, they'd find a bit of privacy
near the loch, or just outside on the wrought-iron
bench Guthrie had brought from the widow's cottage
and placed near the castle wall, or a nice, secluded,
shadowy alcove, like the one they presently were in.

Ethan, being the big guy he was, crowded the con-
cealed, stone hideaway, which was fine with Amelia.
It reminded her of a brick oven cutaway, or a mini
hearth, with an archway and a stone slab for a seat.
Amelia had placed pillows on top for cushions, and
with the barely there glow of torchlight flickering in
the passageway, it gave the most perfect, medieval
ambience.

To go with the most perfect, medieval warrior, of
course.

Neither, though, had voiced aloud their fear of
what would become of them, no matter what the end
scenario was. Not once. The fear was there, though,
constantly, ever-present and lying just below the surface, and any good therapist would take great pleasure in knocking their heads together for a good
wake-up call, to try and hammer sense into both of
them, to make them talk about it. Not keep it bottled
up inside, hoping it would just go away, or fix itself.

A clear vision came to her, of her and Ethan, each

sitting on tall stools beside each other, before a live audience, facing Dr. Phil while he asked, "So, how's that working for you?"

"It's not," she'd answer.

Dr. Phil would raise his eyebrows and shrug, and the audience would chuckle . . .

"Amelia," Ethan said, breaking into her thoughts. He traced the bridge of her nose with his finger. "What's troubling you this eve?" He tucked her hair behind her ear.

Amelia gave a soft laugh. She was about to make Dr. Phil proud. "The same thing that bothers me every eve, Ethan, and every morning, every night, every afternoon." She looked at him, his chiseled face cast in shadows, the one silvery eye with the moon scar beneath it staring back at her. "What's going to happen to us?" She sighed. "If you go back to your time—even if that could be managed—we'd never see each other again. If nothing happens, and you remain enchanted forever, I grow old and die, and you stay the same, living on forever." She shook her head. "I'm not sure I could bear being sixty while you remain a young, virile, thirty-one-year-old, give or take a few centuries. It's almost like you're a ghost, but not." She looked at him. "It's like we're doomed no matter—"

Ethan leaned in, closed his mouth over hers, and simply breathed. One big hand slid over her jaw, tilted her head, and his lips nudged hers open and he kissed her, long, deep, drawing the worry out of her and swallowing it whole. The way he held her face when he kissed her, it felt as though he were blind, and touching her cheekbones, her chin, her brows, as his only means of discovery. With an erotic suckle of her bottom lip, he pulled back and stared at her.

"Amelia," he said, that deep, medieval voice making her shiver, "no matter the outcome, I've lived a more fulfilling life in the past several weeks with you than I did the whole of my days whilst in my time. I'd do it again, too, if it meant spending one more twilight hour with you." His gaze seeped far into her soul. "Whatever happens, we'll take it on together, aye?"

He was right, of course. They'd do their best to wrangle the problem, and they'd cross that bridge when necessary. She took a deep breath and smiled. "Aye."

Ethan grinned. "You're verra cute when you say that, by the by."

Amelia leaned her head against the alcove's wall. "Maybe we should all carry a lucky rabbit's foot." She glanced at him. "You know? A good-luck charm."

Ethan chuckled. "That brings to mind a long-ago memory. When I was a lad, my grandmother had us all carry around a talisman to ward off evil. In case anything happened upon us in the wood. Verra superstitious, Madeline Munro. Too bad we stopped carrying them around once we grew up."

Amelia held his hand, traced his strong fingers, then turned his hand over to feel the calluses there. "What were the talismans?"

"Slivers of yew bark." He grasped her hands and put them around his neck, pushed her hair to one side, and pressed his mouth to her throat. The warm wetness of his tongue, followed by the gentle movement of his lips against the sensitive skin of her neck made her insides quiver. His hand angled her head just to the right, and his finger trailed over her collarbone.

All at once, Amelia froze. She blinked, then jumped so hard she knocked her head against the stone wall. Grabbing his head in her hands, she lifted his face. "What did you say?"

Ethan stared at her, the sexy curve of his mouth lifting into a grin. "When? For the life of me, all I can recall is tasting your verra soft throat."

Amelia let out a gusty sigh. "What was the talisman you carried around as a little boy?"

Ethan blinked. "A sliver of yew bark. Why?"

Amelia's heartbeat quickened, and she stood slowly. "Oh, my gosh."

"What is it?" Ethan asked.

Rubbing her temples, she paced in the passageway. "In my room, and then in the forest that day, when the whispering ghost sent me outside to the forest in the dark," Amelia said. "It kept repeating the word *you*, only the word was drawn out, like *youuu*." She looked at him, his expression puzzled. "I think it may have meant *yew*, as in the yew tree." She looked at him. "I don't know, it may be crazy," she said, "but I think we should all carry a piece of yew bark. My guess is that is the message the gentle spirit was trying to tell me—along with trying to send you back in time, which seems impossible, but, I mean, we're dealing with spirits and enchantments and malevolent beings who can throw spiky balls of hail and turn rooms to frost." She smiled and took a breath. "A little *woo-woo* protection couldn't hurt."

Ethan stood, an endearing smile making his mouth curve into the cutest grin. He stepped forward, slid his hands over her hips, and pulled her against him. Bending his head, he moved his mouth to her ear. "Then yew slivers we shall have, Amelia," he whispered. He took her earlobe in his teeth, then kissed her just below it. "And you'll have one, as well." He looked at her then, his face in shadows, his voice deep and rich. "Now cease so much talk and worry over specters and kiss me, woman. Before I fade away."

Amelia needed no further urging. She had a sexy Highlander in a dark passageway, for God's sake. First thing tomorrow, they'd make a trip out to the gazillion-year-old yew tree, shave some slivers of bark, and everyone would stuff them in their pockets to ward off evil.

Sounded like a plan to her.

With a firm but gentle shove, Amelia backed Ethan against the passageway wall, and pressed against him. She wanted to touch him, run her hands over his stomach, which, by the feel of it through the rough-hewn linen plaid he wore, seemed to be quite the washboard. But there didn't seem to be an easy entrance into that bolt of fabric wound about him. The only way, she figured, was up the hem.

The thought made her shiver.

Instead, she moved her hands over the length of his muscled arms, up to his neck, wound her fingers through the magnificent long hair that fit him so well, and pulled his head down until their mouths touched. With her hands she grazed his beard-roughened cheeks, fingered his throat, his very sexy Adam's apple, and sighed when his hands moved over her hips, then slipped around to her backside and pulled her against him, trapping her between his thighs. She groaned against his mouth, and his lips moved back to her ear.

"Have I mentioned today just how much I loathe your rules of wooing?" he whispered, his voice gravelly, strained.

As he pressed into her, all six feet, seven inches of hard, raw male—especially that specific part of him down there, she mentally noted—she cleared her froggy throat. "I uh, think I can pretty much tell, Ethan," she said, her own voice raspy.

His hands moved to her head, one on either side, and he lifted her gaze to his. Still pressed against her, he traced her bottom lip, nudged it open, angled her head, and then when it was just the way he wanted it, lowered his mouth and kissed her like a man who had hours to spend on just her lips. Then he pulled back, his eyes hazed with desire, and smiled.

Just before the twilight ended.

Later, in the great hall, Amelia shared with the others her idea on the yew bark. Every single warrior had carried it as kids, they'd said, and were willing to do so again.

"Guthrie brought those movies you asked for," said Rob, pointing to a stack on top of the DVD player.

Amelia walked over to the stack, flipped through several, nearly picked *Die Hard*, and changed her mind.

There was enough testosterone lingering in the air to supply another World War. She'd watched just about every beat-'em-up, blow-'em-up movie that Hollywood had made. They'd even watched *Brave-*

heart. Now *that* was an experience all its own, watching a movie about a guy that her guys knew and fought with. They'd roared at some parts—mostly the battle scenes—cursed in others, mumbled in Gaelic during others still. Quite the surreal moment, all in all. During the end, when Wallace suffered during his execution, the men fell silent. Again, a few muttered things in Gaelic, and Amelia thought later she'd ask Ethan what they'd said. She had a feeling it wasn't very nice, and that it was geared toward Longshanks. Or, as the Munros fondly called him, *Wee Wanker.*

Nope, Amelia thought, she'd had quite enough testosterone for one week. They'd watched Abbot and Costello, all the old monster classics, and a few off-the-wall flicks. To see six big guys wearing kilts and broadswords hang on to the edge of their seats while watching little Nemo find his way home was truly a treat.

Endearing, actually.

But tonight was chick night. Most guys would balk. She wouldn't tell them. "All right, fellas," she said, making her selection. "You're going to love this one. I promise. It was the staple of my teenage years." She eyed Ethan. "You'll appreciate it."

He quirked a brow.

And by the time the first dance scene of the movie started, Ethan shot her a look. "I see where you acquired your skills," he said, referring to the little victory dance he'd caught her doing weeks before.

So by the time *Dirty Dancing* wound up, Amelia had six medieval guys all vying for turns to learn the dance steps, of which she, ZuZu, and their other friends had practiced ruthlessly on the front porch of her granny's plantation house, on a daily basis until they had it down to perfection. Aiden, of course, was the most eager of the warriors.

She'd be in big trouble if the Munros ever left the twenty-first century.

And with the music blasting as the credits rolled, Amelia put aside her worries of enchantment, of evil ghosts and good ghosts, and about sending her new-found family back to the past. Especially the very one she was in love with.

To the hollers and suggestive whistles of the others, Ethan good-naturedly did the best he could to keep up while Amelia showed the Munros just how she'd perfected the naughty dance moves.

Ethan lowered his head and said, "We'll try this at tomorrow's twilight."

Amelia could hardly wait.

Chapter 27

Ethan sat with his back against the wall, across from Amelia's room, in the passageway. So far, she'd slept soundly.

He wished he could do the like.

Earlier that day, they'd all traipsed out to the old yew tree, where Amelia had stripped a long sheath of bark. They'd returned to the keep, she'd sectioned the strip into seven slivers, and when the gloaming arrived, they'd all stuffed a piece into their belts. Amelia had pushed hers into the pocket of her trews. She'd seemed rather satisfied that the friendly ghost, as she called it, had guided her toward something protective.

He prayed the old lore his grandmother had believed in so heartily had truth to it.

Leaning his head back, Ethan stared at the darkened rafters and considered. Never had he envisioned an encounter with a soul such as Amelia Landry. She'd entered his home, somewhat fearful yet bold enough to storm forward and brave the darkness. She'd taken their cause and made it hers. By Christ's blood, she'd *believed*.

And he loved her all the more for it.

And although he knew in his bones an end to their time together drew close, he couldna deny himself the contentment of her company. Even knowing the wobbly and odd state of his existence, Amelia gave freely of herself, and whilst they'd agreed not to voice aloud their endearments to each other, in case the malevolent being took rebuttal, she showed him with every touch, every laugh, every deep, fervent kiss just how much she loved him. Had she no' spoken a word, or moved her mouth against his, even once, he'd know her heart. Just by looking into those crescent-shaped eyes.

The thought of giving her up ripped his heart in twain.

With a hearty sigh, he rubbed the back of his neck and stared at her door. More than once, the thought of begging her to wed him had crossed his mind. Each time, he'd dismissed those thoughts. They were selfish, by the by. Why would a vibrant woman of the modern world want to be strapped to a nearly nonexistent lad who had only an hour each day to physically touch her? He'd been afeared of her answer, so he'd kept his stupid mouth tightly closed and not asked the bluidy question.

He'd take what he could now and be damned grateful for it.

All at once, Amelia's door flung open. "Ethan!"

He jumped up, and in two strides stood in her chamber. She stood at her desk, bent over at the waist, scribbling something on her parchment. "What is it? Is aught amiss?"

"No! Yes! Just come here!"

As he drew closer, he peered at the small of her back, exposed by a barely there tunic that had ridden up. There, just appearing at the top of her black trews, which hung loosely at her hips—verra fetching, he thought—was a . . . painting? A painting on her body? How could that be? Bluidy saints, it looked like the tail of a damned lizard—

Quick as that, she turned and jumped up on her bed, her legs tucked under her bottom. She patted the spot beside her. "Come here. Sit." She grinned. "The good ghost just visited me."

Ethan admitted that indeed 'twas passing odd to be visited by a spirit, no matter the demeanor. But by Christ's robes, whatever lay beneath her trews intrigued him a bit more at present . . .

"Ethan, come here!"

He blinked, then sat on the bed beside her. Her eyes were ablaze with excitement.

She waved her parchment. "I think the friendly ghost has just given me a verse to send you back in time."

Ethan blinked, and his air nearly left his lungs. He narrowed his gaze. "And why are you so pleased about that?"

She grinned. "Because, if I'm reading the words right, you and the guys will be sent back to wrong a right. But *after*, everything will be okay."

Ethan quirked a brow. "That's what the friendly spirit told you?"

With a soft laugh, Amelia shook her head. "Of course not. But I don't want to read the words out loud, you know"—she looked at him, the corners of her outer eyes tipping upward—"before you're ready to go back. With the others to help you. See?"

Ethan nodded. He didn't see as much as she'd like,

though. "I canna read well, but let me see the missive, lass."

Amelia nodded and held the parchment up for him to see the words. Luckily, 'twere easy enough. Slowly, he read them to himself.

> *Once as they were*
> *'twill now be again.*
> *Wrong to right,*
> *hearts alight.*

Ethan looked up. He scratched his jaw. "I'm no' sure where you're getting that everything will be okay."

Amelia smiled and pointed. "See this last line?"

He did, and nodded. "Aye, but what's a blazing heart—"

"Shush!" Amelia said, waving her hand at his mouth. "Don't say another word." She grinned. "Just trust me."

Ethan considered. He had no choice but to trust the one person who had not only the sensitivity to see and believe in him and his men, but the courage to give her heart freely to a man not from her time. He nodded. "Done. Now, what is your strategy?"

She pulled her legs up and hugged her knees. "Tonight, at the yew tree, during the gloaming hour." She smiled. "All of us."

Ethan sighed. "Verra well, Amelia. We'll do it." He then remembered the paint. "What's that painted lizard's tail poking from the top of your trews?" he said, pointing to her bottom. "Just there?"

Suddenly, she laughed. "That's the result of a wild

twenty-fifth birthday." She raised one lovely eyebrow. "Can't see it, though."

Ethan sighed and rubbed his eyes. "Dunna tell me. One of your blasted wooing rules, aye?"

She laughed, and he wondered if he'd ever convince her to change her code of chivalry.

As she sat there, a naughty look upon her lovely face, he highly doubted it.

Her lips moved, then, but her voice didna speak. He leaned in close. "Aye? I didna hear you."

She shook her head, pointed at her lips, and mouthed three words that made him swallow a bluidy lump in his throat.

I love you, she mouthed silently, then shyly bit her lip, grinned, and looked down at the parchment.

Ethan stared at the woman he loved, unable to touch her, unable to haul her onto his lap and kiss her soundly, or better yet, lay her down atop her bedcovers and love her in truth, until they both gasped for air.

Amelia Landry. A woman born centuries after he should have been dead. Yet they sat together on the same bed.

A miracle, he thought. And when she glanced back up at him and smiled, his heart ached with more love than he ever thought imaginable.

He prayed then that he could keep her forever.

"Come on, guys, get a move on," Amelia said, later that evening. She fingered the slivers of yew bark in her hand. She'd cut the slivers earlier that day, but had to wait until the gloaming to give a piece to each warrior. "Chop-chop. It's almost twilight."

Torloch walked beside her, and Ethan on the other. Tor glanced down at her and frowned. "What the bluidy hell does *chop-chop* mean, by the by?"

Amelia smiled. "It means hurry your sorry arse up, that's what."

The guys chuckled.

"Ah," Tor said with a grin. "That I get."

"You look unnerved," Ethan said, close to her ear.

She looked first at him, then the other warriors trudging across the meadow with her. Guthrie walked in the back, a bit slower with his limp. Rob stayed beside him. "I suppose I am a little nervous," she said. "The forest is sort of dark and scary this time of evening."

"Did you bring your big flashlight?" Aiden asked. "If things work as you hope, you and old Guthrie will be heading back to the keep alone."

Yet another thing that had her on edge.

"Are you having second thoughts, Amelia?"

She glanced at Ethan's face, darkened from the gloam's light. "Of course I am. My stomach is full of butterflies and I'm scared I'll never see you again." Tears suddenly stung her eyes, and she felt glad for the twilight's bizarre glow. She didn't want them to see her cry.

But she might do just that.

"Amelia," Ethan said. "Dunna think that way."

She nodded. "You're right. Besides, if this is going where I think it's going, you'll be able to save a life— one that didn't deserve to be taken away." She smiled, although she thought it came across weak and paltry. "That's what counts."

They continued across the meadow, to the dark edge of the forest. Once there, the light that filtered through the canopy of trees still shone bright enough that a flashlight wasn't needed yet. They all walked in quietly and started down the path to the old yew tree.

At first the sounds of the approaching night soothed Amelia. The rush of the burn in the distance, the pine martins tweeting in the treetops, the gentle breeze rustling the leaves above; they were familiar sounds, and she now thought of them as home.

Then the wind picked up.

Not so fierce at first, but the closer they got to the yew, the stronger the wind became. It didn't effect the guys, other than Guthrie, but they knew what caused the upwind.

Amelia's pace quickened. "Let's hurry, Ethan," she said. "I'm not in the mood for any more hail."

"I'm right here," he said, and he was, walking as close as he could without melding into her. "The hour is almost here, Amelia. 'Twill be fine."

Without another word, they all power walked (they didn't swing their arms, though) until the gnarled trunk of the yew tree came into view. Once there, they stood in a circle, Ethan standing close to Amelia.

"Why did we have to come here to read the verse?" asked Rob. "Wouldn't anywhere have been just as fine?"

Gilchrist punched his arm. "The old yew is protective, witless," he said. " 'Tis the best place, by the by."

"Ah," Rob said.

"So this is the bad spirit's doin's, aye?" asked Aiden. "A lot of wind?"

The wind picked up even more.

"Och, damn," he said. "I'll keep me mouth shut."

Then the twilight came, and Ethan immediately pulled Amelia into his arms. He pressed his lips to her temple and kept them there for several comforting seconds. The warmth of his body, the fierce strength in his arms as he held her settled her, made her feel safe. " 'Twill be fine, lass. Dunna worry."

She looked up. "That's a tall order, handsome, but I'll try." Quickly, she handed each warrior a sliver of yew bark. "Put these somewhere safe, so they don't fall out and blow away."

They each did just that.

Guthrie stood back a ways, leaning on a walking stick. "Do ye need any help, lass?"

"No, that's okay, thanks." Amelia fished the piece of paper with the verse on it out of her jeans pocket. She unfolded it, looked at it, and then looked at the guys.

And emotions overwhelmed her.

Dear Jesus, what if she never saw any of them again?

She took a deep breath. This had to be done. Not only could their enchantment be broken, and they could live out normal lives, an innocent life could be saved.

Another deep breath, and she did the one thing she knew she'd be very, very bad at.

She said her good-byes.

One by one, she put her arms around each of the Munro warriors and hugged them tightly. She felt just like Dorothy leaving Oz, and saying her good-byes to the Scarecrow, the Tin Man, and the Lion.

She held it together until she wrapped her arms around Aiden's neck. He hugged her fiercely and whispered in her ear, " 'Tis a kiss I'll never forget, Amelia Landry." He pulled back, and right in front of Ethan, kissed her square on the mouth. He smiled, then, and wiggled his brows. "Dunna worry, lass. I'll be seeing you."

With a deep breath, and then one more to steady herself, Amelia turned to Ethan. His arms came around her, encircled her, and he buried his face in her neck. "When did this become farewell?" he whispered.

The wind picked up fiercely then, leaves kicked about and scattered. She held on to Ethan tightly. "I know this is the right thing to do." She moved her mouth to his ear. "But I'm scared."

He pulled back and looked down at her. The wind whipped his hair about his face, and a long strand caught on his lip. His jaw flexed, and his eyes gleamed silver in the twilight. He looked every bit the fierce Highland warrior that he was.

He took her head in his hands and brushed a kiss across her lips. *"Grú mo chroí,"* he said, his rich accent washing over her. *"Go síoraí."*

Amelia smiled and tears burned her eyes. "I love you, Ethan Arimus Munro." She kissed him back. "Forever."

Just then, a rustling sound started, and it grew louder in spite of the wind. She looked around, her ponytail slapping at her eyes and across her cheek, and as the sound came closer, Amelia peered down the trail.

Her heart leaped into her throat and she made a noise—not quite a scream, not quite a squeal.

Rats.

They crested the small hill by the hundreds, like a

black cloud on the ground moving swiftly toward them. Amelia hollered, then literally crawled up the length of Ethan.

"Hurry, lass!" yelled Gilchrist, who hated rats as much as she did.

Ethan balanced her. "Amelia, stop wriggling so. 'Tis a vision, is all."

Hanging off of Ethan's side, with her legs wrapped around his waist and legs, she squealed. "The hail wasn't a vision! These suckers are real!"

As the rodents gathered around Ethan's legs, he began to squirm. "Damn me, but you're right."

"Read the missive, lass!" hollered Gilchrist. "I beseech you!"

Amelia looked over her shoulder. Guthrie stood, looking at them as though they'd all lost their minds.

Maybe they had.

"*Ah-meh-lay-ah!*" shouted Gilchrist.

"Okay!" She held on to Ethan, and with the other, pulled the verse close and read it out loud.

Nothing happened.

The wind turned gale force now, and Amelia wrapped her legs even tighter around Ethan. "Nothing's happening!" she yelled over the noise.

"Try it again!" yelled Aiden. "Louder this time!"

"Love, I've got to put you down. You canna come with us."

"Oh, my God!" she said as Ethan lowered her. He unsheathed his sword and started swiping at the rats, which helped somewhat.

Amelia hurried and repeated it. Once more, nothing. She kicked and swatted at the filthy enchanted little rodents, and jumped up and down to try and keep them away. It wasn't working very well.

She glanced at the guys. Hair and kilts were flying everywhere, rats went sailing through the air, and had it not been such a freaking crisis, she would have thoroughly enjoyed herself.

"Let me see the missive, Amelia!" Ethan hollered over the wind.

She handed it to him, fought the urge to climb right back up his side, and watched his lips form the same words she'd just spoken.

Only, in Gaelic.

Suddenly, the wind stopped and the rats disappeared. The sky grew gray, and a thick, soupy mist rolled toward them from . . . somewhere.

Ethan looked at Amelia, and their eyes locked. God, she wanted to touch him so badly, but she wrapped her arms around herself and simply stared at him.

Just before the mist engulfed them, he mouthed the words *I love you.*

And then the blackness swallowed them whole.

Chapter 28

Amelia's eyes fluttered open. Silence and darkness enclosed her, but slowly; the more she stared, the pitch lightened, and a heavy mist, so thick she couldn't see anything but white, took the place of the dark.

Then, slowly, the mist faded. Not all the way, but only wispy sheets slipped by her.

She looked around. She stood right by the yew tree.

No rats. No wind.

No Ethan.

That funny spot inside one's throat that burned when something drastic happened? When tears wanted to flow and the potential crier held them at bay? Hers burned now. Her insides ached. Her heart hurt.

Jesus, they'd really gone back.

For a second, all Amelia could do was stand there and try to breathe. Reading the verse in Gaelic—medieval Gaelic—had worked. Of course it had. The original enchanter would have been from Ethan's time. She'd not have spoken English—which might be why the only time her spirit had gone all wacko had been when Ethan had spoken to Amelia in Gaelic.

Go figure.

Emptiness consumed her, like a big hole had been chiseled right out of her chest. Would she ever see Ethan and the guys again?

After several deep inhalations and exhalations, Amelia started back down the path, toward the keep. She wondered briefly how long she'd been standing out by the yew, in her weird blackout. From the filtered daylight, it seemed to be very early morning. She glanced around. Where the heck was Guthrie?

As she made it to the edge of the wood, Amelia stopped. Something felt different. Kooky different. She looked up and around. The treetops swayed, but she felt no wind on her cheeks. She took another big breath.

Not one single Highland scent came to her nose.

With a shake of her head, she continued on.

It wasn't until she left the wood and stepped out into the meadow that she noticed something else bizarre, and stopped again.

Her rental was gone.

So was the path she'd driven in on.

All at once, she noticed several more things, and her heart started to pound faster and faster. A small stone church sat off to one side of the keep. An enormous stable was set back from the church. Another stone building, more like a pavilion of sorts, stood off in the other direction.

Her eyes widened.

No way.

She wasn't supposed to go back to the fourteenth century. That hadn't been the plan at all. She wasn't from here. She hadn't anything to do with the original enchantment, or the murder.

So why was she here? Maybe she wasn't. Maybe she was having another of those weird dreams.

Amelia took off running. Good Lord, if she wasn't dreaming, then she hoped no one else saw her first. She didn't like the idea of smoldering on a big stick in an even bigger fire. She had to find Ethan, or one of the guys. She needed to let them know she'd come, too . . .

Just then a movement caught her eye. Her insides froze, and she dug her sneakers into the sod and stopped, wishing hard for a tree, a bush—anything to hide behind. But she was in the meadow, wide open for all to see.

Through the mist, a figure emerged. Dark cloak, big cowl pulled down far enough to see the face. The same cloaked figure from her dream . . .

The figure moved quick and fast across the meadow ahead, and then to skirt the side of the keep. Amelia took a deep breath, hoped with all mighty hope that the adrenaline in her body either flushed out or distributed so she wouldn't have a heart attack, and then followed.

Amelia kept her eyes trained on the figure, and when it stopped, so did Amelia. Whoever it was went into the small church. Amelia eased onward to the keep, stopped, and before she could catch her breath, the cloaked person emerged from the church with another. A girl, very tiny from what Amelia could see, with auburn hair and wearing a long blue gown. The cloaked figure towered over the girl. And then they both started walking toward the mist-shrouded knoll.

A bad feeling crept over Amelia. The kind where one's skin prickles and butterflies slap at the inside of your stomach. Not the sweet, happy butterflies, but the mean ones. That feeling.

Without hesitation, Amelia followed the pair. If she was having a dream, it definitely was of the informative sort. If she wasn't dreaming . . .

Just before the pair reached the top of the knoll, they stopped.

Everything happened rather fast after that, as things do in dreams. The young girl reached out her hand, took something from the cloaked person, and—Amelia squinted her eyes—*drank* something? Drank or ate something. Either way, something went into the young girl's mouth. What on earth were they doing? The young girl seemed perfectly at ease with the other.

More mean butterflies . . .

Just then, the pair began to move again, and it was at that exact same moment the mist thinned out at the top of the knoll.

Exposing an upside down wooden L.

At first, Amelia's mind froze. Then, as realization of what she was actually witnessing set in, her insides turned to ice, and then numb.

That tiny young girl was Devina, Ethan's wife. Amelia *knew* it, felt it in her bones. She'd bet her own life on it. With a loud yell, she started to run toward them. "Hey!" she shouted, dodging the rocks and thick clumps of heather. "Hey, stop!"

Neither person on the knoll heard; neither turned in Amelia's direction. She pumped her arms and legs, running as fast as she could.

Then the young girl slumped to the ground in a heap, and as Amelia dug into the side of the knoll, running up the small, narrow footpath, the cloaked figure withdrew something—Amelia couldn't tell what from where she was—and bent down at the girl's very still body.

Sweet Jesus, she'd just witnessed Ethan's wife's murder.

With her lungs burning, Amelia continued to run and yell. "Hey! Get away from her!"

The cloaked figure didn't even flinch.

Finally, Amelia tumbled to the top of the knoll. She stood, and the figure had looped a rope around the girl's neck. Amelia rushed forward, hollering, ready to fight. "What are you—"

Amelia fell straight through the cloaked figure. It was then she realized she hadn't felt the fall at all, not the damp earth beneath her palms, or the rock she'd landed on. Nothing.

Mist slithering around it, the person threw one end of the rope over the top of the upside down L, caught it, wrapped both hands around it, and began to pull. The girl's body started to rise.

Oh Jesus! No!

Amelia, fury raging within her, repeatedly threw herself at the cloaked figure, every time she simply fell through. She jumped, waved her hands, and screamed so hard, her voice started to crack.

No one heard Amelia's screams as the poor young girl—Devina Munro, Ethan's wife—hung limp and lifeless from the end of a rope . . .

Tears of anger and frustration ran down Amelia's cheeks, and she tried several more times to stop whoever from doing what Ethan had been blamed for. Amelia didn't want to look, but forced herself to meet the lifeless gaze of Devina.

She was looking straight at her as she clawed at the rope around her neck, her body wriggling.

Panic struck Amelia, and she began to scream, punching at the figure, kicking—but it was like fighting air. All those years of martial arts training, multiple degrees in black belt, and none of it helped her stop the murder of Ethan's young wife. Just a girl . . .

It was then the mist cleared, just a bit, that Amelia saw within the depths of the cowl concealing the murderer's face. She blinked. *A woman?* Reddish hair surrounding a pale white face, definitely female. As big as the figure was, and with such apparent strength, Amelia had assumed the cloaked person was a man. Amelia didn't recognize her, but she felt pretty sure it was the same person who'd enchanted Ethan and his men. But why?

The cloaked woman picked up a sword—Ethan's, Amelia assumed, and a width of plaid cloth, and jammed them together into the wood. Just like Ethan had said his wife had been found.

With a curse, Amelia took off down the knoll, across the meadow, and around the loch. Completely breathless when she reached the keep, and surprised to see the great hall door opened. It may have been open before and in her haste she had missed it. Catching her breath, Amelia hurried inside, frantic to find Ethan, Aiden—any of the guys. She nearly slipped, and when she glanced down, she saw the floors now strewn with long, dried weeds, or hay, all pressed down. *Bizarre.*

At the far end of the great hall, where the sofas,

love seats, and recliners usually sat, stood an enormous long wooden table with several chairs lining each side. At first Amelia saw no one. Then, through the kitchen archway toddled an older woman, wrapped in a plaid with a light-colored overlay, carrying a large, steaming pot.

"Excuse me?" Amelia said, carefully making her way over the weedy floor. She walked up to the woman. "Hello?"

The woman set the bowl down, regarded the table, and turned around and walked back to the kitchen.

She hadn't even known Amelia stood two feet away.

Suddenly, a thundering sound just outside the great hall made Amelia turn, and just as she did, Rob came bursting through the door. His face was white as dough, and he ran toward the stairs.

Amelia, grateful to finally see someone she knew, ran to meet him. "Rob! Thank God you're—"

"Ethan!" he hollered.

And ran straight through Amelia.

Amelia sucked in a breath, shook her head, and then followed Rob, who looked a bit rougher than usual, up the steps.

Just hearing Ethan's name from Rob's mouth made Amelia's heart thump hard. They reached the second floor, and Rob burst into a room. Amelia ran right in behind him.

Somewhere, a voice carried through the small open window Ethan Munro stood at.

Rob ran through the door, hollered something in Gaelic, and then reached Ethan's side, pointed out of the window, and yelled some more. Ethan answered in the same manner, a grave expression on his face.

He, like Rob, looked a little different. Raw, perhaps, or just rugged Highland male. She didn't know which.

Amelia ran to the window, beside both Munros. "Ethan!" she yelled, and waved her hand before him. He continued to stare out the window.

Then they both turned, and had Amelia not jumped to the side, they'd have walked right through her.

And as she hurried after them both, a perplexing thought crashed over her. No one could see or hear her.

So this is what it feels like to be a ghost . . .

Chapter 29

Even as Amelia raced around, following Ethan's every footstep, watching firsthand the vast confusion and rushing about in the Munro Keep, dodging as many warriors as she possibly could to prevent them from walking through her invisible self, one thing in her mind stood out, one thing she knew with assuredness.

The melee, the uproar of warriors, the swearing and hollering and hurrying about and gathering of weapons—was worse than a re-creation of the morning of Devina Munro's murder.

It was really happening. And Amelia, as unseen as a spirit, stood in the middle of it all. Watching, like a silent witness in a dream. And unable to do a damn thing about any of it.

A sense of hopelessness washed over Amelia, the energy and fight from before draining out of her with each breath. She no longer tried to make the others see her. They wouldn't. She was in the fourteenth century, but not really. The verse that sent Ethan and the others back in time had given Amelia a free ride. A nonobligatory trip to observe the senseless murder of a young girl.

Amelia wanted to sit down and weep.

As people hurried about the great hall, Amelia leaned against the wall and tried to swallow past the lump that grew larger by the second. Why had they come back if not to save Devina's life? It didn't make sense. And she'd been so sure . . .

Suddenly Ethan began barking orders at his men. Aiden, Sorely, Torloch, Rob, and Gilchrist all stood behind Ethan, along with several other warriors. Armed, their swords sheathed in big leather scabbards on their backs, they stood, faces drawn tight. Veritable medieval M-80s ready to explode. And then they filed out of the great hall and into the mist.

Amelia followed, and kept her eyes trained on Ethan. His mouth pulled tight into a fierce scowl, he surged forward with a determined walk. The sexy, twenty-first-century swagger was gone. Now fury fueled his gait. She all but held her breath as they crossed the meadow and skirted the loch, and then climbed the very same footpath Amelia had earlier.

This time, though, a line of warriors, their lit torches flickering in the mist, stood at the top of the knoll.

And just as Ethan had described, the Munros and the MacEwans clashed. Amelia's heart surged, and her throat burned as she watched a man she assumed to be Daegus push Ethan and then have him held. She glanced at the figure covered by a plaid on the ground, and she felt sickened, knowing it was Devina. Why, after all they'd gone through, had absolutely nothing changed?

And why was she being forced to watch it all?

When the fighting broke out, Amelia pushed back, out of the crowd. To watch a battle on TV, or at the movies, was one thing. Hollywood special effects could really make something look real and gory.

Nothing compared to watching it firsthand. To know these men were really killing one another . . .

Out of the corner of her eye, Amelia noticed movement. How, amidst a battle, she didn't know, but from the top of the knoll, behind the horrible upside down L, a tall figure stepped forward. She was wearing a long black gown, red hair framing a deathly white face.

Amelia's mind scrambled through the conversations she'd had with Ethan and the guys, specifically about the day Devina was killed. This day. They'd gone over a list of wedding guests. One of those guests had been Devina's beloved cousin, whose husband had been killed not a year before.

Marynth. Wearing widow's black. Before that, a cloak.

Devina's murderer.

The Munros enchanter.

With her heart in her throat, Amelia made her way through the fight, skirting around the edge, keeping an eye on Marynth and Ethan.

Amelia gasped and slapped a hand over her mouth as she watched Rob stab Devina's uncle, Daegus, just as he was about to attack Ethan. Gruesome as it was, it'd saved her beloved's life.

Everything happened exactly as Ethan and the guys had described. While Amelia couldn't understand any of the words, the actions fit perfectly. Devina had been murdered, Ethan had been blamed, and a battle had ensued between the two clans.

The only difference was Amelia had witnessed it all. She knew who the murderer was.

She also knew six Munros who had a sliver of yew bark in their belts.

She prayed fervently they still did.

All at once, a new set of warriors crested the knoll. As if in a slow-motion picture, the mist rolled in, and Ethan and his kin gathered in a circle. Through the blanket of white, Amelia saw something they'd not seen. Marynth, rushing out to their small circle, her lips moving fast, something Gaelic pouring out.

And then, out of the mist, a small figure emerged. A young warrior in Munro plaid, running toward Marynth full force, sword drawn. A young boy, perhaps?

Amelia blinked. A young *girl*. And she looked exactly like Ethan, Rob, and Gilchrist.

With Devina's murderer's name on her lips, the young girl, whom Amelia guessed to be Ethan's younger sister, plunged her blade into Marynth's heart, and the tall woman fell in a heap to the ground.

Amelia's breath came hard and fast, and she looked around but saw absolutely nothing. The mist, thick and consuming, rose to engulf her. The curses and shouts had vanished. All was silent.

And then, just that fast, the mist blinded her, and the weight left Amelia's body and she drifted, the blanket of white pulling her fast into a dark tunnel, until the white became a tiny speck of light in Amelia's eye. A pinpoint glimmer.

Then, nothing at all . . .

"Lass?"

Amelia's eyes fluttered open. As her head cleared,

so did her vision. She blinked several times, pinched her eyes shut tight, then opened them again.

Guthrie stood just at the open door of her room, frowning. "You writers sure are peculiar folk. Like I said, you've free run of the tower, lass, so unpack and help yourself. Watch your step, though. The closest infirmary isn't so verra close at all. Supper's every eve at seven. Breakfast is at eight. Lunch, you're on your own." With that, he disappeared into the shadowy corridor.

Amelia stood, dumbfounded. It took several seconds for things to compute. When it did, her stomach got that funny feeling one got when riding the Tower of Terror at MGM Studios. If one dared to ride that, which she did.

Shaking her head, completely bewildered, she glanced around. On the floor beside her, her big Volkswagon-sized suitcase. Next to that, her duffels and computer bag. Her room sat empty, as though no one had ever stayed in it.

As though *she'd* never stayed in it.

Impossible.

She turned around, nearly kicked Jack, who'd parked right by the duffels, and ran out the door. "Guthrie! Wait!" She hurried after him, down the corridor and to the steps. He'd already made it halfway down. "Guthrie!"

The old curator turned and looked up at her, his bushy brows pinched together into a scowl. "Aye?"

Racing down the stairs, she ran straight to him. She panted, out of breath. "What's going on? Where's Ethan and the others?"

Guthrie shoved a long, gnarled finger under the

bill of his cap and scratched. "What others? I'm the only one here. I dunna know what you mean, lass." He looked at her, shook his head, and then leaned toward her and sniffed. "Ye been hittin' the whiskey already, eh?" He chuckled.

Amelia wanted to grab the old guy by his plaid shirt and shake him. "Stop fooling around! What's happened to Ethan? Have you seen them?"

Guthrie stared at her and shook his head. "I dunna know what you're talkin' about, lassy, but I do know that I'm late for me date with the widow." He gave her a hard stare. "First of each month we go to Arthur's for a bit of dancin', and June's special is an open buffet. You were supposed to be here hours ago, you know." He started across the hall. "Supper's warmin' on the stove. I'm off."

"Wait—it's *June*?"

He cocked his head. "Of course it's June." He narrowed his gaze. "Dunna ye look at your flight times?" He shook his head. "Daft lass."

With that, he left.

Amelia just stood and stared, unbelieving. What had happened? Good God, Guthrie acted like she'd . . . never . . . been . . .

With a knot in her stomach, Amelia took a hard, thorough look around the great hall. The TV and DVD player were gone. A single sofa, a coffee table, and a single chair stood before the hearth. The research table containing her time line and note cards was gone. None of it remained.

June 1. She'd only just arrived.

"It can't be," Amelia said out loud. "It just can't." She took a slow turn around the great hall, glanced at the ancient set of antlers above the hearth, and then the pair that made up the light fixtures overhead. With a deep breath, she took off running. She simply wouldn't believe it.

"Ethan!" she hollered, and ran straight out the massive double doors. "Ethan! Aiden!" Pure adrenaline pumped her body out of shock and she ran around the keep, and then down to the loch. A gentle Highland breeze drifted through the glen, sending up that familiar sweet scent of clover and heather. She turned, staring at everything so familiar, yet nothing was what it'd been before.

"Ethan?" she said on a sob.

Only the wind and pine martins answered.

A frown pulled at her face, and anger boiled. No way could it have all been a damn dream. She couldn't have dreamed up the whole thing. Drawing in a lungful of air, she shouted, *"No!"* She heard it echo through the hills.

Once she'd used every ounce of air from her lungs, Amelia slumped down at the edge of the loch, and then fell back in the grass. Her body went limp, as if all the life had been drained.

"No," she said, her voice cracking. "I remember."

Tears burned the back of her throat, and Amelia swallowed several times to clear the lump, but it didn't work. Her eyes welled up, and once the tears overflowed, she let go, and sobs racked her body, and she lay there, shaking in the grass and heather.

She'd lost Ethan. Forever.

As Amelia lay there, staring up at the Highland sky of swirling reds, purples, and grays, she cried. Guthrie's old car hummed up the road and grew faint as he drove farther away, leaving her alone. Alone with memories of a man she'd fallen madly in love with but would never see again.

How long Amelia stayed in the grass, she didn't know. The sky grew darker, but not all the way, as was the way of the summer months in Scotland. The gloaming hour came and went, and although she'd been hopeful that, just maybe, during that magical hour where the fading rays of daylight melded with the first twinkling stars of nightfall, Ethan Arimus Munro would show up. Would just walk right up to her, grab her by the back of her head, and kiss her senseless. But he didn't. No magic happened. She simply lay amidst the clover and heather, listening to the gentle lap of the loch's water against the pebbled shoreline, and the whispering of leaves as the wind eased through the treetops.

The one sound that rose above all the idyllic Highland noises was the sound of her heart breaking.

Amelia fell asleep, there in the heather beneath the winking stars of a midsummer's Highland eve. Time passed, how much, she hadn't a clue, but she awoke to a softness against her nose.

Jack lay beside her head, gently patting her nose with his paw. Amelia reached over and rubbed the soft fur between his ears. He purred like a fine-tuned engine.

With a big sigh, she turned her head in the grass and looked into Jack's big yellow eyes. "Let's go home, boy."

And so she did.

Chapter 30

It'd been three days since Amelia had climbed out of the cab and trudged up the steps into her beachside cottage. She'd pushed her gigantic suitcase into the corner, tossed her duffel bags onto the over-stuffed chair, and had laid her laptop bag . . . somewhere. She'd managed to brush her teeth with a spare toothbrush, praying it wasn't one that she'd scrubbed Jack's little pointy teeth with, pulled off her clothes—the very same ones she'd had on since falling asleep in the grass in Scotland—taken a long, hot shower, and fallen straight into bed.

With only a fresh can of Cheez Whiz for comfort.

She'd not told a soul she was coming home. Not her parents, her brothers, her sisters, or her best friend. Peace was the thing she was after. Peace and solitude. She certainly could have found that in Scotland, but it hurt too much to stay.

ZuZu, though, had a nose like a bloodhound, along with a weird sixth sense. Amelia knew her pal would sniff her out, and by the fourth morning, ZuZu showed up.

And she was armed.

God, she had a pushy best friend.

The lock rattled as ZuZu pushed and jiggled the key, and then she pushed the door open with a bang. "Amelia Frances Landry!" ZuZu's heels clicked across the wood flooring and stopped at the head of the sofa, right by Amelia's head. Her friend squatted down and lifted the ponytail that had fallen over Amelia's eyes, and frowned. "What are you doing home?" She thumped her on the forehead. "What's wrong with you?"

"Too many questions," Amelia said.

"Excuse me? You've been gone only a few days and you say *too many questions*?" ZuZu leaned down and peered into her eyes. "Can we talk about the book?"

"No."

"Amelia!" She smacked her on her backside. "Get up." She pulled. "Come on."

Amelia sat up, stood, and walked over to the fridge. Opening the door, she grabbed the only thing she could find to drink—a two-liter bottle of soda—unscrewed the lid and drank. The carbonation made her throat burn and her eyes water.

"That is gross," ZuZu said.

Amelia glared at her over the top of the plastic bottle. "I do it at your house, too."

ZuZu rolled her eyes, marched over, and took the soda away. "Come on, Meelie," she said, her tone gentler. "I can tell when something's really bothering you. And I can also tell when it's more than book related." She smiled. "There's a reason you fly all the way over to Scotland to stay in a nice, creepy castle, for God's sake, and then turn around and fly right back home. So give." Walking over to the cupboard, ZuZu found a glass, poured Amelia a drink, and handed it to her.

"Thanks." Amelia slid into one of the kitchen chairs and met ZuZu's gaze. "You won't believe it if I tell you, though."

ZuZu sat across from her, rested her chin on her knuckles, and grinned. "Probably not, but I'll still love you anyway. So tell me. You'll feel better after."

So, with a big, deep breath and another swig of soda, Amelia started at the beginning and told ZuZu everything, from her long drive from Edinburgh, to Jack doing his back-arching Halloween-cat-on-a-fence impression, to meeting Ethan and his kin, to the ghostly face in the mirror, to the rats, the hailstorm, all the way back to her supposed travels to the fourteenth century. Finally, Amelia ended the long story with the not-so-surprising ending: that it'd never happened. It had all been a long, delicious, frightening dream.

No other explanation added up.

"Wow," ZuZu said, after a long minute's pause. "To fall in love with someone from a dream." She smiled and patted Amelia's hand. "Must have been some kind of great dream guy."

Amelia gave a wistful smile. "He was."

ZuZu stood up, walked around the back of Amelia's chair, and wrapped her arms around her in a big hug. Then she kissed the top of her head. "It's hard to believe it disturbed you, Queen of NonDisturbia, enough to come all the way back home. I'm sorry it didn't work out at the castle." She sighed. "Actually, it sounds like a phenomenal story." She gave Amelia's ponytail a tug. "So why not make your dream warrior a reality—sort of?" She grinned. "You need to write this, Amelia. Not only would it make a kick-ass romance/mystery/time-travel/ghost story, but"—she gave her a stern look—"your career is on the line." She grabbed her big handbag and plopped it on the table. "No pressure, of course."

Amelia heaved a big, cleansing sigh. How on earth could she have dreamed everything she'd been through with Ethan? She couldn't have. It was way too real. She could still feel his hands on her, for God's sake.

The only other explanation she had, and this from hours of pondering on the subject, was that somehow, when Amelia had been engulfed in that swirling blanket of mist on the knoll, she'd come back to her time, but *earlier*. It had given her enough comfort to at least get up and shower each night.

"Amelia," ZuZu said, opening her bag, "this story deserves to be written. It's too fantastic not to be."

A feeling of rightness washed over Amelia, and it refreshed her in a way she hadn't thought possible. Scottish lore had Ethan tagged as the Bluidy Munro. Amelia knew better. He was a kind, strong, sensual man who loved his kin, and by God, he'd loved her. He'd made her laugh, made her writhe with passion—he'd dirty danced with her, for crying out loud. He didn't deserve to be labeled the Bluidy Munro, a horrifying, bloodthirsty stealer of young girls' souls. And while her version may not be accepted as fact in the world of history, to her, it would be. And it'd be in print. A book is a slice of history, no matter that it's fictional or factual.

By the blood of Christ, she'd do it. She'd write the book.

"What are you smiling at?" asked ZuZu.

Amelia stood. "You're right," she said. "This is the story I'm going to write."

"Good to hear it." She reached into her bag and pulled out her big giant shears. "I won't need these, then?"

Amelia walked over and threw her arms around her best friend. "Not this time. Now, come with me to the store. I've got to stock up on junk food." She grinned. "I've got a book to write."

"Woo-hoo!" hollered ZuZu, clapping her hands together. "That's my girl!"

With that, they did a little dance, shook a little booty, did the bump, and somehow, thinking of writing her own love story with Ethan Munro brought a little more life back into her. It made her feel close to him. Not nearly as close as she'd like, but for now, she'd take what she could get.

Even without all the notes and scenes, and that dynamic time line, Amelia knew the entire story by heart. And by God, she couldn't wait to get started on it.

Ethan sat straight up in bed, body covered in sweat, his heart pounding hard. Bluidy hell, another dream.

How much more could he be tormented?

He'd rather have been slain by Daegus than dream of Amelia each night yet remain without her. And no' just dream of her, by Christ. 'Twas no' what woke him up each night with his heart thumpin' out of his chest.

In his dreams, she was his. His wife. His to love forever. But he'd lost her, that day on the knoll. He hadn't even known she was there until the verra moment the mist blanketed them, and then he'd seen her. He'd thought 'twas his mind jesting him, taunting him. Still, it could have been so. But every night since, he'd go to bed, and every single bluidy night, he'd dream of her lips against his, of touching her smooth skin, of discovering every place he'd been denied before, and of being inside of her, making her truly his . . .

Of breaking every last bluidy rule of wooing the irritating woman had made.

Wiping his face with both hands, Ethan rubbed the back of his neck, paced to the window, and threw open the shutter. Leaning against the sill, he stared into the night.

To remember seven hundred years of living in an enchanted world, and then to be cast back to his own time had bewildered him. At first, he hadn't recalled anything—not until the fight had ended, those eerie enchanted words had fallen on his ears, and the mist had covered them.

Not until he'd laid eyes on Amelia.

And then everything had rushed back. Every single century had flooded back to his memory, the last being the one that pained him the most to think on.

His kin had remembered, as well. Like him, they'd all missed their family, their mother and sire, their younger brothers and sister. But they'd all desired Amelia's time.

Ethan desired Amelia herself.

And his heart ached to think of never seeing her again . . .

All at once, a whisper, soft and barely there, wafted on a breeze and grazed Ethan's ears. At first he thought it indeed was the wind. He turned his head, toward the clear Highland sky, and listened.

Come to me . . .

Ethan's insides froze. The hairs on the back of his neck rose, and he glanced around the chamber.

To the yew . . .

He glanced outside, toward the wood, and a shudder crept over his spine. There, just in the meadow, a wisp of fog floated in place.

All of you . . .

As he stared, the waft of mist slipped into the wood.

Alone, Ethan dressed and eased outside, following the misty presence through the wood. At the yew tree, it disappeared. With a heavy sigh, he considered. He knew what was being offered. At least, he hoped he knew. And by Christ's blood, he wanted to take it.

He had matters to see to first.

Staring at the ancient yew, by the light of the crescent moon he pulled out a dagger, shaved away a section of bark, and started to carve. An hour went by before he was finished. He looked at his handiwork and smiled.

Aye, he had matters to attend, indeed.

A week passed before they were ready. And just like before, the voice pulled Ethan from sleep, almost as if it knew the time was now.

Grabbing his plaid and sword, Ethan quickly dressed, latched his belt, and sheathed his blade. Easing out into the corridor, he went to each of his kinsmen's chambers and awoke them. They'd all managed their matters, as well. They'd said their good-byes, gathered what few belongings they had.

They all met in the great hall, just by the front doors. The fire from the torches had all but burned out, leaving the hall in a shadowy glow. Ethan gave them all a nod. "Then let us go."

Quietly, they left the keep, crossed the meadow, and entered the wood. Once there, the eerie mist emerged from the pines.

"By the blood of Christ," said Aiden. "Look there."

They followed the mist to the old yew, and as they grew close the cloud of white swirled around the gnarled trunk, through their legs, and then around Ethan.

Then it spoke.

Go to her . . .

Ethan glanced at his kin. Their faces held the same mystified look he felt. "How?" Damn, he felt silly speaking to a waft of mist.

And then the waft drifted to his ear, and the whispered words meant just for him came through clearly.

'Twas Devina.

With his heart in his throat, he listened.

Dunna hesitate, Ethan Munro. The wrongs have indeed been truly righted—all but for one. You do no' belong here any longer, and the one you desire awaits you. Your kin must go, as well, as they've been absent from history, like you. Dunna mourn me. 'Twas my time to leave this place, and I am well. The one you truly love tried to save me, but 'twas meant for me to leave. Go, all of you, and remember the verse . . .

Ethan blinked, and the ghost of his young wife, Devina, slipped around them all. He once more glanced at his kinsmen. "If any of you desire to remain, speak now." He stared, and the five Munros stood tall, and stayed silent. With a nod, Ethan reached inside his belt and withdrew the scrap of parchment Amelia had penned the time verse upon.

It had been Devina's spirit who'd told it to her.

And with the mist curling around them, Ethan stared at his beloved's feminine scrawl, written with ink from centuries into the future. His eyes hazed over, and as he said the words, and the mist grew thicker, he glanced at the trunk of that old yew, and at the words he'd carved just days before . . .

The parchment slipped from his hand and fluttered to the ground, and as everything grew deathly silent, the blackness, once again, pulled them into shadows.

Chapter 31

Amelia stared up at the softly whirring paddles of the ceiling fans on her granny's porch. Dropping her leg over the edge of the swing, she gave it another push with the toe of her bare foot. The old chains on the swing creaked, and crickets fought for air time with the summer cicadas. The very sounds she'd grown up listening to.

Somewhat comforting, she thought.

"You want me to squirt some more of that canned cheese in your mouth, Amelia Frances?"

Amelia turned and looked at her granny. "I thought we were out."

"Arthritis creme, we let run out. Canned cheese and Vienna weenies, never." She got up, bones popping with each step, and walked to the swing and patted Amelia on the head. "You look like you could use a little of both."

Amelia sat up and grasped her granny's blue-veined hand. "Just don't tell ZuZu."

"Too late, I already heard," ZuZu said through the screened door, and then made a clucking noise with her tongue. "Shame on you, Granny. That stuff is horrible for you."

Dona, Amelia's granny, grinned. "There's a full serving of dairy in each can, you know."

Amelia laughed.

"Well, now," Dona said. "That's the first real laugh I've heard out of you since you finished your book."

Amelia gave the swing another push. "Post-novel blues."

"It's a fabulous story, Amelia," ZuZu said. "Your best work. You should be proud."

Amelia inhaled the tangy scent of salt marsh and sighed. She *was* proud of the book. It might just be her best effort to date. But it had made her miss Ethan more and more as each day passed. And she was having a hard time picking up the pieces of her shattered heart.

"Is it another boy, Amelia?" Dona asked. "If it is, we'll just get ZuZu there to have another voodoo doll made up."

Amelia gave a soft laugh. "Don't worry, Granny," she said. "No voodoo doll needed, I promise."

Granny huffed, muttered under her breath, and went through the creaky screen door. "I'll bring you girls out some tea in just a minute." She disappeared into the shady depths of the old plantation house.

ZuZu sat down beside Amelia, her flip-flops smacking on the wooden porch floor with each pass of the swing. "I'm really worried about you, Amelia," she said. "Have you told anyone else about, well, what you told me?"

Amelia shook her head. "I know you think I'm crazy." She smiled at her friend. "I'll be fine, really."

ZuZu narrowed her eyes. "I'm not that easily convinced, Meelie. Besides. I think we should go on a little vacation. Maybe a cruise?"

Amelia shook her head. "I don't really feel like it."

ZuZu sighed, and then jumped up. "Oh! I've got something for you." She ran to the screen door, stepped inside, and brought out a thick, white photo mailer. She handed it to Amelia.

"That may make you even gloomier, but I thought it might be important," ZuZu said, and sat back down.

Amelia looked at the mailer and blinked. Postmarked from Scotland, it had a black, scratchy scrawl across the front. She peered at the return address, and then stared up at ZuZu. "This is from Guthrie, the Munro caretaker."

ZuZu nodded. "I know. I thought it might be something you'd left behind."

For some reason, Amelia's fingers shook as she ripped the paper tab across the front. She reached in and grabbed the only thing inside the mailer.

A single photograph.

"A picture? What is it of?" ZuZu asked.

Amelia held her breath as her eyes focused on the photograph. Tears filled her eyes, slipped through her lashes, and dropped onto a glossy, digital print of the Munros' old yew tree. She drew closer and stared, and her heart slammed against her ribs. Amelia gasped.

"Amelia, what is it?" ZuZu said, leaning over her shoulder.

Engraved deep into the bark of the ancient yew tree were the words Amelia would remember for the rest of her life.

Ethan loves Amelia
By the by . . .

"Oh, my God," she whispered, and swiped at her tears.

"Meelie, *what*?"

Then, at the bottom of the photograph, a small arrow, penned deep into the paper. With trembling hands, Amelia turned the picture over.

On the plain white back were two words, scrawled in a bold, ancient script.

Come home.

Amelia barely dared to believe it. So many emotions threatened to choke her; she couldn't form a sensible, coherent word. Tears steadily leaked from her eyes, and ZuZu finally slipped the photo from her.

ZuZu looked first at the picture, then at her. "What's this mean, Amelia?"

Amelia slowly shook her head and took the picture back. Excitement she only half allowed filled her heart. "I'm not completely sure, ZuZu." She smiled at her friend. "But one thing I do know." She glanced at the picture in her hands and her smile widened. "We're going back to Scotland."

"Welcome to Inverness, gateway to the Highlands. I trust your flight was easygoing?"

Amelia smiled at the young Scotsman greeting the passengers as they exited the boarding ramp. "Yes, thank you."

Deep dimples pitted his cheeks as he smiled at her and ZuZu. "Aye, Americans. To Scotland on holiday, aye?"

"Yes," answered ZuZu, giving the guy a big Charleston smile.

"Verra good, then. Have a lovely stay." He tipped his head and smiled at the next passenger.

"God, what a cute accent," ZuZu said. "I should have come with you the first time."

Amelia shook her head. "Come on. Let's go get our stuff."

They made their way through the small airport to baggage claim. Digital signs located above the conveyer belts noted the flight numbers.

"That's ours there," ZuZu said, pointing to the belt from their aircraft. They walked up and stood, waiting for the luggage to start moving.

Amelia sighed. What on earth was she getting herself into? It would have been much easier for her to pick up the phone and call Guthrie, but the keep didn't have a telephone line installed, and Guthrie didn't have a mobile.

Not that he would have told her much, anyway.

What did the photo mean?

She'd not had an ounce of rest on the trip across the Atlantic. The only thing Amelia could manage was to sit and stare at the picture. *Ethan loves Amelia. By the by . . .*

Come home.

ZuZu had booked the earliest flight, which wasn't until the following morning. They'd left at six a.m. Pricey beyond belief, just for booking on such short notice, but there was no way Amelia would have taken a later flight. ZuZu had come for moral support, thank God—for whatever they were in for.

"I am starved," ZuZu said, bringing Amelia out of her thoughts. "I'm going to walk over and get a muffin or something. Want one?"

Amelia couldn't have eaten if her life depended on it. "No, thanks. I'll just wait here."

"Be right back," ZuZu said, and eased through the crowd to a small coffee shop at the other end of the baggage claim.

"Excuse me, miss?"

Amelia looked up and into the eyes of a tall young man. With dark hair clipped very close and a casual pair of jeans and shirt, he smiled, handed her a single rose, and a folded note card, and then walked away.

Amelia stared, stunned. How bizarre. She didn't know that guy. Flipping open the card, she read the one word penned in the center.

Will

"Miss?"

Amelia looked up, and another note card and rose was pushed into her hand by an older woman, who smiled and hurried off. Again, Amelia opened the card. Once again, a single word.

You

She glanced around at the passengers, a few staring in her direction. What was going on?

"Here ye go, love," an older man said, handing her yet another rose and card. He winked, and then shuffled off, whistling. Amelia looked down at the card.

Wed

"Miss?"

Another rose, another card, and Amelia had to juggle things around to keep from dropping everything.

Me

"Here ye go," another young man said, handing Amelia another note and rose. She opened the card.

Lass?

Amelia's heart beat hard against her chest. One by one, strangers walked up and handed her a single red rose. She stood, shocked. She didn't know what to do or say, just simply gathered the roses being handed to her. No less than two dozen, she guessed.

Amelia turned in a circle and stared. The crowd stared back, smiling.

"What in the world?" ZuZu said. "Amelia?"

All at once, tears welled up in Amelia's eyes as she pushed the shock aside. That darn lump was back in her throat, and she swallowed past it. Then she put the words from the cards together.

Will you wed me, lass?

Frantic, Amelia clutched the roses and cards, and searched the crowd of people, who'd stopped to stare.

"Amelia?"

Amelia froze. *Ah-meh-lay-ah.* She began to shake uncontrollably, and her breath stopped dead in her throat. She closed her eyes and prayed, *Please, God, let it be . . .*

She heard ZuZu make a small choking noise.

Then two strong hands gripped her shoulders and turned her slowly around. Out of the corner of her eye, she saw ZuZu drop her muffin and stare, mouth open. She may have said a naughty word.

"I'd have flown to your home across the sea, but as 'tis, I've no' the proper papers." His voice grew closer. "I couldna even bring my sword here. Now, open your eyes, love," he said, that rich, deep accent washing over her.

She did. Tears blurred Amelia's vision as she stared into Ethan Munro's silvery eyes. She couldn't breathe, couldn't move, and God knows, she couldn't speak. A miracle in its own, really. All she could manage was to stare at the six foot seven, fourteenth-century warrior who'd somehow not only managed a trip to the twenty-first century, but to the airport. She watched a muscle tighten in his jaw.

"Dunna say a word, lass, unless it be aye. I couldna bear it otherwise."

Tears trickled down Amelia's cheeks, and Ethan caught them with a knuckle. The feel of his rough finger against her skin made her shiver.

Somehow, she managed to speak. "Aye—"

Ethan swallowed her vow as his mouth claimed hers, pulling her tightly against him, the scent of roses mixing with that of Ethan. That kiss, with Ethan drawing a deep breath as if he could just inhale her in, would stay in her memory forever. Behind her, the entire airport crowd cheered.

He pulled back, slid his thumb over her bottom lip, and stared at her, hard. He repeated the words he'd shouted that day in the meadow. "*Táim I ngrá leat*, Amelia Landry." Over the two dozen roses, he grasped her head between his hands and kissed her ear, then whispered, "*Mo grádh.*"

Shivers ran through her as she asked in a very puny voice, "What's that mean?"

He looked at her with love burning in his eyes. "My love."

All at once, Amelia took notice of just what her warrior was wearing. She blinked. So shocked by his presence, she hadn't noticed. She did now.

Her mouth went dry as sand.

A solid black T-shirt stretched taut over a wall of muscle Amelia had known was there but not really seen, having previously had a bolt of plaid fabric wrapped all around it. Both big arms were encircled by the same etched silver bands. He wore his dark hair down, part of it pulled back at his nape and gathered with . . . something. The T-shirt was tucked into a pair of soft, faded jeans, and below that, a pair of worn leather boots.

"You're ogling."

Amelia looked up and grinned. "Damn straight."

Just then, a loud clearing of throats sounded behind her. She turned, and nearly dropped the roses.

In an impressive line stood five big guys, all wearing jeans, boots, and a different assortment of shirts.

Amelia blinked.

"What's the matter, lass?" said Aiden, giving her a wicked grin. "Dunna think I've ever seen ye speechless before."

With a squeal, Amelia all but jumped up and down as Aiden, Sorely, Torloch, Gilchrist, and Rob rushed forward and embraced her with very tight hugs. Tears came to her eyes as she looked at each warrior.

Aiden grabbed her by the head with both hands and pressed a kiss to her mouth. Then he looked at her. "I fear you're strapped with us, lass," he said, then glanced over her shoulder. He grinned. "And if you dunna introduce me to that fetchin' maid standin' there wi' her mouth drooped open, I shall never forgive you."

ZuZu!

She looked, and her friend stood, drop-jawed, simply staring at the whole scene. Passengers bustled back and forth, in between, passing in front of them, and ZuZu just stood. Staring. Amelia laughed, eased over to her friend, and balancing all the flowers and cards in one hand, grabbed ZuZu with the other. "Come on, girl. I've got some people for you to meet."

ZuZu looked at her, then back at Ethan and his kin, and then gave her a mischievous grin. "Man, I've never been more thrilled to be your best friend."

With a laugh, Amelia pulled ZuZu over to meet the guys. They each gave her a low bow, grasped her hand, and brushed a kiss over her knuckles. Aiden, of course, lingered over those knuckles for just a bit longer.

ZuZu glanced at Amelia and mouthed the word *wow*.

Amelia knew the feeling.

"Well, git your bags and let's go, then!"

Amelia turned to find old Guthrie standing there with a half-grumpy frown on his face. She ran over and threw her arms around him. "Thank you," she said, and kissed him on the cheek.

The old man's face turned red. "I'm verra sorry, lass, not to remember you, but I was a wee bit surprised by the whole bloody thing." He shook his head. "Passing odd, it is. Hurts me noggin just to think on it." He shrugged. "The laird here will explain it all later. For now, let's get going. 'Twasna easy loading up these big fellas. There's four cabbies waitin' out front." He squinted his eyes. "Someone's going to be fittin' tight."

"I hope that's me," whispered ZuZu.

The men roared.

Ethan's hand went to Amelia's lower back, and he pulled her close. "Come, love. Let's go home."

So they gathered their luggage and did just that.

They stepped out into the dim light of a Highland

midsummer's eve. Even at the airport, the ever-present scent of clover reached Amelia's nose. She inhaled and smiled.

She'd come home.

In the cab, Ethan pulled Amelia close, a hand always present on her somewhere. She rather liked it.

" 'Tis a miracle, having you," he whispered against her ear. "I shall never let you go again."

Amelia leaned in to him, felt his warm lips press against her temple. "You'll never have to," she said, and snuggled close for the ride back to Munro Keep.

Home.

Epilogue

Amelia sat before the small dresser mirror and stared at her reflection. For the hundredth time, she took a deep, calming breath.

Her wedding day.

Rather, her wedding eve.

Twilight, actually. The gloaming hour. To her, a more perfect time couldn't have been settled on.

A lot had happened over the past two months. ZuZu, who was by far the most perfect planner in the history of planners, took the planning of the wedding and ran with it. Small, no-fuss, non-froufrou. Easy-peasy. ZuZu had done a fabulous job, including arranging all of the flights for the Landry clan. They'd arrived two weeks before the wedding date, so Ethan and the Munro clan could get to know the Landry clan. The meeting, as Amelia had suspected, had gone off perfectly—all except her brothers, who'd given Ethan every sordid detail of Amelia's childhood. She'd get them back for that.

Meanwhile, her sisters and ZuZu were fought over by five big warriors. Three girls to five guys just didn't equal out, and Amelia knew the girls were eating up the attention. Aiden had set his sights on a very feisty ZuZu. A match made in heaven, Amelia thought.

Standing, Amelia walked over to the small window and leaned on the sill, staring out into the late Highland evening. She'd changed rooms, having found one on the top floor with a window. Breathing in the crisp, autumn air, she watched the light of an early moon glare off the loch's black surface.

When Ethan wasn't busy entertaining her father, or charming her mom and granny, he spent every waking moment with Amelia. They'd had a lot to discuss, she and her medieval warrior. At the base of the ancient yew tree, they'd sat, and Ethan had told Amelia everything that had happened, and she'd shared with him everything she had witnessed, as well. Overwhelming, the sharing of that info.

Ethan's sister had stumbled upon Marynth and Devina in a heated argument—apparently over Ethan. Marynth had confessed to having loved Ethan ever since childhood, and accused Devina of stealing him away. Never, though, had anyone suspected Marynth of the black arts, much less murder. She'd been responsible for all the deaths of any young maid Ethan had showed an interest in, yet Marynth had loved Ethan and his men firercely. She'd made sure the murder appeared to have been committed by Ethan, and then set the beloved Munros within an enchantment, planning to return later and set them free, and to claim Ethan as her own. Marynth hadn't planned on Ethan's little sister to take revenge and kill her. The sliver of yew in the warrior's trews had protected them from the enchantment. Amelia was ever so glad for it.

And poor Guthrie. Because of the yew slivers, the

men had not remained at the tower throughout the centuries—not for a second time, anyway. Guthrie had been oblivious to their existence, and since Amelia had come back to the present a bit early, the old curator hadn't remembered her, either. But once Ethan and his men came to the present, it'd taken old Guthrie more than a little time to adjust to their strange situation. Thankfully he had, though, and was quite excited to be part of it.

Ethan had choked while telling Amelia the story of the good-byes to his family, mostly done in the shade of darkness, alone. He'd returned the lairdship to his sire, who in turn would train his younger brother for his duties. Ethan had gathered what he could; they all had, and brought what meager means they had to the future.

Those meager means had been several gold coins each, which would bring a small fortune if sold to a dealer. Ethan, of course, was worried over how he'd care for his wife and kin once the coin ran out. Amelia had assured him with a few kisses that it would all work out fine. She'd bought the dreaded keep of the Bluidy Munro for rather cheap, she thought, and it wouldn't change owners again, if left up to her. Ethan was smart, quick, and she had no doubt he'd find his niche in the future. As would all the Munro warriors.

"My God, let me look at you."

Amelia turned from her reverie at the window and smiled at her dad. She straightened and did a full turn. "Well? Do I pass inspection?"

A wistful smile touched her father's mouth. "You look as beautiful as your mom did on our wedding day."

Amelia smiled and raised her brow. "Mom had a bouffant, Dad." She held her hand several inches above her head. "Hair stacked up to here."

Her father grinned. "I know. Sexy, she was. Just plain sexy."

Amelia laughed, and threw her arms around her dad's neck.

He chuckled and kissed her head. "You're happy, aren't you, sweetheart?"

Amelia pulled back and grinned. "What do you think?"

John chuckled. "Ethan's a fine boy. I like him."

She kissed him on the cheek. "Good. I do, too."

They laughed, and her dad held out his arm. "Ready?"

Amelia grasped his elbow and gave a nod. "Absolutely. By the way," she said, "nice tux."

John Landry grinned and gave her a tug. "Come on, you."

With a deep breath, Amelia fell into step with her dad. Down the dim passageway they went, and butterflies—the sweet ones—fluttered inside Amelia's stomach. Somewhere down below, a flute played the most whimsical, sweet tune she'd ever heard. Definitely medieval.

When they reached the stairs, Amelia looked out over the great hall. Lit only by candle and torchlight, the soft, wavering yellow glow gave a romantic feel. Tea lights lined the path she'd walk to the makeshift altar at the hearth, and bows of Scots pine covered every surface in the hall, the smell strong and crisp. Once they reached the bottom steps, Amelia lost her breath. The Munro guys, all dressed in their fresh-scrubbed plaids, complete with swords strapped to their backs, stood tall and ridiculously handsome on one side of the tea lights. On the other, the Landrys. ZuZu, Maggie, and Erin all wore pale rose-colored gowns, empire waisted with a white lace overlay. Simply gorgeous, her sisters and best friend. Her mom and granny wore burnished gold gowns, not alike in cut but similar in color. They were adorable.

Her brothers, like their father, wore black tuxes. Good-looking devils, all of them. Even old Guthrie had fancied up for the occasion, and wore his own dress kilt, his knobby and bowed knees knocking beneath the linen.

Her granny's eyes had twinkled at that.

Then, the vicar, who stood at the front with his back to Amelia, stepped aside and faced the small crowd. Ethan stood tall, his hair down and partially pulled back, his plaid buckled, cinched, and in place.

He took her breath away.

As the flute changed tunes, Amelia and her father started across the hall, down the little aisle of tea lights, and with her heart pounding, she met her future husband at the altar.

Ethan tried to breathe a normal breath, but by all the bluidy saints in heaven, he couldna. It hitched in his throat, and he tried to clear it once, but even that didna work. Mayhap, he thought, it'd be that way for eternity.

His bride was just that fetching.

Nay, he thought, watching her as she crossed the hall with her sire. Fetching was Amelia wearing those short trews and strange little slippers that slid between her big toes and flip-flopped against her heel when she walked. Fetching was Amelia in a sundress pulled taut against her breasts, wearing a pair of high rubber *wellies*, which she was wont to do when they hill walked.

Ethan drank in the sight of his Amelia wearing a straight, simple shift of satin, sleeveless, with a low neckline, and like her sundress, pulled snug beneath her breasts by a slender sash of Munro plaid. Her hair, that glorious fair, streaked mass, had been piled high on her head, although several long hanks had escaped and now framed her face. Another slender strip of Munro plaid adorned her throat like a choker, with a small red gem dangling from the center, and like gems hung from her lobes.

His soon-to-be wife was beautiful, and she took his breath away.

Finally, her sire delivered her safely to him, and placed Amelia's hand in Ethan's.

"She's yours now, son," John Landry said.

Ethan gave a nod, and then drew Amelia close. "I know," he whispered to her, and she blushed.

The vicar said his piece, and blessedly, he did so with haste. He turned to Ethan, gave a nod, and Ethan cleared his throat and looked into his beloved's eyes.

"Dunna matter the century, I shall keep you safe and love you binding, *mo grádh*." He stared at her hard and deep, grasped her left hand with his right, and bound a slip of Munro plaid, complete with a sliver of yew, around their wrists. "*Go síoraí.*"

Somewhere behind them, he heard several female sniffles. He couldna blame them. He felt like doing the like himself.

Amelia looked into his eyes, those wondrous, odd-shaped pools of silver luminous in the shimmering light of the torches. She picked up the end of the strip of plaid, and smiled. "No matter where you go, I'll follow, *mo grádh*," she said, her voice shaky "*Go síoraí*." And she completed the binding of their wrists, leaving each one hand free.

"Aye, 'tis done," said the vicar. "Go and be one."

Ethan looked at his wife, slid his free hand around her neck, and pulled her close. Against her lips, he whispered, "My thoughts exactly, vicar," and then wiggled his brows and lowered his mouth. He felt her smile there, with their lips pressed together, and amid the whistles and shouts, they shared their first kiss as man and wife.

'Twould be the first of many, by the by.

Then their loved ones crowded around, hearty slaps on the back from Munros and Landrys alike, and sweet hugs from the new females of their unioned clan.

Soon tables were laden with food, catered in, Amelia had said, along with wine and lager and some fruity stuff in a large bowl. Amelia had said it was punch. Ethan didna get it, but 'twas tasty, after all.

ZuZu came over, gave Ethan a hug, and then kissed his bride on the cheek. "Everything was just beautiful. I'm so happy for you two."

Amelia smiled, and Ethan thought she'd never looked more radiant. "You did a wonderful job, Zu. A fairy-tale wedding I'll remember until I'm old and gray." She cocked her head in that enchanting way she had when puzzled. "How did you find a flute player?"

ZuZu lifted a brow. "I didn't hire a flute player."

Ethan and Amelia shared a knowing look. Indeed, he knew someone who played the flute like an angel.

Devina.

And with that, the music started up, and merriment was had by all. He dirty danced, to the delight of the crowd, with Granny Dona, who could move quite well for her aged years.

The twins, Maggie and Erin, and ZuZu taught his kin something rather odd called the Robot. 'Twas vastly amusing, truth be told, especially seeing big Tor wrestle the moves, but they were having a pleasurable time, laughing, doing the Robot. Dirty dancing. Shaking their *booties*, so Amelia had said.

His new father- and mother-in-law danced happily, bumping their hips and swinging each other about by the arm. He rather liked the idea that they were still so much in love and didna mind letting others know it. He planned to do the like with their daughter.

He planned to start verra soon.

As in *now*.

"Come, love," Ethan whispered, when the others were busy with their merriment. "I've somewhere to take you."

Amelia looked into his eyes and grinned. "Thought you'd never ask."

With that, they eased out the front door, first him, then moments later, Amelia.

He'd promised the twins, Seth and Sean, lessons in swordplay to make sure no one followed.

Ethan felt assured they'd oblige.

He met his wife under the stars, and wrapped a plaid about her shoulders. "Come on, love. Hurry."

And they did.

"Where on earth are we going, Ethan?"

Ethan glanced down at her, the slice of moon giving off just enough glow to light their path, and to show the glimmer of mischief in her husband's eyes.

That wasn't the only thing glimmering there, either.

" 'Tis a surprise, wife."

And darn it, he could keep a surprise to the end.

Finally, they made it to the wood line and entered the forest. Amelia's breath frosted in front of her, but it wasn't freezing cold out. Beneath the wool plaid Ethan had wrapped her in, it stayed toasty warm. Having Ethan's big body pulled close probably helped, too.

Finally, with the moonlight filtering in through the canopy of pines and birch overhead, Ethan led her to his surprise.

She gave a little gasp. "Ethan! You devil!"

"Your brothers helped."

On the massive flat rock, several thick blankets were piled high and spread about, pillows set here and there, and big, thick, unlit candles encircled the rock. Below, the burn rushed over stone and hurried into the darkness. Off to one side, a long box covered with another plaid, and a smaller box atop it.

Amelia looked at him. "You've been busy, laird."

He didn't answer. His eyes settled over her, and he grasped her by the hand and pulled her onto their makeshift bed. Amelia's heart skipped a beat when he said, "Take off your slippers."

She did, and scooted them off to the side.

Ethan knelt, pulled a lighter from his belt, and lit each candle, one by one. When he was finished, he kicked off his boots and socks and tossed them aside. Without a word, he unlatched the leather scabbard at his waist and slid the whole thing, sword and all, off his shoulder and propped it against the long covered box. Then he took the plaid wrap she wore and eased it from her shoulders, leaving it to pool at their feet.

With a gentleness that stunned her, Ethan took her hands in his, rubbed his calloused thumbs over her knuckles, and brought them to his mouth, where he pressed his lips to them. His eyes bored into hers, so deep she felt it to the bone. "You make it passing hard to breathe, Amelia," he said. He lowered her hands and left them at her sides.

And then with both of his large hands, he held her head still, tilted it back and to the side, and with one hand traced her lips with his thumb, tugged her lips open, and lowered his head.

He kissed her then, slowly dragging his mouth across hers, and the sensation of the movement gave her shivers, made her hungry. He tasted her deeply, and she kissed him back, sliding her own hand between their bodies and touching his mouth as it moved, sensual and possessive against hers. He groaned when she did it, and moved his hand to the small of her back, over her bottom, and pulled her against him. His other hand loosened her hair, bound together by a few pins that he found and discarded, threading his fingers through and pulling her head to the angle he desired.

Amelia gave Ethan free reign, every hungry touch she anxiously awaited, and when he found the zipper at the back of her dress, he pinched the small metal piece between his fingers, eased his mouth to her ear, and whispered, "Do I just pull?"

"Uh-huh," Amelia managed, desire making her body tingle, so fierce she wanted to crawl inside him.

Slowly, Ethan eased the zipper, and cool air brushed her bare back, and then he slipped his hands inside the gown, bringing warmth, caressing her ribs, her back, over the silk of her panties. He lowered his head and nuzzled her neck. "Christ, Amelia," he managed, and took his time exploring her skin with his rough hands. The sensation of those calluses, caused by gripping a sword for more than half his life, against her skin made her tremble, then reach for his belt.

"Ethan, help me."

He did, and soon the belt went flying through the air.

Taking her hands in his, Ethan lifted her fingers to the brooch at his shoulder. "Unclasp it," he said, "like so."

He helped her, and the plaid fell from his shoulder, exposing a chest cut from solid rock. She dragged her hands over each hard line and plane, and then pushed the material lower, over his abdomen, tracing the muscles etched there.

As Ethan slipped Amelia's gown from her shoulders, over her breasts, she pushed his plaid over his hips.

Quickly solving the whole *what do they wear under those things?* mystery. Indeed.

His hands followed the satin material of her gown down her body, and as those calloused palms closed over her breasts, he released a sigh that shook her to her soul. He whispered something in Gaelic, and hoped she'd remember to ask him what it meant later. All she wanted now was to *feel*.

They both stepped out of the pooled material at their feet, and Ethan pulled her close and lowered her to the stack of blankets. He laid her back, his arms bracing his weight as he simply stared at her, bare, all for the slip of lace the lady at the wedding store had called panties.

Again, he whispered in Gaelic as his eyes wandered over her, and one hand followed the path his eyes went, and all Amelia could do was hold on to his arms and let him.

Every inch of her felt alive, wherever he looked or touched burned, and low in her belly, she ached—an ache so great it bypassed any pain by yards and yards. While his hands skimmed her breasts, down her side, over her hips, she writhed, desperately wanting him to ease the ache inside.

Unable to help herself, she trailed her fingertips over his chest, down the rippled muscles of his stomach, and he sucked in a breath when her hand went lower, over his hips and muscular buttocks, and then closed over the very part she knew would take away the thing driving her crazy . . .

"Christ in heaven, Amelia," he muttered, his deep voice so thick with desire she could barely understand him. He loosened her grip and took both of her hands in one, trapping them above her head; then he lay overtop her completely, his hips settling in just the right place. Still, it wasn't quite there . . .

With a slow, agonizing pleasure, he pressed his mouth to hers, tasted her mouth at the corners, tasted with his tongue, and then moved to her collarbone, and then lower, to her breast, and when his mouth closed over the sensitive skin she arched her back and tried to free her hands, but he held fast.

"Steady lass," he whispered against her stomach.

He kissed her hip, her belly button, and then each rib. Painfully slowly. *Heaven*.

Almost.

"Ethan, please," she said, her own voice deep, and, God help her, pleading.

Still, his explorations continued. With a gentle hand, he urged her hips to one side, twisting at the waist, and his fingers traced the dragon tattoo at her lower back. Another muttered something in Gaelic, and he turned her back over to face him.

Finally, Ethan turned her hands free, and Amelia dug her fingers into his back and kneaded the muscles there, dragged her hands over scars she hadn't known existed but fully planned to investigate another time.

The next time . . .

And then he kissed her. Sensual, soft at first, then turning starved, he tasted her like a man who'd not had sustenance in centuries. Amelia wriggled beneath him, coaxing him, arching into him . . .

"Wrap your legs about me, lass," Ethan whispered in her ear, and then whispered something else in Gaelic.

She did, and Ethan covered her mouth with his, and at the same time pushed deep into her, reaching a place she'd sworn never to give again, unless it was to the love of her heart.

Ethan claimed her then, and as they moved together, the candlelight throwing flickering shadows onto their faces, he lifted his head and stared. Desperately, they found each other's heart, they found their release as well, deep, long movements that seemed to go in slow motion, and they didn't break their stare, not once. Sensations built, broke, and exploded, and she held on, unwilling to let go. So powerful a moment, tears streamed down Amelia's eyes as she gasped for air.

As they slowed, drank in the cool Highland night air, Ethan remained inside of her, filling her body and her soul with love. He pushed the hair from her face and pressed his lips to her temple, her eye, her lips.

And then suddenly, he had that small box in his hand. How he'd managed it, Amelia didn't know. She looked at him, his face close, precious to hers.

"Open it," he said, that deep brogue washing over her.

Surprised at the strength she still had, Amelia lifted the lid from the simple silver box. Inside, two silver bands lay side by side.

Amelia thought them to be the same color as Ethan's eyes.

"Take them out," he said, and suddenly his voice sounded strained. "And read the inside."

With her heart still pounding from their lovemaking, Amelia turned first one band, then the other to the moonlight. "Ethan loves Amelia." She smiled, tears falling down the sides of her face. "By the by."

Wordlessly, he took the small one from her and slipped it over the third finger on her left hand. Amelia smiled through tears and pushed the bigger one over Ethan's same finger.

He wrapped his arms around her and rolled, pulling her on top of him, remaining inside her. "We're one, lass," he said, and pulled her head to his and kissed her. *"Mo grádh."*

My love.

Amelia's heart soared with happiness. Never had she thought she'd find a treasure like Ethan. She traced his brows, that fascinating moon scar beneath his eye, the bridge of his nose, the sensual curve of his mouth.

"I'll love you forever," she whispered, and lowered her mouth to his.

And as their kisses grew frantic, and they moved together once again, they both knew they'd been given a true gift, indeed.

By the by . . .

ACKNOWLEDGMENTS

I probably sound a bit repetitive with the people I thank for all of their help and support, but it's really their fault. *Honest.* They just continue to be so darn helpful and supportive! So to the following, I'd like to say thank you. Again. Many times over.

My editor, Laura Cifelli, and my agent, Jenny Bent; I can't say enough about these two. They're always there to help, answer questions, inspire, and keep me in check. They've helped make me a better writer, and, I am lucky to have them both in my corner. Thanks!

My mom, Dale, and my dad, Ray, who are always so proud of me and enthused with my work, and to my husband, Brian, and my kids, Kyle and Tyler, who make me laugh and feel proud to be a wife and mom, and to all of my family who have been there over the years, through crazy adventures and just *life*: Sheri, Jerry, Tracy, Jordon, Ann, Brenda (and all of her kin!), Paul, Trey, Leah, Donnie, Jessica, Brett, Hank (that's wacky Henry Heller III, by the way not to be confused with his fabulous and handome, witty, scholarly father, Hank Heller, along with his spectacular wife, Bonnie, who keeps all those Hellers in line), Sabrina, Odette, Nikki, Will, Vince, David, Gail, Troy, Joyce, Brenda R., Bonnie R., Rusty, and Dave and *all* their kids! *Phew!!* Thank you!

Especially to my baby sisters, Sheri, Tracy, and Nikki, who are all silly crazy-fun goof balls whom I share many an unforgettable memory with. I'll grow old with you nutty girls any day!

The Denmark Sisterhood. These crazy womenfolk of mine make me *laugh*, and should the afternoon teas whe have *ever* be secretly recorded, we'd either all be in *big* trouble or become ridiculously *famous*! Thanks to Dona, the matriarch and a most fine writer, indeed (who recently had a very prestigious goat named after her!), Pat, Elaine, Beth, Meghan, Brandi, and Tyler. You guys are the best!

Kim Lenox is my very best pal and critique partner. Always there to encourage me, share loads of laughs, brainstorm, and to just be silly, I am ever so glad to have crossed paths with her. She is a fine writer and a kind spirit, who has really become a sister to me. (She is crazy funny, too!) Thanks for everything, Kim.

These next several crazy girls are my sister-friends. Wicked funny, terribly, *sincerely* demented, and more fun than a barrel of sea monkeys, they have cheered me on and supported me throughout my writing journey. They are some of the grandest women I know, and I am proud to call them all friends: Betsy Kane (what a *nut*!), Molly Hammond (she is *crazy*!), Eveline Chapman (*just not right!*), and Valerie Morton (she is a *riot*!—and her hubby, David, is the *sweetest* guy ever!) I am a better person for knowing all of you. Thanks guys!

These next gals are so supportive and funny, and their praise for my characters and stories (and some even inspire more characters) make me glad to be a writer: Christy (who is the inspiration for all things wacky!), Karen (I borrowed her beautimus eyes for Amelia!), Allison (who works hard to save the ta-tas), Holly (whose hubby is the inspiration for all things guy-related), Renee (who has more energy than any normal human), Shay (who loves Tristan—for real!), Karol (lover of books who eats a lot of candy corn. Seriously. *A lot*), Lesley (who blesses my books before reading them), and Felicia (who is just plain sweet!). Thanks, guys!

To all the fantastic readers, especially those who have taken the time to write to me about my stories, thank you! Your praise encourages me and fills me with pride. And to megareader and pal, Rita-Marie Hester, who with the persistence of a stealthy Dober-man, sneaks into her local bookstore and arranges my books in a most strategic, highly promoting man-ner. Thanks, Hester!

And one more special thanks to my mom, Dale, who is always so happy to talk book ideas with me. I love you, Mom!

Man—what fantastic people I know!

Read on for a sneak peek at
Cindy Miles's next book,
coming soon from Signet Eclipse.

Odin's Thumb Pub and Hotel
Northwest coast, Scotland
November, present day

"Right. Fifty quid then, lass."

Allie Morgan blinked. "Pardon me?" Quid? What the heck was that?

The cabdriver, a tall, lanky guy, around thirty, with a pair of soft brown eyes, grinned. "Your fare. Fifty sterling pounds." He winked. "Quid."

With a smile, Allie nodded. "Gotcha." Digging in her backpack, she pulled out the bills and paid the man. "Thanks for a spectacularly wonderful drive."

The driver's grin widened. "Aye, and thank you for the spectacularly wonderful tip." He stuffed the bills in the console and inclined his head. "Stayin' at Odin's, then, are you?" he asked.

Allie gave a nod. "I sure am."

The cabbie studied her for a few seconds, then shook his head and grinned even wider.

"What?" Allie asked, gathering her bags. "What are you smirking at?"

The driver chuckled. "Oy, lass, I'm sorry." He lifted a brow. "Have you met the owner yet?"

"Gable MacGowan?" Allie shook her head. "Not in person. Why?"

He studied her a bit more. "Damn me, but he'll not be expecting the likes of you."

Allie grinned and opened the door. "He's not expecting me at all. I'm three days early. That's why I just paid you a hundred American bucks to drive me here from Inverness."

The driver laughed. "Right. Let's get your bags, then."

Allie shook her head, pulled her stocking cap over her ears, and stepped out of the cab. A fierce gust of coastal November wind hit her square in the face and she shivered. Slinging her pack over her shoulder, Allie grabbed her overnight bag and the camera bag, and shut the door. At the back of the cab, the driver pulled out her one suitcase.

"I'll take this in for you," he said.

"No, that's okay. It's not heavy." Allie grasped the handle. "Thanks, though."

With a shake of his head, the cabbie slid back into the front seat. He glanced at Allie and cocked a brow. "You know it's full of spooks, aye?"

Allie gave him a big smile. "I sure do."

With a laugh, the cabbie waved and drove off.

After a deep breath of crisp, briny air, Allie quickly took in her seaside surroundings. White, traditional croft-style buildings, and others of weathered stone, lined the single-lane main street that rambled down to the wharf. Each establishment had a battered sign outside noting its business: a baker, a fishmonger, a small grocer, a post office, a few B and Bs, and a chip shop. With the notion to explore later, after she'd settled in, Allie turned and stared up at the sign hanging high above the single black-painted door of the white-washed inn and pub. ODIN'S THUMB was written in Old English script at the bottom of the sign, with a colorful picture of an imposing Viking longboat, the sail a deep red with black stripes, and the long, wooden bow a big ole thumb. She smiled. *Perfect.*

After balancing her gear on both shoulders, Allie opened the door to the pub and was all but blown into the dim interior of Odin's Thumb. She set her suitcase off to the side and plopped her bags down beside it—

"I'm not staying here another minute!" a woman's voice shrieked.

Allie jumped, then stood there, against the wall, and took in the scene. Had she been any other woman, she'd probably have run screaming, too.

It was, after all, quite an interesting sight to behold. She almost had to pinch her lips together to keep from laughing. Instead, Allie simply observed.

Amidst the muted lamplight of the pub, flickering candles floated overhead, suspended in midair. A lady's old-fashioned parasol opened and closed rapidly, also in midair. Beer mugs and wineglasses zipped—yep, in midair, from one side of the room to the other, coming precariously close to the head of the shrieking woman and sloshing ale everywhere. A suspicious-looking mist slipped around the bar stools, over the head of the woman whose face had turned dough-pasty, and at the same time the chairs began lifting and slamming back down on the floor.

"Arrrgh!" screamed the woman, who batted at the mist swirling about her and ran for the door.

"Wait, Mrs. Duigan, dunna go," a deep, graveled and heavily accented voice said, the tall figure hurrying after her. "I can explain."

Mrs. Duigan paused briefly.

Just before the dozens of fish appeared in midair, their tails flapping back and forth.

She let out one final scream and pushed her way out of the pub.

The tall man—pretty darn good-looking, Allie thought—followed the frightened woman.

Allie peered out the door and watched Mrs. Duigan slam her car door and speed off. The man stared after her. With his back to Allie, he tilted his head, as if looking up to the sky, shoved his hands into the pockets of his dark brown corduroy jeans, then looked down, staring at the sidewalk.

"Oy, we're in for it this time, aye?" said a male voice behind her.

" 'Twill be worth it, no doubt," said another.

"I dunno," said yet another. "He looks powerfully angry this time."

Allie turned, and noticed the fish had disappeared, as had the floating candles and eerie mist. A handful of mischievous-looking spirits stood in a half circle, staring at her. A very-much-alive little boy stood in their center. His auburn brows furrowed together over a creamy complexion.

"Who are you?" the boy asked Allie.

Allie looked each ghost in the eye. A friar. A pair of rather cute English lords. An old knight. A dashing sea captain. A noblewoman with a large hat on her head.

The sea captain's mouth quirked into a grin. "Indeed. Who might you be?"

The heated look he gave her, from the top of her head to her feet, then slowly back to meet her eyes, left little wonder just what he was thinking. Allie winked. "I can tell already you'll be a handful."

The sea captain grinned.

"Alys Morgan?"

Allie turned and came face-to-face with the man who'd followed the woman out of the pub. He had a great accent, she thought. "Allie," she said, preferring her nickname. Now, up close, she blinked in surprise. Good-looking? No way. Not even close. Ruggedly beautiful fit more closely. Tall, at least six foot two, with close-clipped dark hair, a dusting of scruff on his jaw, green eyes, and generous lips, he was broad-shouldered and . . . utterly breathtaking.

His eyes held hers, intense, studying, evaluating. A muscle flinched in his jaw, and Allie thought she'd never been more intimately weighed in her entire life. Her mouth went dry, and she finally cleared her throat. "Gable MacGowan?" She smiled and held out her hand.

He glanced behind her briefly, and when her gaze followed, she noticed the ghosts and boy had gone.

Ignoring her hand, the man gave a short nod and grabbed her bags. "Gabe. And you're early," he said, and inclined his head. "This way." He turned and headed toward the back of the pub. Not once did he turn around to see if she'd followed.

Hurrying past a long, polished mahogany bar, complete with the high-backed stools that had moments before lifted and slammed against the wide-planked, wooden floors, Allie glimpsed the barely there figure of a bartender wearing suspenders and dark trousers, wiping down the tables with a white cloth. He tipped his soft hat by the bill and grinned, and she returned the smile and shrugged.

When Allie turned, she plowed into the very broad back of Gabe MacGowan. "Oops. Sorry."

Gabe stared down at her, those green eyes hard and set. He didn't frown, nor did he smile, and yet the electricity that snapped in the air all but made Allie shiver. He remained completely aloof. "Dunna make friends with them. I'm paying you to make them leave."

Allie met his stare, mostly unhindered by his intensity. Instead of frowning, or telling him to stick it where the sun don't shine, she gave him a wide, friendly smile. "I'll keep that in mind."

He stared a moment longer, then turned and headed up the narrow staircase, the old wood creaking with each of his heavy steps.

Allie grinned behind him, thinking things could be a lot worse than walking behind Gabe MacGowan as he climbed a set of stairs. She wondered why such a gorgeous guy had a somber, unfriendly personality.

She'd tell him later that the one thing to remember when dealing with the unliving is you couldn't make them do anything they didn't want to.

Allie turned and glanced over her shoulder. The ghosts from before stood at the bottom of the steps. Grinning.

The sea captain, a tall, handsome man with dark sandy hair pulled into a queue, gave her a roughish smile and a low bow.

As she turned and hurried after Gabe, Allie decided right then and there that the decision to cross the Atlantic to oust a handful of mischievous spirits from their old haunt had been the smartest one she'd ever made.

Getting to know the ghosts of Odin's Thumb would be exciting. But deciphering just what made Gabe MacGowan tick would be something else altogether . . .

Spirited Away

Cindy Miles

Knight Tristan de Barre and his men were
murdered in 1292, their souls cursed to
roam Dreadmoor Castle forever.

Forensic archaeologist Andi Monroe is
excavating the site and studying the legend
of a medieval knight who disappeared.
But although she's usually rational, Andi
could swear she's met the handsome
knight's ghost.

Until she finds a way to lift the curse,
however, love doesn't stand a ghost
of a chance.

**Available wherever books are sold or at
penguin.com**

HIGHLANDER IN HER BED

Allie Mackay

She's fallen in love with an antique bed.
But the ghostly Highlander it comes with is
more than she bargained for...

Tour guide Mara McDougall stops at a London
antique shop, and spots perhaps the handsomest bed ever.
Then she bumps into the handsomest man ever.
Soon Mara can't forget the irresistible—if haughty—
Highlander. Not even when she learns that she's
inherited a Scottish castle.

Spectral Sir Alexander Douglas has hated the Clan
MacDougall since he was a medieval knight and they tricked
him into a curse...the curse of forever haunting the bed (the
very one that Mara now owns) that was once intended for his
would-be bride. But Mara makes him feel what no other
MacDougall (or McDougall) has—a passion that he never
knew he'd missed.

Available wherever books are sold or at
penguin.com